He and Neve w_____t they wanted in _____ when their bodies touched, when their gazes met, it was almost uncontrollable.

"It was a mistake," he rasped out.

"I know."

"Because you want more?" Rock said, seeing the knowledge in her eyes, shattering his reason.

His hand cupped the back of her head, her hair silky against his palm. She closed her eyes and nodded.

Shifting so she was flat against him, he shut his eyes, the rush of sensation so intense that he had to grit his teeth and his breathing constricted. She moved, sending a shock wave of heat through him, and he clutched her head, the feel of her almost too much to handle.

* * *

Be sure to check out the next books in this exciting miniseries:
To Protect and Serve—A team of navy military operatives and civilians are called to investigate...

* * *

If you're on Twitter, tell us what you think of Harlequin Romantic Suspense!
#harlequinromsuspense

Dear Reader,

Problem #1: an international gunrunner wants her dead... Cue problem #2: her brother's best friend and a former marine, sexy, dangerous alpha male Russell "Rock" Kaczewski.

My heroine, Petty Officer Neve Michaels, USCG, stationed in San Diego, California, has been targeted by a dangerous international arms dealer, the White Falcon, leaving her only one option—neutralize the threat and take him out. Before she can go on the offensive, Rock, who doesn't know the meaning of the words *butt out*, refuses to let her go alone. It makes it even tougher that she's deeply attracted to him, but they're incompatible. Rock has set down roots and Neve wants to travel the world.

You just read about my wounded hero and tough heroine in the desert in *A SEAL to Save Her*, but now we're going to the polar opposite: the Darién Gap, a remote, roadless swath of jungle between the borders of Panama and Colombia. It's probably the most dangerous place in the western hemisphere, with the threat of kidnapping, treacherous jungle, impenetrable swamps, drug traffickers, guerrillas, government troops and no marked trails.

The hardest part of this trip isn't the thick and dangerous jungle, the almost-impossible op or the murderous weapons broker—it's the threat to their hearts.

Happy reading!

Karen

HER ALPHA MARINE

Karen Anders

HARLEQUIN® ROMANTIC SUSPENSE

Recycling programs
for this product may
not exist in your area.

ISBN-13: 978-0-373-40252-6

Her Alpha Marine

Copyright © 2017 by Karen Alarie

Printed in U.S.A.

www.Harlequin.com

Karen Anders writes a suspenseful and sexy mix of navy and civilians investigating murder, espionage and crime across a global landscape. Under the pen name Zoe Dawson, she's currently writing romantic comedy, new-adult contemporary romance, urban fantasy, syfy and erotic romance. When she's not busy writing, she's painting or killing virtual mmorpg monsters. She lives in North Carolina with her two daughters and one small furry gray cat.

Books by Karen Anders

Harlequin Romantic Suspense

Five-Alarm Encounter

Coltons of Texas

High-Stakes Colton

To Protect and Serve

At His Command
Designated Target
Joint Engagement
Her Master Defender
A SEAL to Save Her
Her Alpha Marine

The Adair Legacy

Special Ops Rendezvous

Visit the Author Profile page at Harlequin.com.

First in. Last out. You need someone to take a hill, hold the line, a piece of real estate or scare the hell out of the enemy? Call in the devil dogs. Thanks for serving. This one's for you all.

Chapter 1

Death will come for you on swift wings.

Looking over her shoulder, especially an injured one, wasn't a walk in the park. Neve Michaels had been chafing at the restrictions ever since she fractured her clavicle and bruised two of her ribs during a rescue mission gone wrong.

But someone stalking her made it ten times worse.

Her doctor was impressed at her dedication to PT and the amount of flexibility and strength in the injured arm, and told her that the healed break was now the strongest bone in her body.

She was now ten weeks into recovery after surgery and feeling almost back to normal, but still had six weeks left on her recommended medical leave. The terrible bruises from her shoulder to her elbow and down her torso had faded. She was back in the pool, even doing the crawl. Getting back to her crew aboard the Jayhawk helicopter and performing her Search and Rescue swimmer duties for the United States Coast Guard was all she thought about…

With the exception of the rescue that haunted her. She'd been reprimanded in the past for bucking protocol, and her commander wasn't happy about her broken collarbone. He'd had a thorough investigation conducted on her, and she'd been cleared of any blame in the rescue.

There wasn't a day that went by that she didn't remember their faces. She had deep remorse and shame, those feelings combined in a troubling sense of guilt. And that guilt ate at her with a terrible sense of foreboding. She wasn't subject to disciplinary action because the investigation deemed the storm and other factors were at fault, but Neve felt—and she thought her commanding officer might guess—that she would have been in better condition if she heeded the pilot's suggestion they wait just a bit for the winds to die down.

She just wanted to get back to active duty and put the tragedy behind her.

Even though she was expecting it, the knock on her front door made her jump and rise quickly to her feet as if she was facing a threat. Her heart pounding, she approached the door like it was a live grenade. "Who's there?"

"The Avon Lady," was the deep, husky reply.

She sighed when she opened it. She had expected her brother Tristan would be standing there ready to take her grocery shopping. Instead, she found Russell "Rock" Kaczewski, her brother's best friend and business partner.

Gorgeous, frustrating and wholly commanding Russell.

She got a sense of danger she couldn't quite pin down whenever she came within sight of this man, and it had nothing to do with getting hurt—at least not in the physical sense. Neve couldn't seem to drop her guard one iota around him.

There were times when she didn't understand the way he looked at her or the way he acted. At one moment, his intense gaze would rake her, and then in the next it was banked and indifferent. He confused her, and she'd be lying to herself if she didn't acknowledge she thought about him in a way that heated every molecule of her body. But he maintained his distance and kept his attentions toward her platonic. Which suited her fine. Getting tangled up with Tristan's friend, his *best* friend, wasn't smart; he was a take-charge man just like her father. Too many complications and problems could come of it.

His brotherly behavior toward her was just fine. *Brotherly.* Yeesh. She *certainly* did not feel the same way about Russell as she felt about Tristan or Thane. At all.

He was tall, six-five, with a heavily muscled, 240-pound, ripped body. His impossibly broad shoulders and shredded arms were encased in a tight-fitting, short-sleeved black Henley T-shirt, a few of the snaps undone to reveal the enticing column of his strong neck and the smooth skin of his wide chest. His equally impressive lower half was in a pair of worn-out jeans, snug in all the right places. He smelled delicious, an earthy and subtle blend of wood and fruit. His face, covered in a sexy-as-all-get-out short black beard, no mustache, was made of more angles than curves with animal magnetism in every line. He couldn't be described as cute or even handsome. Neither was the right word. Russell wasn't pretty. He was striking, serious even when he smiled, and looked like he'd been to hell, kicked asses, took names and knocked the ash off his boots before coming back. As easy as a walk in the park.

There were two features that Russell possessed that were the exception to the pretty rule: his eyes, an incandescent, deep, aching blue, and his thick and silky hair, the color of midnight and cut long enough in the front to spike over his forehead.

Feeling her resolve weaken, Neve seriously thought about confiding in him. But getting close to Russell wasn't a very good idea. She'd call Tristan later today and mention the situation.

She'd felt trapped for the two days after receiving the plain white envelope outside her door with a piece of paper inside. On the paper was a single line: *Death will come for you on swift wings.*

"Your voice is pretty deep for an Avon Lady…but I hope you brought all the eye shadow colors to model for me," she shot back at him.

He gave her a classic Russell smile—tight, bland— then a split second later, he narrowed his eyes. "What's wrong?" He was instantly alert, and that was also quite intimidating and, dammit, so sexy. Russell had been a marine. Or, according to him and her brother, was still one—once a marine…always a marine. He'd retired five years ago and opened up Rockface, a chain of sporting goods stores. He'd convinced Tristan to join him as a partner and to leave the marines when his last tour was up. Now they were running it together. Just like they had been working together in a two-man US Marine Scout Sniper team.

She'd never seen her brother Tristan happier. He was settled down, engaged to Amber Dalton, a blonde beauty and tough-as-nails NCIS agent he'd met and fallen for while they were working on a friendly fire incident at his last billet, Mountain Warfare Training Center at the foot of the Sierra Nevada.

"Nothing's wrong," she replied, trying with all her might to give him no reason to worry about her.

He tilted his head and said, "Are you sure, Neve? You look spooked." He leaned in, brushing her arm and shoulder to get a better view of the apartment as if he was expecting some kind of threat behind her. She responded automatically to his warmth and strength, swaying toward him. When he pulled back, the air of danger only intensified as he studied her face.

"I'm fine. Just didn't expect you." She never liked it when someone saw her emotions. "Where's Tristan?"

"He's in Vermont, Stowe to be exact, with Amber. Did you forget they were going on that buying trip and taking the time to visit with her family?"

"Oh, God. I did. I totally forgot. He told me a few days ago. It must have slipped my mind." Yes, he had. That was the day before she'd gotten the disturbing and alarming warning.

She'd looked up the saying on the internet and discovered it was part of a supposed curse written near the entrance to Egyptian king Tutankhamun's tomb. But there was never any proof the door had actually been inscribed with those words. It was a myth. In fact, it was rumored that the archaeologists who had found the tomb were all cursed and died because of that. She didn't believe in curses or myths.

"Are you ready to go?" he asked.

She nodded and grabbed her bag from the side table. After closing the door, she locked it and tucked the keys in her jeans pocket. At least this would be a quick trip to grocery shop. She really didn't need that much.

Russell made way for her to go first, the touch of his hand at the small of her back much too provocative, and the hallway much too narrow to accommodate her, let alone Russell's powerful frame.

She sensed his subtle appreciation of her as a woman. His awareness was in the ease of his touch, the light pressure of his fingers and the unspoken admiration in his eyes. Unnerving and charming, flagging him as both a gentleman and a rogue, contrary but apt descriptors for him.

They left her apartment complex, Spanish-flavored, charming red-and-orange stucco buildings with black wrought-iron and quaint balconies, situated not far from downtown and affording her a view of San Diego Bay.

They headed to the I-5, a major highway that ran from Mexico all the way to Canada.

"Whole Foods, please, Russell."

He sighed and glanced at her. "Why can't you just call me 'Rock' like everyone else?"

"I don't know. You always seem to be Russell to me." Before she could stop herself, she glanced in the rear-view mirror as they pulled away from the high-rises, watching for anything suspicious.

"You just like to argue with me." He glanced at her, and she could feel that scrutiny again. She pretended to look for something in her purse. Russell was one of the few men she'd been attracted to who she argued with this much. She'd left behind her high-school boyfriend when she'd enlisted. She didn't want to be tied down, and Doug was never leaving Dutch Harbor. After him, there had mostly been casual dating and an occasional one-night stand.

"Maybe, and maybe you just like to argue with me."

"I can't be forced into calling you something that doesn't work for me." She pulled out some lip gloss and smoothed it on. That, too, seemed to hold his attention, his eyes briefly dropping to her mouth.

"You don't seem to mind me calling you 'Fins.'"

She shrugged. "That's your choice, and I have no problem with that." The truth of the matter was that "Russell" was more formal and "Rock" was too personal. She preferred to keep it formal between them. "Fins" was much less personal to her than her first name. He always pronounced "Neve" with a soft inflection that drove her crazy.

One hand was on the wheel of his cherry-red Lexus SUV. The other was lying against his well-muscled thigh. He had beautiful, strong looking hands, his fingers long and tapered, the tips blunt. She wondered how they would feel— Nope. *Stop it!* That was a road best not traveled.

She would be so glad when she could stop relying on other people to drive and she could pick up her own groceries. Tristan was adamant that she wasn't to do any heavy lifting until she was fully shipshape. And, to be honest, the only reason she went along with him was to be sure she healed as fast as possible. It was in her best interest. Loving her Search and Rescue job, she hated being out of commission.

"How is Dex doing?" Dexter Kaczewski was Russell's younger brother, a Navy SEAL who had just recently had a harrowing experience with getting attacked in Afghanistan. Then he'd had to go on the run with

Senator Piper Jones from her own Diplomatic Service detail. Once she'd finished her husband's Senate term, she'd moved to be with Dex here in Coronado.

"He's great. He's just got back from deployment. They're giving him another medal."

"Of course they are. How is Piper?" Neve couldn't stop checking the rearview mirror to see if they were being followed.

"So we're going to have a wedding in the family. I'm going to be…ah…an uncle."

"You're kidding me?" She smiled for the first time in weeks. "Oh, my God, that is so exciting."

"Yeah, he deserves to be happy. I was surprised he even gave her a chance. He's been burned so many times."

"Are you ready to be an uncle?"

He took a few moments to answer, and his voice was infused with pleasure when he said, "I am. Ready for the rug rats."

The tone of his voice made her stomach jump as if he was saying he was ready for children. That was a really, really deadly and pothole-ridden road with land mines, and she wasn't going down it. Maybe never.

"She gave in to my brother, which had to be tough. Dex is career SEAL, gone most of the year, but she looks strong enough, as strong as my mom, to handle his deployments and not know where he is."

"That wouldn't be for me. I don't like secrets."

"For us military guys, it was necessary."

She nodded, understanding. She just didn't want to handle not knowing. She'd grown up with her parents keeping the dangers of fishing the Bering Sea from her and her siblings. It wasn't until she was older that she realized the risk involved when her father set foot on his boat. She preferred to be open and honest when possible, but she acknowledged the need for secrets and that sometimes they were appropriate.

"More power to them. After being a military brat and then a marine, I've had enough of moving around. I'm happy to have laid down some roots."

"I'm just getting started," Neve said. "I've worked in some interesting places, like Panama. I speak Spanish fluently, but I have a knack for languages anyway. Helps in the job."

"I bet. You're ready to see the world, huh?"

"Yes. More than ready." She was prepared and set to get out there and make her mark.

Russell pulled off the I-5 when they got to Del Mar and turned into the lot of the Flower Hill Shopping Center.

Parking his vehicle, he got out and opened the door for her, reaching to help her out. There was that gentleman part, except it only made her impatient. Neve ignored his hand. She didn't want to touch Russell, and she refused to act like she was eighty years old.

Another car pulled up behind them, and she forced herself not to look. She was probably paranoid, but that note had been creepy. She followed Russell's delectable backside as he walked toward the store and pulled out a shopping cart.

She was sure he wouldn't even let her push it. "I can—"

"I've got it," he said in that authoritative tone that grated on her nerves.

As they progressed through the store, she barely had to lift a finger. It seemed Russell not only remembered her preferences, but recalled what had been picked up on her last trip.

"Oops, forgot the peanut butter," he said, and left to head around the aisle. That's when she noticed *him*. He was lingering around the salad dressings like he couldn't decide what kind of ranch to get. A shiver went down her spine, but just when the tension had built to an almost unbearable degree, he slipped around the corner at the end of the aisle. The winged tattoo on his neck and the reference to wings in the note weren't lost on her. She didn't get a good look at his face.

"Got it. You like the Jif brand, creamy, not crunchy."

She made a small, involuntary sound and spun at his voice, her heartbeat hard against the wall of her chest.

Russell stared at her. And her gaze drifted over his face, the hard angle of his jaw, before finally coming back to his eyes, so seductively dark blue, so intensely focused on her. Suspicious.

She reached for the peanut butter and forced a smile. "I'm out. Thank you! I so love peanut butter. Smooth is my favorite. It's amazing how you remember that." Smooth. Something she wasn't being right now. He eyed her, his mouth tightening and his eyes narrowing. He tilted his head, watching her; his eyes never wavered, and she was desperate to distract him.

"Oh, I need crackers," she murmured, then rubbed at her shoulder. His expression cleared some and sympathy replaced the doubt there. He wet those full lips and turned to get the crackers. "The buttery kind," she called after him, and he gave her a quick wave.

The jar of peanut butter still in her hand, she twisted to find that the aisle was empty. Man, she was losing it. There was no one following her. It was probably some Halloween prank. Releasing a breath, she rubbed her hand over the label, over the word *creamy*, and wondered if his skin would feel smooth over the firm hardness of his golden-hued muscles.

This time, when he returned, she was ready. He set the crackers inside the cart, and they moved on to continue their shopping. As they were checking out, the man who had been looking over the salad dressings was just exiting the store.

He turned and made eye contact, holding her gaze for several seconds, then he left. Had that been a come-on? It hadn't felt flirtatious.

They made a quick trip to the drugstore to pick up a prescription for pain meds. By the time they got back to her apartment, she was tired and was happy to let Russell carry all the bags upstairs and put the food away.

She settled on a bar stool and watched. He also remembered where everything went. As soon as he was done, he straightened, then came around to where she was sitting. "You need anything, Fins?"

"No, thank you."

"I can cook something for you. You look wiped."

"No, I'm not hungry, but I appreciate it."

"All right. You have my number. Just call me if you need me."

"I will. Thanks again."

He nodded, but still looked reluctant to leave. She slipped off the stool, getting another noseful of his enticing scent. She opened the door and he walked out.

"Good night, Russell."

"Night," he murmured.

She closed the door on his retreating back and went to shut her sliding glass door and lock it, but before she could reach it, she heard a brush of a shoe. Her reflexes rusty, she dodged awkwardly away as a knife sliced the air where she'd just been standing.

With automatic precision, she grabbed the attacker's knife hand and twisted, bringing him to his knees. But before she could disarm him, he punched her in her sore shoulder and sent her to the carpet. With the butt of the knife, he dealt her a stunning blow to the head and raised the blade for a killing strike to her heart.

Neve rolled, and his weight came down onto the carpet. She jabbed out with her foot, catching him in the ribs, and grabbed a lamp, smashing it over his head. He dropped the knife and she snatched it up, bore him to the ground, straddled him and placed the weapon against his throat.

Blood dripped from the knife handle gash on her forehead into her attacker's face, the tip of his captured KA-BAR combat knife embedded in his neck, right below the wing tattoo. "Who are you? Why are you in my apartment attacking me?"

"Vendrá la muerte para ti en rápidas alas," he whispered in distinct Panamanian Spanish.

She ripped off his mask, her mouth going dry and her eyes widening. *Death will come for you on swift wings.* It was the man from the supermarket.

"¿De que estás hablando?" she asked, demanding to know what he wanted.

"Si me matan, más vendrán. No puedes escapar," he said, making it clear he was sent to kill her, indicating that if she killed him, more would take his place. She couldn't escape. Her mouth went dry.

"¿De qué?" she asked him. *From what?*

"Nos. Muerte. El Halcón Blanco se vengará. Tú. Toda su familia va a morir." His response had been chilling.

Us. Death. The White Falcon will be avenged. You. Your whole family will die.

"*¿Venganza? Para qué?*" she asked him. Revenge for what? Was he threatening her whole family?

There was a knock at the door, and her momentary distraction cost her. Pain exploded as he slammed the broken lamp into her temple.

Suddenly he was on her, grappling for the knife. She yelled for help and heard the sound of splintering wood even as she fought her attacker. The knife descended, her injured shoulder and arm trembling with the effort to hold him off, her strength failing even as the blade inched closer to her heart.

Then the weight was gone as her attacker was grasped in a powerful headlock and the two males—Russell and her attacker—wrestled for control.

She heard bones break and the bodies whirled toward the open balcony door. Close quarters, powerhouse fists flying. Punching through the screen. She couldn't make out who was who in the dark. They jockeyed for position, and one man's arm sliced the air as the other jumped back. Who had the knife? Russell or her attacker? Then in one fluid motion, after another feint from the oncoming man, the retreating guy grabbed his wrist; then, more sounds of broken bones and the cornered guy clotheslined the attacking figure. He flipped off the balcony, and his scream was abruptly cut off as he inevitably hit the pavement. *Please don't let it be Russell!*

"Russell!" She struggled up off the floor, her head reeling as the man turned and for a moment was silhouetted in the dark, the knife dripping blood. Then he came into the moonlight, and she stumbled toward him with a soft cry.

"Russell," she whispered as they met in the middle, and she couldn't look away. His eyes were wild and he cupped her face, his hands hovering over the stinging cuts.

Her gaze drifted over his face, over the fall of his silky, dark hair, the hard angle of his jaw before finally coming back to his eyes so intensely dark, so intensely focused on her. *Oh, no.* She could lose herself in those blue eyes, drown in the way he looked at her, and with an awful, sudden certainty, she knew it wasn't impossible for it to happen, even against her will.

Please, no. Get a hold of yourself, Neve. It was too crazy, and simply not an option. It didn't make any sense. She would be strong in about an hour. She would remember how to be independent and closed and immune.

But right now, she was so damn glad he was all right.

"You're okay," he rasped. His voice was warm and soothing and wonderful—but it only added to the thick lump in her throat, to the hard pressure against the backs of her eyes. His look only intensified, making the tears fill, spilling onto her cheeks. She couldn't, *wouldn't* do this. Honest to God, she *couldn't*.

"Aw, don't, Neve. Babe."

It was a plea, nothing less, and hearing it from him only made her feel stripped inside.

It would be okay, just for this brief time, to be relieved that he was alive and her attacker was dead. That they were both alive. Maybe, she thought, a lick of panic twisting through her, she could just let herself, for one moment in her life, just feel for him.

Taking a steadying breath, she opened her eyes, an ache snaking around her heart. She had to be realistic. This was only a respite in the wake of the brutality and a brush with death. It wasn't forever. Even if she wanted it, she couldn't risk anything happening that would jeopardize Tristan and Russell's friendship. It would be complete, crazy madhouse madness. Besides, he wasn't really the guy for her. He was grounded, rooted here like a rock, his business tying him down. She needed to be free to move.

She had to consider her brother and not fall into the attraction game with Russell. She liked her autonomy too much, and she would ruin everything anyway. It was feasible it wouldn't work out, then she'd hurt them. Break their friendship because Tristan would most definitely side with her. That would kill the both of them and, in turn, kill her.

It was just too complicated.

He brushed at her tears with his thumbs. She got ambushed by his closeness, his care, the gentleness of those big, beautiful hands. His reaction did her in. She got such a rush of heat that it made her insides turn over. Clutching his shirt in her hands, she closed her eyes and leaned her head against him, her heart flip-flopping crazily in her chest, her lungs jammed up and unable to function.

He made a soft male sound in his throat, as if she was killing him, then his strong hand cupped the back of her neck as Russell murmured something. Running his hands up and down her back, she let go of him and simply melted against him. Her heart struggling to keep on beating, Neve turned into his arms, certain she was going to fly apart, and the feel of his warm skin nearly took her down.

"Hey," he whispered softly. "Hey." Holding on to her with one arm, he pulled out his cell phone, made a quick call to Austin Beck at NCIS, then wrapped her up in a tight, enveloping embrace. His fingers tangling in her hair, he clasped her head against him as he brushed her forehead with a soft kiss.

She held on to him until she heard sirens in the distance, held on to the very last minute until she had to let him go.

Let him go for good.

She needed a clear head to do this.

Horrified at her attacker's declaration, Neve was determined to figure this out and stop the White Falcon at whatever the cost.

Chapter 2

"You and your brother are trouble magnets. First him, now you. I didn't help to save Dex's ass to have his brother's end up in a sling. You okay? You look like hell," Special Agent Austin Beck said after he had arrived at Neve's building just before the local cops.

Rock discovered someone had called 911. The police were there briefly and left the investigation in the hands of Austin. He and Rock had become close after Dex had disappeared. Rock had been in contact with both Austin and his father and had been instrumental in helping Dex apprehend the men responsible for attacking Dex's soon-to-be-wife, former senator Piper Jones.

"I'll make it," Rock said with an off-kilter grin, glad to see Austin, but not thrilled by the circumstances.

"Do you know the dead guy?" Shortly after Austin got there, he notified the Coast Guard Investigative

Service Office—CGIS—and they were sending out an agent to coordinate investigative efforts since an active-duty coast guard member was involved.

"No. Like I said. I broke down the door to get to her. He was trying to kill her."

Austin had the knife secured in an evidence bag, which he held up. "With this KA-BAR?"

"Yes. I disarmed him, and it was accidental that he went over the balcony. Believe me, I would have liked to have gotten some answers out of this guy."

Rock didn't like the way Austin looked at Neve, who was sitting on the couch still dazed. Austin's eyes roamed over her, taking in her bruised and battered face, the tear tracks on her cheeks, the paleness of her skin—the shape of her legs, the curves of her body and the wild, out-there beauty of her face.

"Cut it out, Beck," Rock growled. Actually, snarled was more like it.

Austin grinned and shook his head. "Ah, that's the way it goes."

"No. She's Tristan's little sister. That's all. She's just been through a lot lately." The impossibility of a relationship was easily reinforced. He meant it when he'd said he was done moving around. After years and years of new places and new people, he was quite happily ensconced in his life. Ready to move onto the next step. A long-term relationship, marriage, children, the whole enchilada. Neve wasn't in the same place in her life. He'd be smart to remember that.

Austin nodded.

"Got it."

There was a commotion at the open door and a man with Asian-American features, close-cropped dark hair and a short, well-maintained goatee walked through, dressed in a black leather jacket and motorcycle garb. He pulled off a pair of black leather gloves and slipped them into his back pocket.

He reached out his hand. "Special Agent Davis Nishida, CGIS," he said, first clasping Rock's hand and then Austin's with a strong handshake.

"Russell Kaczewski, Marine, retired, and I'm Special Agent Austin Beck."

"Okay, that explains why NCIS is here." They filled him in on what had happened.

"I was waiting for you to question Petty Officer Michaels," Austin said.

"Appreciate it."

Agent Nishida walked over to Neve, introduced himself and crouched down. *Hell.* She was still trembling, and she looked up to the task, but exhausted, with circles under her eyes and her skin pale.

"Can you tell me what happened?" Agent Nishida's tone was gentle, his voice husky and concerned. Maybe his interest was a little too piqued. Yeah, and maybe Rock was freaking jealous of every man who looked at her sideways.

She explained everything from the beginning, and Rock got all tied up in knots at the description of how close she'd come to death. Then, proud of how she had fought him off and gotten the drop on him. She was a ballbuster.

"Do you know the dead guy?"

"Yes," she said, twining her fingers together.

"You've seen him before?"

It was imperceptible, but Rock saw the look she gave him before she said, "He followed us to the grocery store today. I saw him there watching me. I thought it was just my imagination."

"What is your position in the coast guard?"

"Rescue swimmer."

He blinked a couple of times, and it was clear Agent Nishida's estimation of Neve climbed a notch. "That's impressive. So, he wasn't after classified or intelligence information."

Rock's second call after NCIS had been to Dex, who showed up and greeted Austin at the door. Rock walked over as he approached. "Geezus! What the hell happened here?"

Rock explained everything quickly to his brother. Neve was still sitting on her couch; the EMS had taken care of the cuts on her temple and gash on her forehead, the shallow gash across his ribs and his own facial abrasions.

"I need you to wait for the manager and get this door fixed for her. Then call me when it's all done."

"Of course. Damn, bro, I'm glad you're okay and that you were here."

"She left her purse in the car or I wouldn't have been. She came close to… Dammit." He swore viciously under his breath. A cold sensation spread through Rock's middle, and his insides bunched into a hard knot. How could he survive if anything happened to Tristan's little sister? How could he face his friend and look him in the eye? Losing her wasn't an option.

"But you were here, and she's safe. Have you called Tristan?"

Rock noticed Neve give Agent Nishida a white envelope. He wondered what she was telling him. "No, not yet. She got all upset and didn't want me to, but I will later on."

Agent Nishida offered her his card. "Let me look into this, and I'll be in touch when we have more information. In the meantime, we'll try to get an identity. Let me know if you think of anything else. I'm glad you both are okay."

"Thank you and I will."

Agent Nishida motioned to Austin and he nodded. "Call me, Rock, if you need anything," Austin said. Rock shook their hands before he and Agent Nishida walked out, discussing the case. He noticed how the CGIS agent gave Neve another appreciative glance.

Dex walked over and said a few soothing words to Neve, and she rose and hugged him hard. He held on to her for a few minutes. Rock wondered if he had the same sick feeling in his stomach.

Well, that sucker was dead, and Rock couldn't feel one lick of remorse. But Neve was holding something back. He was sure of it. Her vigilance in the car and her jumpiness told him she wasn't exactly forthcoming, and he had to wonder about that. What was she hiding?

He walked across the room and said, "Do you need help putting some stuff in a bag?"

"What? Why?"

"You're coming home with me."

"I am not." She looked as flimsy as a wet paper bag. Her special effervescence—that rare kind of energy that could light up a whole room—was gone. It was as if her bright spirit had been extinguished, and she looked fragile. All he could do was think about keeping her safe. What the hell had happened here?

"Yes. You. Are. Pack a bag, and if you need help tell

me. Otherwise, I will do it for you and carry you out of here."

"I second that," Dex said.

"There you go. Two six-five guys against one five-eight woman. Go."

"Bullies," she grumbled. She hunched her shoulders and turned away, her body tight, as if she was trying to ward off pain or…fear.

He watched her stomp off, and his brother gave him a sidelong glance. "I don't envy you tonight, bro."

"The manager's number is on the fridge. I appreciate you coming over and taking care of this for her."

"No worries." He slapped his brother's back. "She's okay, man. You can relax."

Rock got the gut feeling that he wasn't going to relax anytime soon, his emotions all twisted up. Neve was in danger, and this attack was just the tip of the iceberg.

"I've got to give Piper a call and fill her in. I'll be right back." Dex headed for the ruined door to the hall.

"Okay." He went over to the sliding glass door, needing space. The cool gush of air was welcome against his heated face and neck. He rubbed at his eyes, his head congested with thoughts he shouldn't be thinking, but could never seem to control.

There was a whole lot of stuff that had gone under the bridge, and he was sure he'd put it all behind him. Slipping his right hand into the back pocket of his jeans, he leaned against the wall, the longing tugged at him so hard, it hurt.

He'd harbored the secret for a long time—five years, to be exact. He and Tristan had been the same age—twenty-eight—when he'd first set eyes on his best friend's baby sister.

Ah, damn, he still felt the impact of that first look at her. He'd been divorced for eight years; he'd gotten married too young, right out of high school, and the marriage hadn't lasted through his deployments. He wouldn't hold the cheating against her; once he'd gone off to war, his feelings for her had cooled quite a bit.

Tristan introduced them when they'd been on leave, and Rock knew that his life would never be the same. He had tried to get past it, dated here and there, but his heart had never really been in it. It had nearly killed him to realize that he could never have her; Tristan was just too important to him. He would never break the moral code he lived by. Never touch a friend's sister. Ever.

It had been one hell of a vow. Heartache? He could fill reams with what he knew about it. The constant ache had become a part of his life. And that was why sometimes, like tonight, he hated facing reality. Usually when he got like this, he went to the gym and lifted, or ran like hell. Yeah, his body reaped the benefits, he thought, a flicker of humor lifting one corner of his mouth. He was ripped and honed.

Leaving the balcony when he heard Neve still protesting, he stepped on glass and looked down. It was a picture frame, and he bent and picked it up. His chest tightened as he studied the picture. It was a snapshot of her and Tristan. She was laughing, and he had his arm loosely around her neck. He set the frame back on the table.

Yeah, reams wouldn't be enough to hold his heartache. And secrets? He had them by the bushel. Most of them were stored up in a whole lot of pain.

He lingered on her face in the snapshot, the hole in his chest getting bigger.

And it was a secret he would take to his grave without ever giving it up.

* * *

When Rock tried to take Neve's arm, she sidestepped him, and before he could open her door, she pulled it open herself and got into the passenger seat.

He sighed. Yeah, it was going to be a long night.

He pulled up to his home, located on a cul-de-sac, opening the garage and parking his SUV inside. He tried to help her out, but she wasn't having any of it. Neve was back to her old self. Which should make him happy. Right? Distance, anger, discontentment between them was good.

She went up the three small stairs into the house and he closed the garage door, locking the car. Shutting the door behind him, he entered the kitchen. Neve was standing at the wide sliding glass doors that led out to the patio and the pool.

"Neve."

Their eyes met in the glass, and hers looked bruised and battered. She folded her arms over her chest. "Can I use your pool?" Her clipped tone was clearly broadcasting she wasn't open for conversation. "I could use the extra PT."

He suspected it was more about releasing some of the tension that had built from being attacked. "Of course you can. I can barbecue us something to eat." She licked her lips, pink and enticing, her bottom lip full, the top a perfectly enticing bow. He wanted to lick it. Suck on her.

She gave him a short nod, still not giving him an inch, but that was all right. He would rely on sniper doctrine. He would plan to take the least traveled, most difficult route to ferret out what was going on with Neve. He was used to lying in wait for hours on end. His patience was legendary and honed. He would apply the fundamentals.

Nothing mystical, nothing magical. She would tell him what he wanted to know.

"I'll show you where you're sleeping."

He went to pick up her bag, but she beat him to it.

"Lead the way."

He headed toward the stairs and climbed them to his room. "I'm not taking your bed...bedroom, Russell." Her voice was breathless but firm.

He felt like there was something hard pressing on his lungs at just the thought of her in his bed. "I insist." His voice was firmer.

"I don't want to displace you."

"It's only for one night, Neve. Dex can handle your door."

"Dex is handling my door?" Her inquiry was punctuated with definite anger in her voice. What the hell? She was so damned stubborn.

"Yes."

She frowned, playing with the strap of her bag. A quiet Neve didn't bode well. Her head came up and her gaze riveted on his face, her eyes narrowed. "You don't think I'm capable of handling my own business, do you?"

"It's not that," he assured her.

She set her bag on his bed and, uh-oh, she put her hands on her hips. "What is it, then?"

"I'm making you do this so I know that you're safe and cared for. Tristan..." He trailed off. This was about his fears and worries over her safety, and until she told him what she was keeping under wraps, he would handle his own worry his way.

She threw up her hands and grabbed up her bag again,

reaching inside and pulling out a bathing suit. "Oh, this is for Tristan, is it? Peachy."

"Yes." He sighed. "Damned peachy." He studied her, not liking the awful tension he sensed in her. He really didn't need to see her in fewer clothes. That wasn't going to help. "He's my best friend, and I told him I would take care of you if ever the need arose."

His gaze locked on her face, he waited. Finally, she drew in a deep, shaky breath and straightened, folding her arms tightly across her chest, never a good sign. "Was that like a marine buddy pact when you were in combat?" she bit out, a depleted look in her eyes.

"Yes, it was."

She lifted her chin and gave him one of her cool looks. "I can take care of myself, Russell. Now march out of here and let me change. I need to swim."

By the time Rock had arrived back home from a run, the last light of dusk was fading from the sky and the full moon was sitting high above the eastern horizon. His body was wet with sweat, the muscles in his legs ached and his lungs were on fire. He had pushed himself every step of the way, hoping a grueling pace would keep his mind focused, would keep him from thinking.

All that had happened had thrown him for a loop; his first instinct had been to bulldoze his way in. Contact with Neve always made him crazy. But he would have to endure it. He just kept reliving that moment when he'd burst through the door and that descending knife was so damn close to her heart. He'd gone berserk.

Slowing to a walk, he swore and shook his head as droplets went everywhere, hitting his shoulders and his overheated upper body. But that wasn't the only thing that was eating a hole in his gut. It was Neve. It would always be Neve, and no amount of running or lifting weights was going to get her out of his system.

He was feeling things he didn't want to feel. And she had no damned business telling him she could take care of herself when all the help she could ever want was standing right in front of her. It hurt to think she didn't either trust him enough to confide in him or didn't care enough to.

Frustration bordering on anger churned in his gut, and he punched in his alarm code with more pressure than was warranted and jerked open the side door to the garage.

After stripping off his soaked tank top in the hallway, he fired it into the washing machine on his way past the laundry room. He glanced out the door to find her still swimming strongly across his oval pool. The lights made the water sloshing over her look like liquid midnight against a pale, heavenly body.

Ripping his gaze away from her, he took the stairs three at a time and headed for his bathroom, hoping a shower would put things back in perspective. If it didn't, he was in big trouble.

But there were things he couldn't ignore when he stripped down and stepped into the shower enclosure. Like the fact that he was fully aroused, that his pulse rate had nothing to do with the five-mile run, that his lungs kept trying to seize up. He braced his arms on the tile surface and closed his eyes, letting the hot water pour over him. He tried like hell to shut down, but those constant feelings kept washing over him in waves, making his pulse run thick and heavy. Gritting his teeth against another rush, he clenched his hands into fists, trying to stop the response. He didn't want to feel as if his skin was rubbed raw every time he took a breath.

He'd thought he'd had everything under control, and he had damned near lost it all. He simply did what he had to do, but the bastard who had attacked her was dead. No answers there. He didn't think, didn't let his thoughts stray.

But his thoughts didn't listen to the marine part of him and meandered right into the sensual territory.

He'd needed to hold her against him to make sure she was still warm and breathing.

Now that was working against him. The memory of her heated skin sliding over his, his hand entangled in her hair... And he remembered in absolute living detail the erotic memories making all hell break loose inside him. His mind, his body—it was if someone had flipped a switch.

He clenched his jaw, his whole body primed and throbbing. And he could only let his imagination run free, fantasizing what it would be like to be deep inside her.

Realizing he was having very dirty thoughts about Tristan's little sister, Rock swore and roughly adjusted the temperature setting, the shock of straight cold water doing little to ease the heaviness between his thighs. He didn't want this. Damn it, he didn't want this. Feeling as if the walls were closing in on him, he turned off the water, then dragged his hand down his face. This was getting him nowhere. There wasn't enough cold water in the world to wash away what he was feeling.

How disgusted Tristan would be with him, he thought, as guilt mixed in with his fantasies about Neve. He could never let Tristan down. His mission was clear.

He opened the door to the shower, rounded the glass

block wall and reached for a towel. Deep in thought about what his next step would be, he heard a gasp and his head came up, water dripping from his wet hair down along his neck and across his chest. He froze for a split second. Neve was standing there, one arm out of her suit, a dark-tipped breast buoyant and.plumply full against the blue fabric, her hand under the second strap.

All he could think was that she had a beautiful body. Toned and honed with strong lines that made him breathless and only aroused him more. Her muscle definition was awesome, not juiced, just sleek and cool-looking, like she'd worked for it. She was pure, kick-ass gorgeous. Her long, dark hair was wet, but no less luminous; the glossy strands shone against the dark fabric of her suit.

Her deep, jet-black eyes, tipped with impossibly long, thick lashes, flowed down his body, and then her heated gaze widened. Elegant, black eyebrows lifted. She jerked up her eyes and her suit at the same time he grasped the towel off the rack and dragged it across his... Oh, damn.

There was no way she missed his aching hard-on.

She flushed as he wrapped the towel around his waist. "Well, now we can say we're past that awkward seeing-each-other-naked part."

He tucked in the end. In spite of the tension, he managed a laugh. She gave him a cheeky smile. "One more thing to check off my list," he said as she stepped back. "It's okay. You can have the shower. I'm done. I'll get dressed and get the food going."

Still aroused, his erection throbbing, he went downstairs and fired up the grill. Then, when it was ready, he got two steaks out of the fridge and set them to grilling. His senses were sizzling like the steaks as he imagined her in the shower, all wet and slick, those tantalizing breasts all soapy as she washed her delectable body. Back inside, he shucked two ears of corn and got them into the water, then made a salad.

He heard her footsteps on the stairs, then moments later she appeared in the kitchen.

"Is there anything I can do to help?"

He poured her a glass of wine. "Sip and sit," he said as he handed her the wineglass and went out onto the patio awash with moonlight. Year-round, San Diego's weather was mild, and it was so beautiful in September. Several trees in his yard were adding orange and red to the landscape, along with the colorful and fragrant sage.

The only sound was the rustle of leaves, and something scurried through the underbrush, probably a gecko, the only sign of life.

"This is beautiful, Russell. You've made a nice life for yourself."

He wished he could say he was content, but it would be much more fulfilling if he had someone to share it with.

"Yeah, the chain has taken off. It's been a surprise to me. I had no idea I was any type of businessman until I set my mind to it." He had shocked the hell out of himself. Rockface was thriving, and he was enjoying the heck out of managing it. He was even installing a climbing wall in his downtown store.

"Tristan loves working with you. It's so great to see him so happy. Amber is so good for him."

"Speaking of Tristan—"

"I will take care of talking to him." She looked at him, her eyes bleak. "The assassin threatened my family, Russell. I don't need you to run roughshod over me, regardless of what he asked you to do."

"I'm not running *roughshod* over you. But there is safety in pairs, Neve."

She stiffened and choked on her wine. "What?" She stared at him for an instant, almost as if she were paralyzed. "We're not a pair, Russell. That wouldn't be smart for either one of us."

His gaze locked on her face. "I don't back down from a fight when my friends are involved."

Finally, she drew a shaky breath and let it out. "I've got to handle this. Our lives hang in the balance, and it's my fault." She rose and stepped off the patio and stood silhouetted against the light. She paused and took another swallow of wine, then spoke, her voice barely audible. "It's terrifying to think something might happen to my family because of me." She avoided eye contact with him.

"Neve. Please let me help you."

She turned and faced him, giving him a wan smile. "I think I've put enough people in danger for today." Her face ashen and her hands visibly trembling, she came back to the chairs and sat, not a trace of animation in her. She clasped the armrest. Her attempt at a second smile failed.

He had forced himself to remain disengaged during her responses—not allowing any kind of feeling to surface. But now, as she sat there, the vibrancy beaten right out of her, he experienced a rush of rage. She was out of her element here, wouldn't confide in him, which hurt, and her life was in danger.

He'd accidentally killed for her. But if she was threatened again, he would have no problem deliberately killing to keep her safe.

He would be watching her from now on, and eventually he'd find out what was going on.

After dinner, she said her good-night and went to turn in. At the bottom of the stairs, she said unevenly, "I appreciate everything you've done, but I'm okay. I'll handle things from now on."

Then she turned and went up the stairs, and Rock watched her go, his lungs suddenly so tight it was impossible to get air into them.

A rush of emotion jammed up in his chest, and he returned to the kitchen and poured himself a shot of whiskey. He went back out to the patio, staring at the expensively designed landscape. He'd never sleep with her trapped in his head, not without help. Damn her and her pride. He really didn't have any options here. Neve had put on a brave face. She wouldn't accept his help. There was no way he was going to leave her alone and vulnerable.

So that only gave him one alternative.

He was stepping in whether she liked it or not. And it was too damned bad if he trampled on her pride.

Closing his eyes, he took a deep, uneven breath. He had let himself get far too close. But it wasn't nearly close enough.

Yeah, the secret he carried would stay buried. It had to. There was too much at stake, and it would complicate and tangle things up way too much.

No one would know he was watching her.

No one would ever know that he was deeply in love with her.

Chapter 3

Neve settled into Russell's big bed, the scent of him engulfing her until she could barely breathe, let alone sleep. She picked up her laptop and booted it up. She was sick with dread and worry about what that man had said. She'd thought about nothing else since he'd told her the White Falcon wanted revenge and was gunning for her family. She had to discover what this threat was and neutralize it.

Russell couldn't understand how she'd had to fight tooth and nail in her family to be taken seriously. When she'd gone into the coast guard's swimmer rescue program, she was bucking some pretty big odds. Eighteen weeks of relentless physical punishment for a chance to become one of the elite and most fearless first responders on earth. Such a small percentage of men ever finished, so a woman had to be stronger, faster and better to compete. Out of a class of fifteen with only two female candidates, she was the only woman in her graduating class of three. She'd had to prove herself over and over, and she wasn't about to let down her guard now. Staying strong was what was important in both her professional life and her personal life. She couldn't lean on anyone and always had to remain strong.

She rescued people. She didn't need rescuing.

Russell was just being his protective self. Part of her wanted to let him in, all the way in, but that would make her too susceptible to his charms. She had already somehow gotten her whole family into danger. She wasn't going to add Russell to the mix, too. She would figure this out. This was her problem, not his.

She typed the words *White Falcon* into Google. The results that came back were predictable. Images for white falcons that surprised her. She had no idea there were albino ones. But nothing that would pose a threat to her or her family.

Opening up her email, she quickly typed:

marcodecruz@zmail.com
Hello, Marco, I need to talk to you urgently. Let me know when I can call you.
Neve

She pressed Send and closed the laptop. If anyone knew any information about this White Falcon, Marco would. She'd hauled him and three DEA agents out of the Pacific when one of their drug busts on the sea had gone south when she'd been assigned to a cutter. Marco had told her he was her forever friend. Panamanian, a slick street fighter and a steadfast ally of the DEA, he told her he'd owed her his life and for her to let him know when he could repay her.

She lay down in the dark and closed her eyes, but all she could see was Russell in his full, naked glory, sporting that impressive erection. That image was burned into her brain, and it just got that much harder to get him off her mind.

But he was just like her father. He didn't believe in her abilities, didn't give her the benefit of the doubt. He'd saved her life tonight, and she felt a twinge of remorse for not at least thanking him, but she couldn't seem to get the words past her tight throat.

She was grateful and she was crazy about the man, but she wasn't going to get tangled up with him for many reasons, no matter how beautiful he was.

Oh, God, the man was beautiful.

She fell asleep and spent the night dreaming about white falcons with malevolent red eyes fluttering outside her window, and toward dawn a very erotic, wholly arousing dream of Russell in his bed with her and the sheets pulled off her naked, writhing body, his head between her legs, giving her an intense amount of pleasure.

She woke up throbbing.

As the room brightened into day, she pushed off the covers, dressing carefully, her shoulder stiff and aching, the skin around her cuts tight and painful. In the mirror, she saw that she had a black eye, and bruises on her arms and torso where her attacker had held her and kicked her. She leaned against the bathroom sink for a moment to get control. All the times that she'd ever been hurt had been job related. Most of her feelings after those incidents were about failure stuffed into a heavy layer of guilt and self-recrimination.

But she'd been attacked by someone who'd wanted to end her life, and she didn't know why. A killer who was associated with an unknown someone she didn't know how to fight. The uncertainty and the fear overwhelmed her for a moment. She dropped her head, and with quick anxious breaths breathed carefully around the panic.

This threat wasn't just against her. It was against her whole family. Thane, her oldest brother: tough, opinionated, an alpha male, teacher and naval hero. Tristan, also a hero, decorated, another alpha and so strong and capable. Nova, her twin; they were eerily connected, like two beating hearts joined as one. Smart, sarcastic, bold and beautiful, a crack helicopter pilot who had saved countless lives. And her mother, who had given her Inuit blood and features, born of a proud and rich culture of hardship and survival that ran through her blood and was embedded in her bones. A sweet, happy homemaker, a huge support for her family and her husband who was away so much. Then, her father, big bear of a man who had shaped her into the woman she was today, a Bering Sea fisherman, stoic, honest to a fault, tight-lipped and with integrity to spare. So damned good at what he did, braving the elements and the odds year in and year out to support his family. She loved them all, and her throat got tight just at the thought of losing any of them. She squeezed her eyes closed and maintained her composure only by sheer, stubborn will.

She would prove that she could do this, save her family just as she'd been forced most of her life to prove herself. First on her father's fishing boat, then the challenge of the coast guard, one she welcomed. She could blame her dad for her need to strive for excellence. Now her mettle would be tested again and she wouldn't fail. Get to the task first and complete it with dazzling competency. She didn't need to ask for assistance; it made her feel helpless in the process.

She opened Russell's medicine chest, searched around, carefully avoiding the box of condoms, and found ibuprofen. Popping three pills, she washed them down with a swallow of water from the tap.

Packing her bag, she walked out of Russell's bedroom, pushing away all her thoughts about him, even as she felt a twinge of jealousy as to who he was using those condoms on. Then that made her think of his gorgeous body again. She swore softly at the way that image made her knees weak. It was necessary to get her head screwed on right.

Neve entered his bright and spacious kitchen. The aroma of something hot and cinnamony, mingled with the smell of freshly brewed coffee, made her mouth water. Seeing his kitchen in the bright light of day, she was suddenly floored. There were splashes of bright colors, lush, healthy plants everywhere and the granite countertops were as neat and inspection-ready as any marine barracks. Even the whimsical ceramic frog near the phone was full of organized pens and pencils. The stainless-steel fridge sported an array of Post-it-notes, flyers, Chinese food and pizza menus and what looked like…childish artwork.

She hadn't noticed any of this last night because she'd been too mired in her own reactions and thoughts from the afternoon's events.

She got closer to the drawings and smiled at the depictions of cars and robots. She read the name at the bottom: "Georgie," penned in colorful crayon. That had to be the artist. Her heart melted as she thought that there was someone in Russell's life named Georgie who proudly drew for him.

Curiosity gave her a moment's reprieve from her heavy thoughts of death and Panamanian hit men with wing tattoos.

The door leading to the garage opened, and she heard the sound of footsteps and the opening and closing of a door. Then Russell, glistening and bare-chested with only a pair of snug black running shorts on, his well-muscled thighs bulging beneath the hems, came into the kitchen.

He stopped and smiled and said, "Good morning."

Wow, the man had a knockout smile, and those shorts left very little to the imagination. She whipped her eyes back up to his only to meet his deep blue gaze and see the glint of knowledge that said he knew what she was looking at and thinking about.

He cleared his throat and sidled by her as the timer on the stove started chiming. Donning oven mitts, he opened the oven, pulled out what looked like coffee cake and shut it, setting the pan on the stove.

"Perfect timing," he stated.

"That looks good enough to eat."

He raised a brow. "Think a jarhead can't cook?"

"No, just one more thing I didn't know about you."

"There are a lot of things you don't know about me," he said cryptically, his voice a husky rasp, hitting her hard where it hurt. Damn the man. "My mom made sure both Dex and I knew the basics. This is her recipe, and I loved waking up to this smell."

"Yeah, it's wonderful how smells bring back good memories."

"And bad, sometimes," he said.

She nodded. Too true.

She was relieved when he ran upstairs and took a shower; they ate what turned out to be the most delicious coffee cake, and he took her home. He insisted on walking her up to her apartment, but she just needed him to go. The new door was in place, thanks to Dex. She went inside but stopped Russell at the threshold.

"Neve—"

"I'll be fine. You get back to your life. I'm sure you're very busy."

"I'm always here for you," he said.

She closed the door and leaned against it, her eyes darting around her apartment. Just as she set down her purse and dropped her bag in her bedroom, her cell phone rang.

"Chica," Marco said when she answered. *"¿Qué pasa,* beautiful?"

"Marco, thank you for calling."

"Yeah, sure. Anything for you, *chica*. What's so *urgente*? Marco is here to help."

She took a breath. "I was attacked last night."

"Santa mierda! You are okay?"

"Yes, thanks. I am, but the man who tried to kill me is dead, and I don't know why he targeted me."

"This is very upsetting to me. Why do you think I can help?"

"He spoke Panamanian Spanish."

"What did this *hijo de puta* say?"

"That I couldn't escape, that he would have revenge against my whole family."

"¡Basta ya! Tell me all the details. Exactly what he said."

"Marco, he mentioned the White Falcon. Does that mean anything to you?"

There was utter silence on the other end of the line, ominous. The skin on the back of Neve's neck prickled.

"Dios mío." His breath hissed out, and she bet he was making the sign of the cross. He always did that after that phrase. "Are you sure that is what he said. *El Halcón Blanco?*"

"Yes. I'm sure. What does it mean, Marco? Tell me straight. Don't hold anything back."

"Muy, muy dangerous. *Muy* ruthless. Did this hombre have a wing tattoo on his neck?"

"Yes."

"Dios mío, chica. You must get protection for you and your family. *Rápidamente.* This White Falcon is a gunrunner, Egyptian-born, very bad. Did you receive a plain envelope with the line 'Death will come for you on swift wings'?"

"Yes."

"Esto es malo. This is bad. He will never stop coming after you."

"Why? I have no idea what he thinks I've done to him."

"What has happened recently in your life? Have you been to Panama or Colombia?"

"No. I broke my collarbone trying to save three people from a terrible storm off the coast about ten weeks ago. I haven't been anywhere."

"These people. What are their names?"

"Just a minute." She went to her laptop and opened it up navigating to the official report. "Cadoc, Galina and Tai—"

"Saad?"

The surname jumped off the page at her. "Yes."

"*Santa Madre de Dios!* That is…*Dios*…was his brother and two sisters. He blames you for not saving them. He must have taken all this time to track you down, and now that he's found you, you are not safe, none of you are safe. But, he will come after you first, there is hope there."

"Marco, do you know where he is?"

"Yes, but only rumors, the Darién Gap, a very bad place. I am ready to help. My life is yours, *bella.*"

Two days later, Neve settled into the conference room in a comfortable seat across from Special Agent Davis Nishida and Special Supervisory Agent Kai Talbot at the NCIS San Diego office. "We've looked into this White Falcon threat, and Agent Nishida has talked to Marco de Cruz. The White Falcon is Ammon Blanco Saad. He changed his name to Set after the deity of disorder and violence. If you ask me, he's an egotistical maniac with visions of grandeur, and that makes any slight toward him personal. That is why he is coming after you, even after you attempted to save his family. He's part Egyptian, part Colombian, and an international gunrunner who is married to Lizeth Maria Sosa Torres de Set. She's the daughter of Raúl Torres," Kai said. "His wife's crest is a falcon. Combined with his Colombian mother's last name, that's where he gets the moniker.

"His wife is one of the most powerful people in the Latin drug world, leading one of the largest trafficking rings in Central America. She's transporting thousands of pounds of cocaine into the US and is on the DEA's watch list. But her money laundering has her marked by the US Treasury's Office of Foreign Assets Control, or OFAC."

"What does this all mean?" Neve asked, her stomach lurching, dread settling in the pit of her belly.

"The hitter was identified as Juan Ramos, assassin for hire and a dead end. We have no hard evidence that Set put a hit out on you or was involved in the attempt on your life. I think his motive is clear. He is blaming you for the deaths of his brother and sisters."

"What happened during that rescue, Neve, so we're all aware?" Agent Nishida asked.

"I have a copy of the report." She handed them a sheaf of papers.

She swallowed back her guilt and discomfort. Retelling the story wasn't going to be easy. "It was off the coast during a terrible storm. I had an argument with the pilot. He didn't want to risk me or the crew, but I argued that I could handle it."

That storm spooked her. It reminded her of what her father used to have to fight against while crabbing and the pressure of being a woman rescue swimmer. She hadn't been sure the pilot's bias against her winching down to the survivors didn't have to do with her being female. She didn't want those people to die because of some sexist pilot.

"The wind took the helicopter and me with it like a feather in the breeze. I slammed against the side and fractured my collarbone, but I didn't quite realize it at the time.

"They winched me to the surface, and one of the survivors was already floating face-down. I tried to get her in the basket first, hoping that they could revive her, but her brother panicked and took me under. The seas were so rough, and I was fighting him for my life. I almost drowned and my arm was going numb. But I was able to get away from him. After that, I lost track of him in the waves. His body was recovered an hour later, but the sister who had already drowned…they never found her. His other sister had severe hypothermia. She didn't make it."

What had happened was so tragic. It was unfair to her, but he wanted to blame someone and grief affected people differently.

"We're opening an investigation and will actively pursue this, but at this time we don't even know where they are hiding," Agent Nishida said, dragging her out of her thoughts.

"The Darién Gap. Marco told me that's where they have a compound." She knew of the stretch of wilderness; she'd even hiked it once. She'd worked the Panamanian waters on the California-based Coast Guard National Security cutter *Crockett* for two years before her acceptance into the swimmer rescue program, nabbing drug runners in narco-submarines, self-propelled semi-submersibles that stuck close to the coastline and carried tons of drugs from South America to the US.

"That's also problematic, Neve. The DEA and ATF have an active investigation on them, although they don't know exactly where they are. It's hampered by the dense wilderness, the sheer number of baddies in the area and their ability to hide. Now that we have a definite location, thanks to Marco, we can begin searching, but that could take months. It's a dense area with plenty of obstacles for any kind of force, along with the red tape we have to hurdle to get permission from Panama."

"You're basically telling me there's nothing you can do."

"Other than putting your family members into protective custody, and that is in the works, we'll investigate this hard, joining with the DEA and ATF, working it out. In the meantime, as a precaution preliminary to moving your family members to a safe house, the local police will up the patrols in your area. Have you notified your family?"

"Yes, I contacted them after Marco told me why he thought I might be targeted. My brother Thane is in the hospital from a hit-and-run. The cops don't think it was an accident. My parents are in their early fifties, and Dutch Harbor isn't a hotbed of criminal activity. The local police have indicated they will patrol their home. How can I keep them all safe? I can't wait days, let alone six months."

Kai's face showed her frustration and concern. "We're taking this seriously, Neve. I promise you. It just takes time."

"Thank you for looking into this for me. I appreciate your efforts." She got up from the table and both agents exchanged a glance, one filled with discontent and worry.

"Call us if you need us," Kai said, rising and setting her hand on her arm. Neve nodded and realized that she had to do something. Because she'd been unable to help Set's family, he had targeted her and her whole family for death.

This was now up to her.

As soon as she was out of the building, she put in a call to Marco, now hyperaware of her surroundings. Looking over her shoulder was something she was going to have to do until Set was in custody or dead. When he answered, he said, "What's the plan, *chica*?"

The thought of losing her family, or even her own life, while the DEA and ATF took their time building a case against the White Falcon and his notorious wife made her sick and terrified. There was no way she was going to sit back while this threat was active. There was only one thing she could do. "I'm going to have to kill him before he kills us," she said.

Rock had been trained to kill the enemy. Trained and carried out that mission every day he was in combat. But he'd been shadowing Neve for two days, and what he saw made him realize that she was going on the offensive. She was preparing for battle.

A stone-cold warrior in a body to die for.

Everything she did, every line of her body was poised.

He was pissed because she was gearing up and she was leaving him out. Leaving everyone out. He'd been carrying around all this anger inside him. She had never seen him, not once. He was a ghost that was as close as her shadow. It was what he'd done for a living, and he'd been damn good at it.

Solo. Lone she-wolf.

Well, she was going to get the shock of her life.

Soon.

He'd followed her to the shooting range. He loved watching her as she loaded the M9, chambered a round, then released the magazine and topped it off with another cartridge before loading it back into the pistol. With the spare ammo on her belt and the M9 in her holster, she was ready to go. Thirty shots for ten targets, some stationary, some moving.

In addition to their coast guard training, Tristan had taught both the twins to shoot for protection. But Neve had come here with a different goal in mind—to protect others. Nova was good and Neve was…well, she was even better—a natural, gifted.

She would have made a hell of a sniper.

And damn if that didn't make him hard as a rock.

They would have to go through him first, and he could made himself damn hard to go through.

She took a breath, relaxed, stretched out her right arm and rolled her shoulder, trying, no doubt, to release the kinks she'd gotten from that clavicle break.

From experience, shooting was both a science and a skill, and both were best practiced with cool, calm deliberation.

With smooth, gunslinger quickness, she drew her pistol and started unloading her first magazine. When it was empty, a flawless, tactical reload gave her another fifteen cartridges to run through her M9. *Bam! Bam! Bam!* The 9 mm bullets smacked through the targets, one shot after another. Her second reload found her cleaning up on the moving targets, trying for another shot on each. Three on every target was the goal, as tightly grouped as she could get them.

When she'd run through her ammo, she released the pistol's slide, flipped on the safety, holstered the gun, then pushed the button to inspect her targets.

Then she started the process all over again. That was his cue to get out of there and over to her apartment. Once he was there, he used the extra key Rock insisted she give him just in case.

He went directly to her laptop, which was up and running. After waking it up he checked her email. Sure enough, there were plenty to a guy named Marco de Cruz talking about specs and gear she would need.

As he was reading, he moved his elbow and displaced

the papers near the computer. He found a space-available travel fax for a military transport that would take her to Panama City. Bingo.

From the list of supplies she'd sent, Neve was preparing for war, and he was frustrated and feeling like a big, protective jerk. She was trying to go it alone, but he was determined that she wouldn't. He dialed Austin, and even though he was reluctant to give up the details since this mainly affected Neve, Austin told him everything.

He intended to be there when she engaged the enemy. She might try to keep him out of this, but that's not how a marine handled things.

As the key turned in the lock, he was ready for an all-out war.

He expected nothing less from Neve.

That sweetheart was packing. He just hoped that safety stayed on the M9.

When she saw him, her eyes narrowed and her mouth tightened into a hard line. *"Russell."* Her eyes cut to her laptop and narrowed some more.

"Why don't you sit down and tell me whose ass we're kicking, baby?"

"I don't know what you're talking about."

It was his turn.

"Why do you need so much gear and firepower, and who are you hunting in Panama?"

Her shoulders slumped, and she set down her bag and the gun case. That was a good sign. "Can I get you something to drink? This is going to take a while."

He'd finished his cup of coffee by the time she'd started telling her story. It was only later that he realized she'd been stalling.

He wasn't sure, but the sleepless nights of watching

her like a hawk must be getting to him. He rubbed his temple as a wave of lethargy washed through him.

His eyes felt heavy, and that's when he knew. Damn her.

"Just let me go."

Her voice snagged Rock, those serious black eyes penetrating any wall he put between them. She was damn righteous and determined, and the chips were stacked so high against her, he knew this wouldn't be pretty.

Suddenly, she leaned close to his face, touched his jaw. He clenched it beneath her palm. He was furious.

"I know you think I can't do this on my own, that I need you to handle it. Well, I don't. Just stay out of it."

"I can help," he said slowly. "I've been down there… in the Darién for several missions when I was a marine. I know people."

"I don't want to involve anyone else. Just stay here and let me do what I have to do."

He'd get to her. Drag her back here and sit on her if necessary.

"I'm coming after you."

"Good luck finding me, Russell."

The tenderness in her voice slayed him, had him reaching for something he could never have because it was impossible. Yet he hungered for it.

"I won't need luck," he whispered softly. "I'll find you." His voice thickened, slowed; the drugs slurred his speech and movements. "But that's a dangerous part of the world, Neve. Nasty jungle with disagreeable wildlife, impenetrable swamps, crazed drug traffickers, pissed-off guerrillas, greedy kidnappers, paranoid government police, no marked trails. I'm trained for that kind of thing and you're not. You need me."

She watched his mouth as his brain fogged over, and he wasn't sure if his reaction was the drug in his system or her.

Neve closed the nonexistent gap between them, pressing a fervent, lingering kiss to his cheek.

This kiss was so much more than a goodbye. The woman had more weapons than he thought. She didn't need the M9 to slay him.

Then suddenly she was gone, leaving his heart aching, even as anger slammed through him. Dammit. He could kick his own ass for being an idiot.

"Goodbye, Russell," she said, and moved away as the gray fog turned into a thick, sooty night and took him under.

She tried not to think as she boarded the Navy transport, a no-frills cargo plane with the bare necessities, a metal seat bolted to the side of the aircraft and a seat belt. Traveling this way would keep her off the radar and make it harder for anyone to track her movements. She tried not to remember how she had leaned over Russell, kissed his cheek while he succumbed to her powerful pain meds, dropping into slumber.

Neve swallowed, her heart hurt at having to use such an underhanded way of getting him to butt out.

She'd discovered it wasn't enough.

Neve had to forget about him, forget that she had betrayed him, drugged him and left him behind. It would sap her strength, give him power, and she wanted control in her fist, to exploit her environment, the people in it. She needed an edge, every shred of it.

She knew her path was right, and she'd have to do

this without any help. Get to her enemy first before he got to her.

The plane took off from San Diego airport on time, though in the middle of the trip it was delayed for six long hours, but then finally took off again.

She headed for the entrance to Tocumen International Airport, and as soon as she hit the pavement, Marco drove up in a tricked-out Jeep.

She was at home here in Panama City, having worked here for purposes of training the Panamanian Coast Guard years ago. She loved the city, the friendly and helpful people, and the food. She was apprehensive about tracking down Set, but she was determined to follow through on her own. She put on her game face, the one she used when she had to deploy alone into the nightmare conditions of a raging sea.

As she jumped inside, he said, "Good timing. Nice ride, huh?"

Marco was a bona fide lost boy, one of a gang of them that ran the streets of Panama City when they'd been younger, but were making a difference now that they were older. He had been all of eighteen when she'd first met him, and he was what now…twenty-one? And he was simply beautiful. Silky black hair that tended to curl on the ends, flashing, dreamy dark eyes, a blinding smile, honey-colored skin and a lean, muscular build.

He had the kind of charm and enthusiasm of Peter Pan, the fighting style of Rambo and the chops of a con man on steroids. He was adorable, young still, but adorable.

He drove sedately through the darkened streets of Panama City until they reached his place of business, a small warehouse with his apartment above.

He closed and locked the door behind them, and flicked on the lights.

Marco's adorably admiring gaze gave her a once-over—twice, his smile lighting up his model features. "How's it shaking? You look good, mama."

"No toques," she said and followed her words with a very cool, very steady gaze at him. Her message was clear. No touching.

"Sí, bella." The young man's smile disappeared, but was back in full dazzle when she started to survey the gear laid out.

"Am I all set?" she asked.

"You are locked and loaded, like a badass commando. Bring on the death wings. You're ready."

She was worried about Russell catching up to her in Panama, but Marco guaranteed that he was incognito. That didn't reassure her. Russell was a pit bull—a pissed off pit bull. First and foremost, he was a warrior, a marine through and through, and just because he had "retired" after his name didn't mean squat.

By dawn's early light, she was tooling down the Pan-American Highway in the solid but old pickup truck Marco had provided her, heading toward the Darién Gap, a remote, roadless swath of jungle on the border of Panama and Colombia known as a drug-smuggling corridor between the two countries. She couldn't exactly let down her guard, but as for eluding Russell, that looked like it was in the bag. He had been right, though; this area was dangerous and it rankled that he thought she didn't know what she was walking into. She might be in the coast guard, but she knew what she was doing and had the skills to pull this off. But the area was hell on earth, and she was driving right into it.

Her first obstacle was a police checkpoint in the village of Agua Fría. Access into the area was highly restricted. Marco had been instrumental in getting her cover as a missionary nun. Her forged papers and her Inuit coloring made it easy for her to pass as a native and local. She was fluent in the language, as well, so she breezed easily through the first checkpoint. Her main destination was Yaviza, a small town that marked the break in the twenty-nine thousand miles of the Pan-American Highway. Thirty miles from the Colombian border, it was known as a haven for smugglers, prostitutes and fugitives.

Once she arrived at Yaviza, she got out of the beat-up pickup and locked the doors. She'd get a quick refreshment and come back and load up to move out. Crossing a narrow pedestrian bridge spanning the Chucunaque River, she entered the town and immediately went to a place that resembled a cantina with hopes of getting a quick meal.

The interior was rustic and dark, and she went up to the bar.

"What will you have?"

She asked for a menu and ordered fried fish and rice with a Balboa beer to wash it down.

Before she could turn away and find a table, a deep, male voice rasped in her ear. "Hello, Neve."

She whirled to find Russell, still pissed off and looking like a rabid pit bull off the leash.

Dios mío.

Chapter 4

"Russell," she said a little breathlessly, as if she'd just been kissing him. But she must have miscalculated how much of her pain meds would keep him under. After all, a pill designed for a five-eight woman who weighed no more than 120 pounds soaking wet, couldn't keep down a six-five, 240-pound man.

According to her fax he'd found while snooping, she'd taken a military transport which was notorious for delays. His commercial jet down to Panama was much quicker. He knew she was going to the Darién Gap from all her computer research; therefore, she had to show up in Yaviza sooner or later. With the thick growth of the Gap, she would have to trek it on foot, and this was the end of the highway.

He grabbed her by the arm and dragged her toward the rooms in the back. Too many eyes on them. Hauling her into the room he'd paid for, he said, his voice low and lethal, "That was underhanded and beneath you to drug me like that." He dragged her up against him, his hands around her upper arms, his face tight, his voice snapping with energy and defiance. "What is it with you? You let everyone else know what's going on but me."

"Yes, and still here you are," she said, struggling against him, but he was too afraid to let her go. With anger eating away at him, he swore savagely, so damned mad he could barely see straight. If there had been a bar fight handy, he would be pummeling people right now.

"Can't you understand that being around me is dangerous?" she shouted, then glared at him. Splotches of color bloomed in her cheeks, but her eyes were still guarded and her mouth pinched at the corners. "I have a hit out on me." She took a deep unsteady breath. "I can't stand by while my family is murdered. No one can guarantee that Ammon Set will be caught and brought to justice, and even if he is…he can still make his plans from prison. He's not going to rest until me and my family are dead. He has to be neutralized," she whispered.

His expression grim, Rock wouldn't give an inch. He held her gaze, trying to rein in his anger. "Neve, you don't have to do this alone. I'm a marine, for Christ's sake. We are stronger as a pair watching each other's back," he growled. Then he released a breath, real fear unfolding in him, his voice going soft and husky. "If anything happened to you…how do you think I could look Tristan in the eye?" He shook her slightly. "It would destroy me." It was true. He would never be able to face Tristan again or look at himself in the mirror if he left her here to fend for herself when he knew he was capable, had already handled these kinds of situations.

She stubbornly shook her head, not giving an inch. Her eyes and voice softened, and she looked resigned. "Russell, don't. Please just go back to San Diego. I can handle this on my own."

His anger spiked again, pushing out those tender feelings and replacing them with fear for her safety, making him almost crazy with worry that she was going to get herself killed. "*We* can handle this even better! I'm all you need. I have experience in supplying absurdly accurate intelligence on the enemy and can take them out if need be. Recon and targeted strikes. That's what I trained for and can execute with precision."

She sighed and broke away from him, her arms folding around her as she rubbed her skin. "You don't trust in my abilities," she said, her voice clearly accusatory. She looked away, her eyes sad.

He swore softly, took two steps and tipped her chin up with his finger. "I think your abilities are damned impressive," he said. "But you're a rescue swimmer, Neve, and don't have the kind of experience I have."

She had flawless skin, no makeup. Her face all moist with a sheen of perspiration, she looked younger than she was. Her long, dark hair was pulled back off her face into a tight braid that hung over her shoulder, and the pack she carried looked like it weighed more than she did. She was locked and loaded, and ready to kick ass and take names. She looked up at him, her black, almond-shaped eyes wary and determined.

Then, he lost his train of thought as he stared into that enticing gaze. With her this close, that's when it usually happened. Neve always made things topsy-turvy and mangled, and he'd forget his goals, in life, in love, in everything. She was a force that destroyed him and his training to boot. Following her hadn't been easy, but being here, here with her, was the only place on the planet he could be. Wanted to be... Ah, dammit.

Her breath hitched, and he worked hard at not responding to that little, sexy sound. "There's another reason, and this is the most important. The reason why I drugged you."

"It better be good, 'cause I'm thoroughly pissed off right now, Neve." He had to admire her courage to actually try to lose him. *Him.* Swift, silent, deadly. He might be out of the game, but he was capable of doing this whole damn thing by himself.

She blinked a couple of times, then looked away. "I don't want you involved in something illegal, Russell. That's why I have tried to keep you in the dark. I know you and easily predicted how you would react." She gently covered his wrist and pulled his hand away, then stepped back. "Just *please* go home. I don't want to be the person who makes you a killer. You're not that and never would be." Her voice a soft plea, she went to leave.

His hand shot out and slammed against the wall, blocking her path. He gritted his teeth. Okay, murder wasn't exactly one of the things he'd ever contemplated doing. At least, not in the sense of the cold-blooded type. He was a warrior and had killed men on the battlefield. He was quite aware this was different.

"There's only one catch, sweetheart. This guy is gunning for you. As far as I'm concerned, this is a long-range case of self-protection, not premeditated, cold-blooded murder." She covered her face and took a deep, irritated breath. "I have no qualms about killing him for you. I won't hesitate a millisecond to put him down if it will keep you and your family safe."

"That's just it. I don't want you to have to kill him for me. That's my mission. To take him down. He's left me no choice, Russell. This is not something I decided on lightly. I just don't want to be responsible for you having to do this…for me."

"I'll sleep just fine at night. Don't worry about that." He would. He didn't dwell on combat or the things that had to be done. Ammon Set wouldn't even remain in his memory banks. He'd purge the man from them, just as he took his life to protect this beautiful, courageous, foolish woman and his best friend, business partner and her brother Tristan, his fiancée, Amber, her sister, Nova, her brother Thane and their parents. There was too much at stake here for her to be worried about him.

She was determined not to be swayed, and it made his heart roll over that this was about him. She was refusing his help because she had some skewed notion that she was protecting his integrity or whatever. He was shameless where Neve was concerned.

"My mind is made up," she said, and tried to go under his arm. He reacted by stepping into her and pressing her up against the wall. Her startled expression made him realize that she hadn't expected him to use physical force on her.

"You're not going anywhere without me. My mind is made up, too." Then his stupid man parts started realizing that he was up against all the softness of her body, and he remembered the teasing and tantalizing view of that plump breast and the dark, puckered nipple, and heat balled up its fiery fist and punched him right in the gut and groin.

For a moment suspended in time, they stared at each other; everything he was feeling was obviously on his stupid face because she looked just as aroused as he was. Then the accusation he vowed he wouldn't say to her because it was just too damn volatile popped out of his mouth without so much as a by your leave. "You ripped out my heart when you left me like that," he said, his voice a low rasp.

She went still, then she drew a deep, shuddering breath. "I shouldn't have, but I didn't want you involved. It was possible I wouldn't ever see you again and…I care about you, you big jerk. Don't make this harder than it already is."

The stark truth was in her eyes, and the whole of him had wanted her for so long. To see her confess to the same need made him almost crazy. He'd held back because he was quite aware that Neve had no intention of staying in one place. Unlike him, she wanted to travel and see the world, go onto the next challenge. She wanted the wide-open spaces, and he wanted the white picket fence and the little rug rats. He wanted his children to understand permanency and roots. He wanted to give them a place to grow, learn and live without dragging them to the next place, fish out of water, having to make friends all over again. He'd done that, and he had vowed he wouldn't put his children through it. He had a business and was grounded in San Diego, a city he loved. She was only visiting until her orders changed.

He and Neve were out of sync with what they wanted in their lives, but when their bodies touched, when their gazes met, it was almost uncontrollable.

"We can't—" he rasped out.

"I know."

"Because you want more?" he asked, seeing the knowledge in her eyes, shattering his reason.

His hand cupped the back of her head, her hair silky against his palm. She closed her eyes and nodded.

Shifting so she was flat against him, he shut his eyes, the rush of sensation so intense that he had to grit his teeth and his breathing constricted. She moved, sending a shock wave of heat through him, and he clutched her head, the feel of her almost too much to handle.

His fingers snagging in her hair, he forced himself to remain immobile. Every muscle in his body demanded that he move, and his shredded nerve endings sent raw need shooting painfully through him. She was quite aware what she was doing to him.

It took him some time, but he was able to get himself under control, and he could finally breathe without it nearly killing him. Releasing a shaky sigh, he adjusted his hold on her, drawing her deeper into his embrace, his lungs constricting.

Finding out her reaction to him was as strong as his reaction to her made everything much more intense and complicated. He pressed her head against him as she shrugged out of the pack, her arms coming around him.

Knowing that this was going to go downhill fast if he didn't let her go, he tried to release her, but her arms were too tight around him, the fullness in his chest expanding. She was so damned beautiful and he'd wanted her for so damn long. He wasn't sure how they were going to get out of this and not end up with pain they both didn't need or want.

He was so close to the edge that it wouldn't take a whole hell of a lot to push him over. The feel of her and scent of her drove him closer; he wanted her naked body all over him.

Unable to control the urge, he widened his stance a

little, pressing her against the hard ridge of his flesh, turning his face against her neck and kissing the soft skin. He wanted her to have the presence of mind to push him away.

But she didn't. Instead, she curled her hands into his shirt and navigated him backward until the back of his legs were against the bed; then he was on top of it and she was on top of him. She made a low, desperate sound and twisted her head, her mouth suddenly hot and urgent against his. The bolt of pure, raw sensation knocked the wind right out of him. Her hand tightened around his wrist as she drew it over his head. He shuddered and widened his mouth against hers, feeding on the desperation that poured back and forth between them. She made another wild sound and clutched at him, the movement welding their bodies together like two halves of a whole, and he nearly lost it right then. Vaguely aware there was a tightness around his wrist even as her hand moved, he got lost in the exquisite taste of her, his heart pounding hard with desire and adrenaline.

"I'm so sorry, Russell," she whispered like a prayer against his mouth. "So sorry."

Then he heard a distinctive snick and she was suddenly gone.

When he came to his senses, she was standing over him, and he was handcuffed to the bed.

"What the hell!" he swore, and wanted to kick himself all over again for falling for her seductive trap. He pulled at the cuff, but it was secure against the metal frame of the bed. "Let me go," he snarled.

She backed up; whether from the raw rage on his face or the lethal sound of his voice, he didn't know or care.

"No," she said, bending and slipping into the pack.

"I'm going to kill Ammon Set, and that means if I'm caught, I'm dead. I can't ask you to put your life on the line and commit a highly illegal act for me." She adjusted the straps and then said, "Go back. Don't follow me." Her voice was weary and firm.

She turned away, and he couldn't believe this. She was actually leaving him behind again. His fury mixed in with a healthy dose of panic. For the first time in his adult life, he was terrified, and he'd been in some tight, harrowing spots in the marines, but nothing compared to this. He jerked at the cuff, the metal singing with the force of the pull. "Neve!"

She turned to face him. "Russell, *please…*"

She looked at him as if she was ready for a fight, and he was prepared to give her one.

"I want to talk to you."

"Well, I don't want to talk to you."

His jaw set in determination, he snarled, "Too bad, sweetheart. We're going to talk anyway."

Folding her arms in a defensive stance, she stared at him, her voice taut. "Say what you have to say because I'm not sticking around very damned long."

His breath released in an exasperated sigh, then he said, "You want to know what you're getting yourself into? The Darién is an extremely dangerous place. It's probably the most dangerous place in the Western Hemisphere, most definitely in Colombia. The Darién is filled with so many ways to die—if you're not kidnapped and held for ransom. There's tough, nasty jungle to navigate, with caiman, lizards, jaguars, anacondas, poisonous snakes and frogs, and scorpions, not to mention some of the plant life is lethal. Impenetrable swamps that have to be navigated, drug traffickers who will kill you on sight, Ejército de Libertad guerrillas, unreasonable, trigger-happy government troops and no marked trails. You need me! Now, let me go and I'll forget about this."

A muscle twitched in her jaw, and she drew another deep breath. "You're trying to scare me."

"I'm freaking dead serious."

She narrowed her eyes, a warning glint appearing. She shook her head and took a step back.

"Dammit, Neve. Use your head." He rattled the cuff again, drawing it tight.

"Forget it," she said, looking at him, her expression bleak. "Stay safe." Her voice broke, and she cleared her throat and squared her shoulders, once again adjusting the pack. "I meant it when I said not to follow me."

"Neve!" he called as the door closed behind her. Frantically he shoved off the side of the bed closest to the wall, jerking wildly at the cuff. He had to get free. *Geezus!* He was going to lose her, and that would effectively be the end of him, too. If he lost her, if she died out there because he'd been too lost in his desire for her and had let down his guard *again*, he would never, ever be able to forgive himself.

He might as well put a bullet in his head.

Even as she exited the cantina and followed the bartender's instructions on finding Brayan Muñoz, a guide the bartender said would take her up the river in a dugout canoe called a piragua for a five-hour trip to Boca de Cupé, a remote jungle village, she couldn't get Russell's desperate voice out of her mind. If he'd been angry before, he was now way past that and into fury. She pushed that from her mind and his order for her to come back and release him. The agitated way he'd called her name, limed with a ferocity that was palatable.

She would pose as a Panamanian nun and use Boca de Cupé as her base of operations as she hoofed it into the jungle and searched for her nemesis. It was rumored that Ammon Set had a compound in the surrounding area.

She didn't want Russell involved, though she acknowledged that it would have been comforting to have him covering her back. But if he got hurt, that would destroy her. And she'd have more guilt on her conscience on top of the guilt she already felt for failing to rescue Set's family members. She had to make this right, protect her family.

Neve had noted the intense rage that hadn't yet been banked or neutralized. Dammit, she didn't need Russell in this state, and she regretted terribly what she'd had to do back in her apartment in San Diego, and she regretted what she had done here to him even more. But he gave her no choice.

She disliked hurting his feelings, since the anger was more about that than it was about her being stubborn. He wanted her to lean on him, but she couldn't do that and keep her conscience clear.

She had failed to save Set's family. She wasn't crazy about having to kill a man in cold blood, but now he was threatening her family. That rescue, the loss of those people, weighed heavily on her. The storm had been a factor, but she knew deep down she had been too sensitive and had argued for the rescue in light of the storm's ferocity. She'd been reprimanded and told to rethink her commitment to the coast guard while she healed from the injury she'd sustained. Her commander indicated that being a team member was all about considering everyone involved.

That's what Russell had wanted, too, but she couldn't do it.

She approached the "docks," using that term loosely as they were nothing but a concrete platform and a stretch of dirt embankment with some wooden stairs and skinny boats floating along the shoreline. Produce was being unloaded, mainly plantains, yucca, cassava and manioc roots. She stopped at a vendor and bought a slice of watermelon and a couple of oranges to augment her meager stash. Spotting a man in a blue tank top and brown shorts, she approached him and said in Spanish, "Are you Mr. Brayan Muñoz?" He nodded and smiled, showing some gaps and yellow teeth. He had hair as black as her own, was about two inches shorter and had dark brown skin. His almost-black eyes went over her in a quick inspection, lingering for just a quick moment on her full lips.

"Sister Mary Agnes," Neve said, smiling back. "I would like to take passage to Boca de Cupé."

"That is no problem, Sister. Just call me Bray," he said, gesturing to a twenty-five-foot-long boat with gas and supplies. They would be heading up the Tuira River.

It was Neve's understanding that there would be security checkpoints at El Real and Vista Alegre, and she'd have to contend with SENAFRONT, Panama's elite border security force, which had a strong presence in much of the region.

She pulled off her pack and Bray took it, the air breezing across her back, cool against her moist shirt as he assisted her into the piragua. He stepped in after her, handing her the pack, which she stowed in the middle, taking the forward-facing seat.

When he finally pulled out onto the water after firing up the outboard motor, the simple craft cut into the silty brown water and the wet, humid air.

On either side of her, the forest was a blanket of rolling green, the air thin and the jungle so dense she could barely see a few feet beyond the banks. Each of the buildings had straw roofs common to the Emberá people; they were elevated on thick poles at the edge of the river.

Local natives paddled their own piraguas chock full of the chief crop of the region—plantains.

Behind her, Bray's eyes focused straight ahead, and he adjusted his course to miss a very large, black caiman in the water. Neve looked down at it as they passed. All she could think was that this large, scary gator was basically a dinosaur that never got the extinction memo.

Neve caught her breath at the sight of a beautiful heron with a turquoise beak, yellow breast and light gray wings, along with several of a different species that were larger and a darker gray.

Later they had to stop for a military checkpoint. While there, she ate lunch—lentils and rice—and drank a beer while she waited for the quick approval from SENAFRONT. They searched her pack, but she'd temporarily removed her weapons and stashed them in the waistband of her pants. With the calls of exotic birds and a sighting or two of flashes of color overhead, they continued on and finally made it to El Real, a small village where the border patrol occupied a crude fortification of sandbags and camouflage netting.

Back on the river, the air was so still, the humidity and heat increasing as it slipped into late afternoon. When they were no more than fifteen minutes away from Vista Alegre, Neve felt a rounded barrel in the center of her back.

"I am doing God's work," she murmured in Spanish,

and Bray laughed. "The people of Vista Alegre are expecting me. They need spiritual attention."

"Then you might want to pray for my black soul," he said. "You better hope that you get someone to pay your ransom, Sister, or you'll be meeting God very soon."

He guided the boat to the bank and motioned for her to get out. She hadn't gone two feet when there was another gun in her face. *Great. Just great*, she thought, working at staying calm. The man in front of her grabbed her by the arm, and the odds of overcoming her captors, now that there were four, including Bray, was unlikely. Best to hedge her bets and try to escape later. How she would deal with a ransom demand was another matter. She was well aware they wouldn't pay for her, since she technically didn't really exist with her fake identity, and it was the Catholic church's policy not to pay kidnappers. It was their collective opinion that it only encouraged more abductions. If she fessed up that she was an American, that might be worse. The US government wouldn't be shelling out any dough for her either, per the same policy as the church. She decided to remain mum for the time being, swallowing down her fear and working to remain calm. She was used to tense and dangerous situations. Panicking wasn't going to help and would most likely get her killed.

The man with the gun pulled a burlap sack over her head. He bound her hands behind her back and led her around, chuckling when she stumbled. Kicking and screaming wouldn't do anything but get her smacked around. Besides, by the sound of footsteps, she was getting more outnumbered.

From inside the foul-smelling sack, she heard the voice

of her guide, the backstabbing scum, say she was a nun and they would get a good ransom for her.

Heavy hands forced her to a spot under a tree, the relief from the sun instant and welcome. She swore there were bugs in the sack, but tried to ignore that.

After a brief respite, she was walked, tripping and stumbling, over the jungle floor to a place that smelled of rotting vegetation, sweat and booze. She thought of Russell and his warning. He'd been right; she hadn't expected this to happen. She should have been more vigilant and in the future, once she escaped, she would be.

In the back of her mind, she chanted, *Don't panic, an opportunity for escape will present itself.* She just hoped her escape didn't include white lights and crossing over to another plane of existence.

An engine rumbled, racing nearer, and she flinched at the slide of pebbles and dirt. A door slammed, and a new voice broke past the noise, the command in his tone clear and thundering. He was taking the prisoner.

"This is our captive. Our ransom."

Then she heard a scream, and something hit the ground near her. For a moment she thought Bray was dead. Then he begged for his life. She tipped her head in an effort to pinpoint voices. The mental picture she had wasn't pretty, and through a thin spot in the hood, she glimpsed Bray.

About two seconds later she heard a gunshot.

Chapter 5

The frigid temperatures of a high altitude low opening jump decreased as rapidly as his descent. The land came rushing toward him at 120 mph before he released the chute, abruptly slowing his silent free-fall into the jungle.

Right into drug dealer paradise.

If anyone saw him, he wouldn't feel it when he hit the ground.

As he dropped toward the thick canopy, the wind tore at his black jumpsuit, the fit tight to avoid generating sound, his body rapidly warming as hot air slowed him further. Through his night-vision visor, he saw heat signatures dotting the landscape. Below him was nothing but a dark void accelerating toward his face. It was a personal high. He didn't get excited about many things, but jumping out of a speeding aircraft topped the list.

He aimed for the sweet spot, a small clearing that

would be tough to hit without getting snagged in the dense trees. When his boots brushed the treetops, he pulled the suspension lines of the parachute close, bringing him straight down rapidly.

His feet hit with a jolt that rattled up through his boots, and he tucked and rolled, pulling the black chute with him. He spat out the oxygen mouthpiece, then unhooked his helmet, on one knee, weapon aimed.

He didn't expect company, but preparation was his middle name. Switching the visor to thermal, he surveyed his surroundings, sweating inside the suit and layers of clothes. It showed him nothing but dense forest and a couple of monkeys.

In the dark, he stripped off the jumpsuit, wrapping his jump gear in the chute, then dug a deep hole. Equipment buried, he positioned rocks and foliage over the pile, dusted his hands, then pulled out his GPS and marked the location.

He shifted items in the pockets of his worn black cargo pants, then pulled a khaki shirt over his black T-shirt. He took care with the weapon carrier strapped to his chest and soon had assembled the pieces—a gleaming black death dealer that had put fear into the hearts of the Taliban.

A British-made L115A3 Long Range Rifle weighed roughly fifteen pounds and in his hands was as deadly as anything that roamed this jungle—four-legged and two-legged predators alike. "The Long," as snipers dubbed it, could take out an enemy from nearly a mile away. Silent death.

He'd refreshed his memory of the topographical terrain before leaving the US. Shouldering the rucksack and the rifle, he drew a machete as he started walking.

Even as dawn broke, the rain forest was wet, hot and dark.

Easy in, he thought. Entering the country under the radar kept him invisible, and that's how he expected to remain throughout this op. His passport was stamped, just not in a customs office, but it was real enough that no one would question it. This was drug- and gun-smuggling territory. People didn't ask too many questions.

He had no need to ask any questions.

His mission was locked.

His target clear: Petty Officer Neve Michaels.

He would take out anyone who stood in his way.

Neve opened her eyes to the shadows. She was lying on her side on dirt. Her wrists were still bound behind her back, and when she tried to move her legs, she found that they had tied them, as well.

Her mouth felt as dry as the Sahara, and she worked her jaw where she'd been tapped and it'd been lights out. The walls were moving...and it took her a moment to realize that it was because they were a creamy canvas. She was in a tent.

Then she froze at the movement not far from her face. The dim light didn't reach the shadows, but her breath caught when she saw the small creature moving steadily over the ground.

A scorpion.

She gasped softly and inhaled a little dirt, coughing. The flap of the tent flipped open, and a man walked in. He stepped on the scorpion, crushing it with a sickening, crunching sound beneath his boot.

"Ah, the sister is awake." He crouched. "You don't look like a nun."

The man who had shown up in the Jeep. He'd taken her from Bray. This hadn't been a handoff. Bray and his three-man crew were most likely dead. A petty kidnapper was all he was. But this hombre was a lot more. He wore an olive uniform, and that told her he was part of some type of paramilitary organization. There were a few that liked to make the Darién their hideaway home and conduct illicit activities free of the government's involvement. Even with the SENAFRONT and Colombia's increased interest in cleaning up the Darién, there were still some snakes in the grass.

"We don't wear habits anymore," she stated. She didn't like to feel vulnerable or afraid, or trapped. Right here, right now, that's exactly what she was. Needles of fear traveled up her spine when he released her feet and, playing the part of an innocent, virgin nun, she scrambled up and scurried away from him. Most of the fear on her face didn't need to be faked.

He crowded her and reached out, grasping her braid tightly, fingering the bound strands with a mesmerized look on his face, a look that made every female instinct in her twist with recognition and alarm. "Too beautiful to keep yourself just for God," he said with a leer.

"Please," she pleaded softly. "Release my hands so that I may pray."

"Not just yet. What is your real name? What church are you affiliated with?"

She'd read all about the rebels doing background checks. Thank God she had Marco who was as good with a computer as he was with supplies.

"Mary Agnes is my real name in Christ." Any self-respecting nun would insist that her name was the one bestowed on her when she took her vows. If she gave it up too easily, there would be suspicion. "I was on my way to minister to the indigenous people of the Darién."

He surged forward and grabbed the base of her braid and jerked her head, getting right in her face, the sting of her scalp the least of her worries. "Your birth name, Sister, and stop playing games with me."

"I'm not playing with you. We take new names—"

Screaming in her face, spittle flying, his fingers tightened and she cried out. "Name! Now!"

She jerked back, and not all of it was for show. "Cristina Cabrera." She whispered the alias unsteadily. All she had to do was get free. Play along until then. "I'm not affiliated with a church. My mission is with the Margaret Clift Sisters."

"Is it? Well, you sit tight and hope there is someone out there willing to pay to release you." He looked her up and down. "I find myself hoping there isn't."

He released her and left the tent. She checked her cargo pants pocket, but they had taken her pocketknife. Dammit.

Neve lifted the flap with her boot, then looked out. There was a wall, and she was situated in the middle of a compound. If she was going to get out of here, it would have to be under the cover of night, and luckily the sun was going down. She spied her backpack with all her gear still in it, including the canteen. Had they already searched it and found her weapons? No. If they had, Big, Bad and Ugly would have said something.

She had to get out of here before they discovered that very deadly Glock.

That's all the time she had for recon. Fifteen minutes later, he was back. He strode up to Neve and jerked her away from the corner, dragging her to the middle of the tent. Then he pulled out a very big knife.

She gasped, her heart pounding. But all he did was cut her bonds, then pull out a cell phone. He handed it to her. "You check out. Nice picture and bio on the website. Call your sisterhood and get yourself ransomed or you're mine."

Who the hell did he think he was kidding? He had every intention of taking what he wanted from her. She could see it in his glittering eyes. She dialed Marco. He answered.

"This is Sister Mary Agnes."

"¿Qué pasa?"

She continued in Spanish. "Father Abernathy. I've been kidnapped by…" She looked at her captor.

"Ejército de Libertad."

She repeated it into the phone, and Marco swore softly. "They are ransoming me." She was well aware that most organizations wouldn't pay the requested sum. It was policy, and she was sure they would be sympathetic but firm.

"Tell me what you want me to do, and I am there." His tone was hard.

"No. I understand," she said softly. "There is nothing you can do. You don't pay ransoms. Perhaps you could contact my parents and—"

The kidnapper grabbed the phone and disconnected the call. "Parents?"

"They're wealthy. They will pay you. I promise. Two hundred thousand US dollars."

His eyes lit up, and he thrust the phone at her. "Call them. Make the arrangements."

She took the phone and dialed her apartment. "Mom?"

After she went through the whole spiel to an empty

line, even squeezing out tears, he was satisfied. He took the phone.

"Do your praying, Sister."

This was it. She went to her knees and made the sign of the cross, then pressed her palms together into praying hands and started to whisper under her breath. When he reached out and pulled the ponytail holder out of her hair, she gritted her teeth.

Don't jump the gun.

She continued to mutter and mock cry. When he cupped the back of her head, she twisted and shoved the heel of her hand into his face. He stumbled backward and she was already on her feet, moving as swiftly as possible. If he got those big hands on her or punched her, she was done.

She grabbed his wrist before he could regain his equilibrium, dug her thumb into the apex of his finger and thumb and twisted hard, forcing his arm and elbow backward. Throwing all her weight into it, she lowered him toward the floor, then slammed her knee into the side of his head. He dropped with a grunt right at her feet.

"Maybe you should have been the one to say your prayers," she ground out as she grabbed the knife from the sheath. Unfortunately, there was no gun. She raced to the back of the tent and lifted the flap to look out. It looked clear, and she decided it was now or never. When Big, Bad and Ugly woke up, he was going to take out his humiliation on her.

Slipping under the flap, she crouched and made a direct sprint to her pack. Staying low, she pulled it off the table and backed away, heading toward the wall. The gate would be guarded. As soon as she hit the sun-warmed stucco, she flattened against it. The gate was about thirty feet to her right.

She'd have to find a tree to get over, as there were no handholds. She raced along the wall, thankful for the darkness. As soon as she got to the tree, she shrugged into her pack. Her shoulder and clavicle twinged with her initial pull up, the pack hanging heavy off her shoulders. She had been regaining strength, but she had been laid up the past ten weeks and had lost some power in her upper body.

At the apex of the wall, she heard shouts. *Oh, crap. Time's up.* She was high enough to step onto the wall, which she did without hesitation. Heights didn't bother her. Someone fired; the bullet hit the stucco wall, chipping away a large chunk near her foot. *Oh, major crap.* Before she was a rescue swimmer, she was used to dealing with danger on the water; drug dealers always fired at the coast guard with the intention to kill.

She pushed off, hanging by her fingertips, then she let go so fast, she fell to the ground. Unable to get her legs under her, she landed on her side and for a moment was stunned. The voices were closer, men trying to get up the tree and over the wall. Neve got one knee under her, her shoulder protesting.

Just as she rose, someone grabbed her pack and spun her. She lashed out with the knife, blood arcing and splashing against the stucco wall. He let go with a harsh cry. She took off with crushing speed as men shouted in Spanish to stop her, but there was no gunfire. That gave her an advantage. They weren't trying to kill her, but she wasn't under any such constraints.

She made out frantic shouts as their directions to one another were to flank her. Dear God, they were spreading out. Her only hope was to make it to Bray's boat and pray she had enough of a head start.

She never saw the arm as it whipped out and clotheslined her, hitting her in the chest and knocking the air right out of her. Combined with the lack of oxygen from panicked running, she was stunned and flat out on her back, her pack cushioning her fall, but also adding to the compression of her lungs. For a second she could barely draw breath. She never saw the fist as it connected with her jaw.

Neve woke in a disoriented panic as consciousness came back to her slowly. The pain in her jaw, the same damn place where she'd been hit the first time, making her damn sick of this already, registered with a low dull throbbing.

Cautiously, she opened her eyes and found that she came full circle. Back in the same damn tent, Big, Bad and Ugly's blood still fresh in the dirt. But he was nowhere to be seen. Waiting until her brain stopped dancing in her skull, she shifted and groaned softly. Yeah, that fall had left some bruises, too. But the groan was also a result of realizing that she was trussed up and helpless once again. Her hands were bound in front of her and her ankles immobilized.

She closed her eyes.

She was in some serious trouble.

Neve pushed back at the panic, using techniques she'd perfected from many rough sea rescues that had gone a little shakily. Quietly terrified, her heart pounding, there was no play she could make until someone came for her.

She opened her eyes and caught her breath when the tent flap moved and a set of large shoulders encased in olive green pushed through. The sight of Ugly with a butterfly bandage across his cut and bruised nose sent that panic clawing up her spine.

There was no glitter in his eyes this time. Just stone-cold violence.

He crossed the expanse of the tent and crouched down. As he reached for her T-shirt hem, his quiet calm, even as his eyes seethed with rage, unnerved her completely. He pulled it away from her skin and slipped the knife underneath, slicing the T-shirt open, exposing her bra.

"Please," she whispered, "don't."

He leaned into her face and said, "Pray hard for salvation, Sister."

She closed her eyes again and gritted her teeth as she felt the deadly steel against her skin as the blade slid underneath the tiny bridge of fabric caging her breasts. She wouldn't give him the satisfaction of begging.

Suddenly the knife fell away, and she heard the distinct sound of bone cracking.

When she opened them, a big man, still in shadow, was letting go of a very limp Ugly, his open, dead eyes filling her vision as he hit the ground.

She heard the sound of Shadow Man's boots move in the dirt as he stepped over Ugly's prone body. Looking up into a pair of rage-filled, piercing blue eyes, for a minute, she didn't recognize him.

This man was primed for violence in every line of his body. A marine, a warrior, the man who had just used brute force to save her from something incomprehensibly horrible, and emotionally and physically damaging.

Russell.

Rock.

A slab of carved granite, except lethal and vital.

Ready and able to kill with his bare hands. Dangerous was an understatement.

Even with him fighting mad, looking like he could
break the world in two, all she could think was: *Oh,
thank God.* She was so happy to see him.

But in this instance she realized that she needed Russell. She didn't want to and had fought against it, but
she couldn't deny it. He had been right back there at
Yaviza—they were safer together.

She had a job to do, and she hadn't wanted him to
be any part of it, not if she was to live with herself afterward. She was accustomed to physical danger. That
came from the elements and the circumstances of her
job. But what she had planned for the White Falcon was
nothing short of murder. Cold-blooded, calculated, first-
degree murder.

It felt so wrong to corrupt Russell this way.

He was sweating freely, his T-shirt damp in places.
His biceps thick, gleaming curves of stone. His gaze
traveled over her, and he was all edge, a sharp, dark edge.
In one fluid movement, he stripped off the garment. Her
gaze ran over his heavily muscled torso, more gleaming
delineation that only made her realize how truly powerful Russell was. She had to harden herself against her
own weakness. Sweet Mother of God.

But there was nothing sweet about Russell's body.
Over six feet of raw power and testosterone roped with
muscle and sinew, he was a force to be reckoned with, a
force of destruction evident and eliciting a force of near
unbearable longing—in her.

Something clutched through her, seizing her heartbeat, her muscles. He shouldn't have this much effect on
her, those blue eyes and dark hair, just as much a threat

as his body. She just had to remind herself that he was as binding as the bonds around her hands and feet.

She opened her mouth.

Swearing viciously, the handcuffs dangling from his wrist, he dragged her up against him by her bound hands and in a fierce whisper said, "*Don't* freaking talk, Neve. *Don't* say a *friggin'* word."

The words died before they were even uttered. He was…furious, and she felt sorry for any members of the EDL who got in his way tonight.

The KA-BAR he'd used to slit her bonds still had blood on it, and she swallowed hard. He kept his hand around her wrist as if she was going to bolt. With one swift move he had her ruined T-shirt off, then, like a child, he slipped his over her head, leaving her to push her arms through.

He knelt then, spitting into his hands and mixing it with the dirt. He smeared the mud all over every exposed, hard-packed inch of him.

Through all this, his face was impassive, yet in his dead-calm eyes, Neve saw the intense rage, and the inevitable grew in her mind, tearing at her composure. He wouldn't forgive her, and worse yet, didn't trust her, and that hurt more than she had ever thought it would.

Rising, keeping his gun hand free, he gripped her hand tightly. The warmth of it seeped into her, and she hated it even more that she'd betrayed him not only once but twice. What he still didn't obviously get was that she was trying to protect him.

"Stay close to me." His voice snapped, even in a low tone, something clearly warring inside him. As if he wanted to say something but couldn't spare the time.

Neve's gaze moved rapidly over the compound, her

senses jumping when they silently slipped from the back of the tent. His attention was honed to a keen edge, every muscle of his half-naked body in stark relief.

There were bodies lying everywhere, blood pooled on the ground beneath each. Now she knew why he'd been so quiet and why there were bloodstains on the knife.

A chill rippled over her. This was a side of Russell that Neve had never seen. She'd only seen him interact with Tristan in a close and teasing manner, knew him as the smart, successful CEO. Maybe she had been protecting him for nothing.

He was first and foremost a warrior.

He'd probably done things that would definitely shock her.

It brought home how completely she was out of her element.

Rock didn't let go of his fury, used it to fuel him through the darkness of the jungle.

"My pack." She pulled at his hand, but he didn't let go.

"Outside the compound already," he bit out.

He walked to the gate and they slipped through, stepping over dead EDL. He used speed and recklessness and the rush of danger-induced adrenaline to override the fury that threatened to explode with every step he took. With anger eating away at him, he'd sworn savagely, so damned mad he could barely see straight. He'd demolished that bed, ripped off the mattress, fractured the metal frame like an eggshell and slipped the cuff attached to the metal pole right off so it dangled from his wrist. The cantina owner was furious until Rock thrust money at him. He'd rented a boat, then followed until he found the empty one Neve had been riding in. When he'd discovered the guide's head blown off and his three friends in crime, his blood had run cold, then heated until it was boiling. He'd followed the Jeep's tracks right to the compound and executed a recon until he was ready to assault and eliminate any threat to the stubborn back-stabber inside.

She was also kick-ass. She'd obviously put a beat down on the EDL bastard he'd killed in the tent, from the looks of his nose. She'd scaled a tree and slashed at her pursuers. Fought like a demon possessed.

He wasn't going to be proud of her. He wanted to feel nothing but anger. Rock clenched his jaw and increased his pace, stopping only briefly for her to pull out a shirt and change. She handed him his shirt back without a word so he could cover up his gleaming skin. They then shrugged into their packs. All he wanted to do was out-run the suffocating weight of pure, unadulterated fear.

The night was pitch-black, but Rock navigated by the stars, already having reconned this trip back to the water, and his steps were sure-footed.

The air was still and oppressive and hung thickly, though cooler and almost dense to touch, but the night was far from quiet. He listened carefully as he moved, deciphering his own breathing, hers and their rapid footfalls as they disturbed the small creatures around them as they ran. He was keenly aware this part of the world was dangerous, and it had nothing to do with the predators. The plants could kill, sticky and poisonous, and gloves saved him from having to look where he touched.

They were barely breathing hard when they reached the piragua. He pulled her on board and said, "Sit."

"Russell—"

He grabbed her shirtfront and drew her close to his

face. "Don't talk to me, Neve. Not now." Dammit, this woman made him crazy, especially because of what he'd seen when he'd entered that tent. He had the god-awful urge to press his face into her hair, to somehow reassure her, to—Geezus—reassure himself that she really was okay. That EDL bastard hadn't cut her.

He could feel her breath on his skin, soft and shallow and warm. *Damn*.

Her eyes widened, and she just stared at him like she'd never seen him before. That was a true statement because he was still sweating, his hands shaking. Hell. Thinking back to when he'd found the compound and then had seen her climb up over the wall, jump off with the courage of a lion, how she'd been surrounded and fought them off. After that, he'd waited with a roaring in his ears, a thousand miles away, still reeling from the adrenaline rushing through his system, raw emotion searing across his brain.

Then he had to witness that EDL son of a bitch with a knife against Neve's body.

He shook himself. Flashbacking marines were dead marines, and they sure as hell weren't any good to anybody else. He couldn't talk to her now. There was too much—*too much*—to process. He let her go, and she almost tripped over one of the slim benches before she settled down. He didn't even think about what he must look like with the dirt smeared on him, his over-the-top commando attitude and his gruff, demanding voice.

He just needed her not to say a word or he would explode.

He was losing it, and now was *not* the time, and this was *not* the place to be losing anything.

Rock got in, settling both their packs for even weight

distribution, then started up the outboard, the sound loud in the dark night.

As they cut through the gloomy brown water, he scanned the area while Neve gathered her long, straight dark hair and quickly braided it, then looped it up and secured it with another holder. Movement was sporadic, the flutter of birds moving from branch to branch, monkeys doing the same, and he could see only the tremble of bushes and trees, like short, quick bursts of air. He followed it and saw a dark, slim body rife with sharp, white teeth slide into the water.

He looked behind them. His senses were heightened and pulsing. He wasn't sure if it was the EDL he'd left behind massing to follow and find them that made the hair lift on the back of his neck or some other danger he couldn't see.

The sniper's ability to find what he was looking for was something that was just innate. He'd made a career out of it. He knew the woman had to have hitched a ride upriver from Yaviza and that the small village was rife with untrustworthy lowlifes. He chuckled at the story that some *chica* had handcuffed an unruly guy to a bed, one he demolished and had to pay the hot-under-the-collar cantina owner restitution. He was beginning to like Michaels, a hazard in his line of work.

He watched silently as Russell "Rock" Kaczewski, former marine, handcuffs still dangling from his wrist, dragged the woman—the beautiful, plucky Petty Officer Neve Michaels—along behind him, a fierce protective look contorted his features as he got into her face and she stumbled into the piragua. Even in the dense overgrowth, unseen, the watcher felt Kaczewski's anger singe the air.

Trouble in paradise, my friend?

The sniper rifle slung over his shoulder, he rose as they motored off. They had been unaware of their shadow just steps away. Immediately he followed, sliding down a hillside on the sides of his boots, then hit the ground running, hoping to intercept them when they ditched the boat. Kaczewski couldn't afford to stay on the water. Too open.

But he grinned. It would give them a nice head start.

He pushed himself, his night-vision goggles allowing him to bat at obstructions, jump debris. He grabbed a vine and swung over a creek, hitting the ground, taking a few steps, then stopped.

Closing his eyes for a moment, he listened, separating his breathing and heartbeat from other details—the scent of disturbed earth, the buzz of insects stirred from hiding, monkeys swinging above him. He tipped his head, his gaze sliding over the ground, and he could feel it before he saw the snake wiggle out and shimmy across the undergrowth. The soft whirr of the motor stopped, and he turned in that direction.

"Olly olly oxen free," he murmured, then took off as the jungle swallowed him whole.

Chapter 6

At a sharp bend in the river, the trees and overgrowth thick, Russell steered the canoe to the bank and cut the motor so he didn't have to yell above the noise. Neve looked over her shoulder at him with a frown.

With the motor quiet, the sounds of the jungle took over the night, pitch-black. But with foresight, he'd brought a pair of night-vision goggles. They were neatly tucked into his pack. But with the instincts of a cat and the glow of the moon, he could see well enough.

It was more important they get off the water.

"What are we doing? The boat will be faster."

"And easily visible. I took out a lot of the EDL. They aren't going to let that slide, *Sister.*" He'd overheard what the EDL thug had said to her as he was slicing off her clothes. Posing as a nun. Ha. The only holy he could think of belonged with hell, as in "holy hell."

"It was a good cover," she grumbled.

He bit his tongue, even drew blood. He wasn't going to have an argument with Neve in the middle of a hostile jungle when they were still in the open and exposed on the water. He wanted to yell at her, but that would have to wait. "Don't talk, Neve."

"What is it you want me to do then, Russell?" she asked, her voice sugar sweet when there was nothing but annoyed woman behind every word. "Your wish is my command."

"Sure it is," he said, his tone dry before he could keep his mouth shut. He clenched his jaw, then shook his head when she opened her mouth.

Right now they were up to their armpits in alligators—literally.

They'd pissed off the EDL.

Was she seeing how many crazy, ruthless bastards she could get to come after her? And he had no doubt they were going to be beating every inch of this jungle looking for them.

She already had a whacked-out gunrunner after her. The very reason she'd used to betray him not once, but twice. Used his attraction to her, his concern about her, against him. Drugging him when all he wanted was to help her and then manacling him to that bed. A rush of heat traveled through him in a wave of renewed anger.

Military ops were second nature to him, eliminating the enemy cut-and-dried; even after being out of the marines for five years, he'd never neglected his training. He was still strong and honed. Neve was a damn rescue swimmer. She saved lives, for freak's sake. She didn't go gunning for ruthless bastards who would mow you down one minute and calmly go and eat a sandwich afterward. But she'd done the job. He admired her don't-mess-with-me attitude, though he'd met a few who were far more brutal.

Guns and drugs and thugs—all over the world, those three things were twined together tighter than the knots on a dropped noose. Nowhere thicker than here in the Darién. It was like walking through a live minefield naked with a fever.

The EDL camp had been full of them, and if he hadn't insisted on following her, she would have been hurt bad, as bad as a woman could be hurt. It made him want to jump in the river and wrestle a caiman. He let out a puff of air. She had no idea how...*pissed* he was right now.

"Get your pack on. We're getting off the river. It's not a defensible position and much too exposed."

She reached down angrily and grabbed her pack, sending the narrow canoe rocking.

"Gently," he growled, and she stood still for a moment until the rocking abated, then reached again for her pack.

She slipped her arms through the straps, glaring at him. Well, the feeling was mutual.

He would get through this, cowboyed up, swallowing the hard ball of rage sticking in his throat to lie like a forty-pound weight, ignoring the edge of fear licking at his emotions.

He reached carefully for his own pack and slipped it on without so much as a ripple in the water around them. Then he reached down and pulled the rip cord on the motor and started it again.

He got close to her, the tickle of her hair soft against his cheek. "Get on my back," he said.

She gave him a skeptical look, and he used his thumb

to point above them where a sturdy branch jutted over the water.

As Neve looked up, comprehension dawned on her face, but it was with a dose of apprehension. He nudged her with his hip as he turned and, without saying anything above the roar of the motor, she jumped on his back and wrapped her legs around his waist. He took a moment to get used to the weight of her, which barely registered. With a slight bend in his knees, he exploded out of the canoe, kicking at the motor with his boot as he grasped his hands around the branch.

The dislodged boat wobbled a bit, then motored out from under them until it disappeared around a bend. He could only hope it would go for miles before running aground.

He did a chin-up, his feet dangling above the settling, choppy water.

On cue, creatures slithered into the river with most likely a meal in mind as Rock moved along the branch, hand over hand.

"Oh, God," she said breathlessly. "I really don't want to get wet, and I left my gator knife in my other pants."

He was not going to be amused. He was still too annoyed; nothing had been resolved between them. For all he knew, she could pay lip service to him and then hightail it away from him as soon as an opportunity rose. He wasn't going to take any chances of her fooling him again.

She clung to his wide shoulders, her legs tight around his waist when the sound of cracking coming from his right-hand side splintered the night.

"Grab the branch, my right!"

Neve never hesitated. She loosened her hold and latched

on to the limb, barely getting her delicate hands around the thick bough.

Several caimans floated below them with anticipation, their teeth gleaming in the moonlight. Rock swung himself and hooked his legs on the branch. Then, hanging by his legs, he reached for her, helping her get a better handhold, then a foothold on the branch.

She let out a breath and he grabbed her bag, pushing it into the foliage. He shushed her. They held still, as seconds later two canoes laden with armed men slid over the glassy water. Right past them. They waited until the others were downstream a bit, then Rock moved painfully slow to avoid shaking the trees. Neve was closer to the trunk and started inching her way to the center.

She gripped the trunk of the tree like a lover as Rock worked his way toward her, his size not giving him many options. Then he was in the branches with her.

"Now what?"

"Shimmy, shimmy cocoa puff your way down the trunk. I know you're damn good at that."

She looked at the ground. Several feet below, it was a soggy, watery mess and several yards to higher ground.

"That looks like a surefire ankle break if we're not cautious. I'm up to here on rest and relaxation, so be careful."

If she broke her ankle, this was going to go downhill faster than a speeding locomotive with no brakes.

"That's the watchword, babe. Be careful of our friends at our six who want to have us for dinner."

She whipped to the right. The caimans watched them with dark, beady eyes. "I'd taste really bad," she said. "Much too tough."

"I can't shoot them or we'll have the EDL here, as well as our uninvited guests."

"You really know how to bolster someone's confidence," she said caustically.

He'd instructed her to the point that she looked up at him with pique. "Would you like me to sit on that branch and coach you while you inch down a thick trunk, trying with all your might not to fall to your death? I'd be happy to oblige."

"Got it," he said, his brows shooting up and a smile curving his lips against his will. "Shut the hell up. Proceed, ma'am."

She rolled her eyes. "Ma'am, my ass." Then she looked back at the caimans. "Really, I'm so tough, you'll break a tooth."

He watched as she concentrated, every muscle tense as she worked toward the ground, her gaze flicking to the gators floating in the water a few yards away. When her feet touched the ground, she carefully walked across the soggy earth.

It was his turn, and Rock used his boots and gloved hands to slide down the trunk. He saw that Neve had gotten bogged down, and he waded through the knee-deep, algae-covered vines and water plants to cut her free with the machete.

Wrapping his arm around her narrow waist, he hauled her to higher ground. He didn't pause or let her catch her breath. "The gators are licking their chops."

They ran, pushing through the underbrush, water flowing off their clothes.

Then Rock came to a dead stop as Neve plowed into him.

Every sense was tingling and he turned in a circle,

his eyes trying to penetrate the thick growth around them. Everything in him said there was someone there, watching, listening.

She went to protest, and he covered her mouth, bringing his finger to his lips. Her eyes went wide, and she froze.

Then the moment passed, and Rock had to wonder if he was paranoid. He didn't think so. He grabbed her arm and hacked at the heavy growth with his machete. A mile away from the river, he slowed and signaled her to stop.

"We need to get some rest. Let's make camp over here." He went to a deep, shadowed undergrowth and cleared an area. Creatures rustled the bushes as they vacated the spot. Rock pulled off his pack and delved in for his lightweight two-man tent. He quickly assembled it and then rose. "I'll get some water."

"I've got a lightweight stove and meal packs."

"Me, too. We'll use yours first. I'll be right back."

When he returned, she'd laid both of their sleeping bags at the floor of the tent. He didn't say a word and didn't invite dialogue, but busied himself with purifying enough water for them to drink, then warmed a pre-cooked meal pack—spaghetti and meatballs.

Afterward, they removed their wet boots and socks to allow them to dry, and settled in the enclosed tent. She pulled the holder out of her hair, and it tumbled like a fall of ebony to the middle of her back.

She looked down at his wrist, and when he followed her eyes, he saw she was eyeing the silver handcuff lying on the dark sleeping bag and he said, "Do you have a key for this?"

"Yes. I—"

"No, no conversation, no talking, no nothing, just give me the key," he growled, his jaw firm and tight.

She stared at him a moment and looked like she was going to argue, but he narrowed his eyes and she wearily sighed. Digging in her cargo pants pocket, she held it up to him. He unlocked the manacle and before she could protest, he placed it around her wrist.

"Russell," she huffed, jerking at the cuff.

She'd proved damned resourceful up to now, and he was done with chasing her. All he wanted to do was get to Ammon Set, put a bullet in him and get her out. "Go to sleep, Neve," he said as he opened, then locked the other cuff around the loop of tough nylon at the top of his sixty-pound backpack. "This is just insurance that I know you'll be here in the morning. I'll take the first watch."

She scowled at him, then promptly turned over and gave him her back. Unfortunately, she had to snuggle against him because he was using his rucksack as a pillow. He didn't give a damn as he stared out through the openings in the nylon, effectively keeping out the bugs, but giving him a full clear field of vision. Stretching out his legs, he reached for the weapon he'd pulled out, the deadly sound suppressor already screwed onto the barrel. He set it and a couple magazines of ammo on his lap.

Now that they were safe, he could finally breathe.

After a few moments, his gaze settled on her and traveled over her thick, dark, stick-straight, silky hair. She was a solid, midsize woman, sleek muscle from her shoulders to the rounded muscle of her calf, with luxurious, bold, sloe-black eyes. His hands almost itched with the memory of her tight, firm shape under his palms. He wanted to explore her thoroughly.

He dragged his gaze from her to the jungle, shoring up his guard. No involvement with Tristan's little sister, especially now that she'd made it clear she found it very easy to betray him. He was a fool for even letting his thoughts go down this road. She was determined to see the world, and he was rooted on home soil. Neither one of them would budge.

But that didn't matter. He already had his heart involved here, and it hurt more than he could say that she'd dismissed his help more than once.

His anger had banked into a slow simmer. He wasn't ready to let go of it and let her make her explanations or whatever she'd been about to say when he'd cut her off three times now.

She shifted in her sleep, rolling toward him; her hand went to his chest, her palm lax, and Rock gritted his teeth. It was moments like this when he forgot about all the reasons he shouldn't get involved with her. He snuggled her against him more comfortably. He was still mad at her, but he couldn't seem to help wanting to give her security. He insisted that was all it was, her turning to him to feel safe. It felt too good to have her compact body wrapped around his. It had been a while. Rock hadn't dated anyone recently and convinced himself he just hadn't found anyone he was that interested in, but in reality, it was because he was just too hung up on Neve.

His marriage had been unsatisfying and uneventful. When he received the Dear John email from her, Diane's cheating hadn't even been a blip on his radar. The divorce papers came soon afterward, and he'd actually celebrated by screwing the first woman who was willing, laughing at himself for staying faithful to someone who couldn't care less about him. They weren't compatible, and she hated that he was gone so much. After that, he'd slept around, and that contented him. Then, he'd gone on leave with Tristan and ended up in Dutch Harbor, in his best friend's home where he'd met Neve.

He would never forget it. He'd been up early, so excited about being in Alaska and dying to see the crabbing boat and the town that he couldn't sleep. There had been a noise, the stairs creaking, and he had expected Tristan, but instead, Neve had emerged and taken his breath and his sanity.

Her hair had been really long then, down past her hips. It had been right before she'd enlisted in the coast guard, just twenty and halfway through her college degree. She had ditched schooling for swim fins.

He could remember it like it was yesterday—how she'd met his eyes, so firm and bold, and he'd been lost. So beautifully dark. He wondered if she recalled it like he did.

Neve's hand shifted to his stomach, and Rock's muscles instantly flexed. He moved her hand away from the danger zone and tried not to think about her touching him with nothing between them. He wondered how long he'd last without tasting her again.

The way she'd kissed him told him an aching story. He had much more in mind before he shut those thoughts off.

At least the hard-on she gave him would keep him alert. His eyes went over the handcuffs. People did strange things when they were threatened. He got that, but he couldn't trust her right now.

He perked up as a jaguar padded across his line of vision; the cat had something in its mouth, and he was relieved it had already hunted and killed. He wasn't keen to be on the menu, and a sated predator would leave them alone to a certain extent. He did remember that jaguars were very territorial. "Keep on moving," he murmured, one predator to another as the cat paused and its big gold eyes swung his way. It stared at him for a moment, then turned away and melted into the trees.

Two hours before dawn, he woke her up. He needed to get some sleep. He left her cuffed to his pack, and she wasn't too happy about that, but he didn't argue. Just closed his eyes and went to sleep.

When he woke up, she was still watching the jungle. The pink of dawn blushed across the sky. The sun rose slowly. Giant kapok and rubber trees shadowed the Andean valley, the ground spread with a gray-white mist that wrapped the enormous palms and curled toward the sky, where it hovered, hiding in the jungle canopy.

"I'll get more water," he rasped.

"We should have enough—"

"For a quick wash," he said over his shoulder when he reached the zippered doorway. The air was already steamy as the jungle stirred. He answered nature's call, and when he came back with the water, he set it on the small stove to boil.

She was munching on something and she handed him a packet, which he opened to find granola and dried fruit. Supplementing that with a power bar, he found it took the edge off his hunger. He checked their socks and boots to find them all dry.

He handed over hers. She took them, her gaze trying to connect with his, but he was still not ready to have the kind of conversation that could get much too heated. It was best to leave that for a time when they were much safer and less exposed in the jungle.

With that thought, he froze again, the hair rising on the back of his neck. He finished lacing his boots and rose. "Stay here," he ordered.

"Russell!" she hissed and raised her arm.

He looked around and went to uncuff her. "So help me God, if you're not here—"

"I'm not going anywhere without you." At his skeptical look, she made a pained expression and said, "I promise."

He pocketed both the cuffs and the key, still not exactly trusting her. She could be very easily biding her time before she tried to give him the slip again.

He ghosted out of camp, ignoring the sounds around him, the movement of creatures, the drop of nuts from trees. A small green iguana skittered, then vanished into the thicket. As he crouched and listened, he heard something barely discernable. Someone trying to move stealthily.

Even as he drew his weapon, he got the feeling in his gut, the one that never failed him and now warned him that someone, not something, was out there watching them.

Rock scowled. The land around him was lush and untouched, but as he scoured the jungle floor, he caught something, a piece of disturbed earth near a root of a tree with a direct line to their tent. He could see Neve breaking camp and storing everything away. She was wary and aware of her surroundings. That made him feel a whole heck of a lot better.

His heart sped up. Even as he looked, he could find no signs that there had been a human here, no broken fronds, no footprints, no evidence.

He just knew it in his gut.

Someone was shadowing them, and he had no idea why.

But he did know one thing.

Their shadow was damn good.

Chapter 7

Russell was really starting to get under Neve's skin, and she didn't mean because he was so damn sexy, she thought as she changed her clothes. Russell had changed as well, his discarded clothing from the day before folded on his pack. The fact that he'd kept her from talking to him for all this time rankled. She'd had her reasons, not to mention the fact that she simply wanted to thank him for coming to her rescue.

She wanted to tell the stubborn jerk that she was sorry!

He stalked back into camp, looking like the big, bad marine he was. There were no illusions here. Russell was in full-out assault mode.

"Let's move out."

She checked her weapon and tucked it into the leather holster at the small of her back. "Why did you go out into the jungle?"

Giving her an approving look, his eyes still guarded, he said, "It's nothing." He looked down at his watch, which included a compass. He glanced around and then found his bearings. It was uncanny and…okay, sexy as hell…that he knew exactly where he was going. That was definitely from his training. Suddenly, she was very happy that he was here beside her, even if he was now wary and had actually cuffed her to his backpack.

She could fume all she wanted, but it served Neve right for treating him like she had, even though her motives were protective…of him.

Russell had been clear about conversation, but Neve wanted to clear the air with him.

Trying not to remember what it had been like to wake up all over him, enjoying the feel of a man—no, this man—beneath her was damn hard. It was like sleeping on a rock, though, every inch of him ripped and hard. His nickname was certainly appropriate. He was a rock.

He reached out his hand. "Backstabbing ladies first." His tone was gruff with the anger he still held on to.

She sighed, and her mouth tightened. "You know the way."

When she didn't move, he started walking. "Stay close," he said, and turned away from her.

He climbed over fallen trees, pushed through underbrush, hacked through thickets. They took a rest in the shade of a cropping of granite boulders protruding from the hillside. Red-and-blue macaws were perched on the jagged rock face in little colorful clusters, and as they approached, they shrieked at the invasion. A dozen birds flew into the trees, giving away their position.

They drank some of the purified water and ate another power bar. There was no sign of civilization for miles and miles. She was sure there were villages tucked into the jungle and probably many more baddies out there, especially drug smugglers and kidnappers. She hoped the EDL was far away to the south.

She also couldn't forget Panamanian border guards patrolled the area and also had checkpoints along here.

They might be skeptical she was a nun. They would never believe that Russell was a priest.

She laughed softly at the thought, and he turned to give her an inquisitive look.

"I was just thinking that you couldn't pass for a priest."

He gave a brief laugh and nodded. "That is a stretch on a good day."

"Russell—"

"No, Neve. Not here. I'll let you have your say when we are both in the right frame of mind. I'm not there yet."

"I just want to say I'm sorry," she said in a rush to get it out and off her chest. It had been festering there ever since he'd saved her at the EDL camp.

He pinched the bridge of his nose as if he had a terrible headache, and she bit her lip. She'd really done a number on him. He was affected by her duplicity, and that meant he must have some kind of emotional stake in her. Who was she kidding? How could she keep ignoring the fact that he had a huge, major jones for her?

"Neve, please cut me a break here. I can get you to Boca de Cupé and find the White Falcon for you. I can even kill the bastard, but I'm not having this discussion now. It's too dangerous. Is that clear?"

Geez, he was being so high-handed. But she guessed she could cut him some slack. He had gone through hell with her. Because of her. Her shoulders slumped, and she nodded. "Trust me, I can cut you some slack."

"Trust you?" he said, his voice strained, then his jaw tightened.

He looked away, reality striking home, and a cold feeling settled in her gut. Clenching her jaw against that awful sliding sensation in the pit of her stomach, she forced herself to take a deep breath. It was a full minute before she could speak. "You don't trust me," she said, her voice hollow.

"No," he responded, his voice rough. "I don't."

She didn't look at him. She gazed out to the valley, her arms locked around her middle. Her voice was very quiet when she answered, "I can't say I really blame you."

The silence was brittle, strained. Neve could feel it right down to her bones. Suddenly drained, she rose when he did and followed his stiff shoulders.

It was too true. She had betrayed his trust. She'd lost it when she'd been working so hard to make him back off in the only way she could. Her words had no impact. She felt frustrated and unsettled because she had lost something…precious. Yet she put one foot in front of the other, now keenly aware of how much she'd relied on their friendship, their unspoken bond.

She hated Ammon Set for that, too. For fracturing their connection and making Russell look at her like she didn't deserve his confidence.

Guilt rushed like an invisible force through her. She closed her eyes briefly, wishing with all her heart that she realized the pilot wasn't sexist, but was considering all the crew when he'd made his decision to wait and see. If she had chosen to heed his warning, realizing that it had been too dangerous to go down for those people, she might not have been injured. That was a bitter pill to swallow.

Without her broken collarbone hampering her efforts, she might have been able to save at least two of his siblings. It was as if that botched rescue, regardless of her being cleared or not, set the tone for her whole career. Maybe she didn't even belong in the coast guard anymore.

Maybe she had ruined her vows, her duty, that day she'd lost those people, and now she was disgraced, if not in the eyes of the coast guard, in her own eyes.

Her interaction with Russell drove that home.

How was she supposed to get past those lost lives, lives that had been entrusted to her and the crew?

Not for the first time she wondered how she was going to face her team when she returned to active duty—if she made it back home in one piece.

She felt a bit frantic to think that something would happen to Russell, and that feeling didn't leave her as she followed him, the jungle claiming them once again.

They moved through the jungle at as fast a pace as the machete wielded by Russell could get them. When they heard voices, Russell ducked and pulled her into the trees. It was just the normal everyday conversation of locals, and she said, "We could stop here for lunch."

"Let me do a little recon. Stay here."

She sat, not daring to remove her pack in case they had to run. About ten minutes later, Russell was back.

"It's safe. We eat and then head out."

She nodded. Women wore bright, colorful cotton skirts, and men loincloths and colorful shorts. Some women had intricately beaded tops and others were bare breasted, but all of them smiled warmly.

They headed down the center of town, an uneven

dirt road not more than twenty feet wide. Buildings constructed of wood and thatch, easily ten feet off the ground on stilts, were close to each other.

Russell's gaze scanned the area as he walked, keeping his weapon concealed. They entered the communal hut with large plank floors, rough-hewn tree limbs supporting the thatched roof. They sat on the floor and were served fried fish, plantains and fruit. It was delicious and Neve finished everything.

While Russell paid for their meal and talked to one of the men, Neve got up and browsed the flat woven wall hangings. She wished she had room in her pack for a couple, but refrained from buying any. This wasn't a tourist trip. She was here on serious business.

It wasn't long before Russell motioned to her they were leaving. As they headed out of the village in a casual stroll, the thick jungle closed around them, blocking sunlight, and cooler temperatures created a thick, rolling mist over the forest floor. The beauty of it didn't escape her, but their steps were slower because they couldn't see the ground well.

She swiped her face and the back of her neck as she walked. No breeze, and the sun barely reached the forest floor. As they walked, she heard the rush of water and it got louder as they got closer to the source.

Finally, they broke out into an open area with a small stream and cascading sheets of water from rocks fifteen feet above them. Gusts of cool air and spray from the falls lifted fine hair on either side of her face, and it felt good on her skin.

"Should we camp here?"

He shook his head. "Too likely animals will come here to drink. We're better off heading into the trees over in that direction." He pointed farther to the north. "But this would be a good place to take a quick shower, gather water."

"Shower?" she said, looking around. The area was enclosed by jungle, and there was probably no one for miles. Neve wasn't exactly self-conscious about her body, but it seemed prudent to be constantly on alert. "Is that a good idea?"

"Don't worry. I'll stand guard until you're done, and you can do the same for me. One of us should be armed at all times."

Her eyes caressed the length of him, and it was easy to remember how Russell looked naked—all that hard-packed muscle. For sure, one of them was armed and dangerous. When she met his eyes, they narrowed with a lethal quality that was so much a part of him it cut off her breath for a second. That was all the tell she was going to get. Maybe he hid it well from others, but not from her. Just below the surface he tensed, right along his ribs. He was affected by her, but he had incredible control.

Thank God he did, because she was losing her perspective. Ever since he'd saved her, she wanted to touch him, fondle him, move her hands over the contours of his body. Even when he'd cuffed her, looking so angry, she couldn't help wanting him, draw comfort from how solid he was.

His anger was still apparent, and he wouldn't agree to talk about it. He was worried about letting go of it when they had to pull together to make this work. She caught her breath, thinking about what would be left between them when that anger was burned away, appeased. The very thought jangled her nerves.

There were so many complications, but again, out

here where they were fighting for their lives, they all seemed inconsequential.

Maybe it was true they weren't compatible, but the barriers between them seemed so far away, civilization far. Here, in the jungle, they had to rely on each other, and she wondered at how hard she'd fought to keep him away from her. Now she couldn't deny how good it felt to have him here.

"Let's find a place to set up camp, and as soon as it gets dark, then you can go first," she said, tearing her eyes away from him.

He cleared his throat, running his hands through his hair. "Sounds like a plan."

He headed over the rocks and across the stream. Needing to distance herself, she followed but not as closely as before. Aware of the thickening sensation in her chest, she stared at his wide, retreating back, feeling strangely misplaced.

She was sorry now for how she'd treated him. Caught up in her desperation to not include anyone else in this mess she'd made, it had seemed the logical plan. But she'd lost his trust, and that hurt tremendously worse than anything she'd ever experienced in her life.

Aware this train of thought was only going to make her feel worse, she focused on moving. When they stopped to make camp, she dived into the preparations. The busywork would keep her mind off the feelings buried deep that were now surfacing.

Once the tent was assembled and secluded along with their packs, they each pulled out a clean set of clothes along with some citronella wilderness wash, formulated to keep the bugs at bay and suitable for everything, microfiber towels and washcloths.

She was under no illusions here; getting a shower on this expedition was a luxury.

When they reached the waterfall, Russell pulled his T-shirt over his head and reached for his zipper. He didn't even wait for her to turn around, which she promptly did when he gave her a provocative sidelong glance. "Do you think we lost the EDL?" she asked, keeping away from the kind of conversations Russell refused to have and trying with all her might to keep from imagining him…naked.

"They've probably found the boat wherever it landed. I'd say they have no idea where we are now."

The different sound patterns and the splashing said he was under the flowing water. There was a noise to her left and she whipped around to see what it was. The rustling in the bushes made her stare intently and watch to make sure it wasn't anything dangerous. When nothing happened, Neve realized that turning brought Russell into glorious view.

He stood in profile to her, a body fueled by pure testosterone, his head back and his eyes closed as the water sluiced over heavy, delineated muscles from his broad shoulders, impressive arms, over his wide chest, to his lean, tight waist, sleek hips, hard butt, thick thighs and defined calves. Russell, from head to toe, was breath-stealing gorgeous.

As she stared at him, he brought his chin down and opened his eyes. Turning toward her, his gaze, incandescent blue from the lamp he'd hung on an overhang, slammed into hers. She was unable to look away from him, her chest suddenly aching. The longing caught up with her all at once in one big tidal wave of need, and damn but it hurt. More than anything, more than her next breath, she wanted to step into his arms and rest her head on his shoulder. She wanted to hold on to him and never let go.

She shivered, not from being wet, but from all the feelings welling up inside her.

He stepped out of the spray and bent to retrieve his towel, wrapping it around his waist. "Your turn," he said as he walked down the natural shelf of rocks that created a crude stairway, his body glistening.

He shot her an intent look. "Unless you want to watch me get dressed."

She lifted her chin, her gaze direct. "Why? Do you have something I haven't seen yet?"

He stopped in front of her and gave nothing away. "No, ma'am. I believe you've seen everything I have. So much for privacy."

She wondered if he knew how somber he sounded when he called her *ma'am*. "I was checking out a noise."

"Is that your story?"

"You think I wanted to ogle you?"

He stepped closer, nothing but bare man, one flimsy towel between her and some pretty acute danger, smelling fresh and delicious. "Didn't you?"

"Are you asking me if I think you're completely, mind-numbing magnificent, Russell?"

"No. I am asking if you like looking at me, Neve."

"A woman would have to be blind or swing the other way not to want to look at you."

"I'm not asking about any woman. I'm asking about you."

"No." The lie was barely a whisper. A tremor went through her. He couldn't miss the shaking in her shoulders, and she wasn't at all convincing with her voice low and husky.

A small smile ghosted across his lips. He tilted his head and leaned in as if he was going to kiss her, but he didn't. He just stood there, the chemistry between them sending the jungle heat up a notch. As if she wasn't sweating enough. This conversation was putting her into heated overdrive.

"That didn't sound very convincing. Are you sure?"

The only time they'd kissed, she'd been the initiator and she'd had an ulterior motive. She closed her eyes, seeing that knowledge there. It was clear he was taunting her. Years of fantasizing about Russell's kiss, of imagining how his lips would feel, his body pressed into hers, had cross-wired her brain, and suddenly there was nothing but regret. She was ashamed of how she'd acted, and now she really wanted him to close that last bit of space between them. For him to want to kiss her.

In her fantasies, she hadn't imagined his mouth being so hot, or that the sheer physical heat of his kiss would wash down her body like a flood tide and make her ache for more. She hadn't known her breath would catch and her heart would race, that her hips would rise toward him and her body would yearn for his before her mind had even registered the facts, let alone analyzed them and formulated a plan.

"What was the question?" she asked, disoriented by his presence, aching for him to make the move and frustrated when he just hovered there like the tantalizing bastard he was.

Suddenly she really wanted his forgiveness. But he had refused to talk about the whole ordeal. She could see that he hadn't changed his mind.

Stubborn, it seemed, was Russell's other nickname.

But she grumbled to herself. She wasn't at all blameless. She had manipulated him, and he had every right to be angry. She wanted to have the discussion, argument, fight and get all the pent-up feelings out in the open.

His chest was so close, and she wanted to touch his flexing muscles; it was difficult not to move toward him.

"Weren't you paying attention?" he murmured. There was an edge to his voice. He couldn't be nice here and give her an out. Her hope sank. He was still very angry. The man could carry a grudge. *You did* handcuff *him to a bed! You* drugged *him when he was only trying to help you!*

Nice? What the hell was she thinking?

No. *Nice* was not a word she associated with him. Dangerous, devastating, an explosion going off in her life, a rock-hard wall of granite—that's what he was, not *nice*.

The waterfall pounded behind him, nothing but a swath of fire-engine red microfiber covering him. But she didn't have to envision what he looked like beneath the insubstantial towel. She'd seen Russell in all his glory, and it was everything she could do not to let her jaw drop.

"Um…what?"

"I think that's all the answer I need," he said, then leaned in, and her whole body softened, but all he did was take the gun out of her hand. A thick lock of dark hair fell to his forehead, and it was all she could do to keep her hand at her side. "You better get to it. We need to eat and get some shut-eye before the next trek."

He moved away and set the weapon on a dry rock where he had his clothes. He went to unknot the towel but before he removed it, he looked at her. She turned away and started to unlace her boots. When she looked back around, he had his pants on, but no shirt. He checked the pistol and chambered a round, his biceps flexing. Then she glimpsed ink on the inside of his right arm on the edge of the firm muscle.

He gave her another edgy look, and this one didn't have anything to do with seduction. It was pure badass marine. Russell was rock solid, honed by the Corps's finest into an elite combat weapon, trained to think two steps ahead of the enemy while under fire, underwater, outgunned and outmanned. Nothing had changed.

Except apparently when she'd overcome all that training and guarded warrior. It hurt to think he'd given in, his response a direct result of how much he trusted her... and how much he wanted her.

He folded his arms over his chest and stared at her, daring her to say a thing. Without wasting any more time, she reached for the buttons of her shirt and peeled it off. Underneath was a sports bra. His smoldering eyes watched her without any reaction. He was so damn controlled. *He* was starting to *piss* her off. She crossed her arms over her chest and pulled the bra off and dropped it. His jaw rippled and his eyes ignited. She reached for her waistband, unbuttoned and unzipped, stripping off her pants and her underwear.

Stark naked, she picked up the bodywash, turned her back and headed into the spray. The water was cool, and she gasped softly as it pounded down on her head and shoulders, a refreshing relief after the smothering heat and humidity of the jungle.

While it went a long way to cooling her skin, it did

nothing to quench the fire that burned inside her. She leaned her head back and squeezed a small amount of the concentrated wash into her palm, then lathered up her hair, washing away the grime and the sweat in the clear, clean, cascading water.

After that task was done, the sensation of his eyes boring into her back, watching her, made her shiver. She soaped up a cloth and sent it over her body. If he wanted to watch, she was going to give him a show. She moved it over the skin of her arms, up and around her neck, then across her breasts, her nipples puckering and sensitive to the touch, over her hips and buttocks, then down her legs.

She paid attention to her feet, noticing that she luckily had only two small blisters, when she felt his presence very close to her.

"Neve," he said very softly, "keep still."

She dared to raise her head a fraction of an inch and came face-to-face with a jaguar. The cat was huge, a male, his eyes a feral but gorgeous tawny gold. He stared at her just at the very edge of the light, the reflection of his eyes flashing with a predatory gleam.

The touch of Russell's hand on her arm made her jump. Very cautiously, he gripped her around her bicep, pulling her out of the rushing water, and deliberately put her behind him.

She grasped his tight shoulders and pressed her upper body against him, her breasts flat against his back even as she looked over his shoulder.

The cat rose, making a soft growl in his chest. She wasn't sure if he considered Russell a rival for her as his meat or for territory—the watering hole—or as a male he was just being aggressive.

Russell carefully brought his free hand up to grip the gun with both hands.

She gasped as the cat charged toward them.

Chapter 8

Neve flinched as the gun discharged. But the animal didn't stop. Rock spread his arms and started shouting and waving. The jaguar skidded to a halt and regarded him. Rock just waved harder and shouted unintelligible things, making himself as big as he could. Finally, the cat turned and ran off into the jungle.

Now that the danger was over, he felt every inch of the creamy skin that was pressed to his back, especially the globes of Neve's generous breasts. She was trying to kill him. He gritted his teeth against the onslaught of sensation. They weren't out of the woods yet, and she needed to finish her shower.

Why didn't he put a damn shirt on? Because...he liked her looking at him the way she'd been looking at him. She didn't pull any punches, this woman who had discovered a way to generate a rage in him he'd never even realized he'd had.

She had a hold over him, God knew that. But this game they were playing was like live ammo, and it would explode in their faces. But what a rush it was to defy death.

He'd definitely should have looked away, but he hadn't been able to. Hadn't wanted to, was more like it.

"Are you all right?" he asked, both of them so still they could have been statues.

She took a breath, let it out, and the warmth of it feathered his skin. "I swear, Russell. You are the bravest, most badass, scariest dude I have ever met."

He wasn't sure that was a compliment.

"Let's not temp fate. You need to finish, and we have to get back to camp."

"Does it make you feel more in control when you're issuing orders?"

"I issue orders and expect they'll be carried out when I'm the best bet you have of getting this White Falcon job finished. I want him dead, Neve, and you safe."

"Don't say that."

He turned and grabbed her upper arms. "That's the unvarnished truth. War is hell, Neve, and there's only one outcome here. We're going to be the ones to walk away alive. That's the only win I'm going to accept."

"I wish it didn't have to be so."

"It is so. What did you think was going to happen when you came out here? A walk in the park? A nice, leisurely jaunt through the jungle?"

"No. I'm just determined to save my family."

He took a breath because he couldn't have this conversation with her right now. He was too close to the edge with both his anger and his feelings for her.

His voice softened and he said, "I know. I'm all for that." God, she felt so good against him.

He loved her, and he was going to make the world as safe for her as he possibly could, no matter the cost.

With the iron will he'd used in his missions, he let her go. She stepped back into the flowing water and he kept his eyes off her and on the jungle around them.

When she was finished, she dried off and dressed. She walked past him, then stopped and gave him a coolly artless look over her shoulder. "Are you coming?"

"Off you go," he said.

She didn't hesitate, leaving him to follow behind her in those snug-fitting cargo pants, behind the languid movement of her booted feet and the smooth, rolling motion of her hips. But the image of her beneath the falls was burned into his brain. Miles of bare, naked legs, high, firm breasts tipped with mouthwatering dark nipples, and the most perfect ass he'd ever seen—perfectly curved, perfectly tight. And he was dying, the awful, wonderful feeling from the first moment he met her rearing up again and swamping him in one big crashing wave of want.

Pure lust had never come close to dropping him to his knees. Never. He could handle lust; this was love. And love didn't relent, not all the way from their bathing area to the dense jungle and finally to their tent. It was like a fist around his heart, a heated knot in his stomach.

They made quick work out of the meal, this time Hurry Curry Seasoned Chicken with Rice. He kept the weapon on his lap, and he noticed how she kept giving him glances all through the meal.

Now they were settled in the tent, all zipped up and cozy. "I'll take the first watch, Russell."

"You handling me, babe?"

"No, I'm just offering. You have had enough for to-night. It feels like you're going to jump out of your skin."

"That has nothing to do with jaguars, EDL or any number of other dangers in this godforsaken place."

She was concerned, and even as he liked it, he didn't want her to see him like this. There were a couple of times yesterday when he'd been wild-eyed. "I'm not too complicated, Neve. Right, wrong. Good guys, bad guys. Cut. Dried." Neve had a certain innocence about her, a purity of purpose—not that she would ever see it that way. But Rock knew it, just like he figured she knew what buttons to push.

He rose and crowded her back against the tent. "You know what set me off yesterday. He had a knife on you. His intent was clear."

Her face fell, her skin turning even paler than normal, her soft mouth softening even more.

"Geez," she said, swallowing. "I was sure nothing would push you over the edge."

Except you, he thought, dragging his gaze away from her. Other than not heeding his warning, cuffing him to that bed and cutting him out of the action, she'd been amazing out here, held up her end, done what needed to be done. It wasn't lost on him that she knew her way around hand-to-hand combat and could shoot. She'd handled the Glock like a pro. "Yeah. Exactly. Seeing you like that would push any guy a couple of degrees into wild-eyed maniac."

He knew the signs of going off the rails. It was a warning he needed to heed, right damn now. This ache he had for her, it needed to go away.

He could use some sleep, but instead of capitulating,

he took her hand in his, caressed the back with his palm, so smooth and strong, yet delicate.

This hand had saved lives, sometimes in wind-tossed waves, gale-force winds and frigid temperatures. She did a job that would tax a man and did it damned well. He knew she had the courage.

He wasn't going to kiss her.

He gritted his teeth. *Right.*

He was so glad he made that clear. Ever since he'd broken down her door and saw her trying to hold off that assassin, so little was clear to him.

"All right. Take the first watch," he said. He lowered his forehead to hers and just rested a moment, letting the quiet and the warmth seep into him. At the snick of the cuffs, a boatload of tension drained out of him.

She stiffened and opened her mouth. Then closed it, a sadness coming into her eyes. After a couple of seconds, she leaned back and let out a soft breath. "When are you going to trust me again?" she whispered.

Watching her, his eyes slowly adjusted to the dark night. A full moon was visible in the clearing sky, but he felt it in his bones that rain was on the way. The sound of free-running water, a lot of it, coming from the distance, was unmistakable and soothing.

"I don't know," he whispered back. The anger, the pure-hot rage, had never really left him. He'd just disarmed it and buried it for now like an unloaded weapon much too close to the ammo. But there would have to be a reckoning. He just wasn't sure when or where, just that it was inevitable.

He rubbed his thumb across the back of her hand and let out a heavy breath. His gaze drifted over her face in the moonlight like this was a romantic getaway instead of a fortified camp. He didn't miss a thing when it came to Neve—her thick lashes brushing her cheeks when she closed her eyes briefly, the softness of her breath, the rich beauty of her dark skin and the racing of her heart, and he wanted her.

He also wasn't ready to trust her. Not quite sure whether she was paying lip service to needing him or just waiting for the moment to leave him behind. He couldn't take any chances with this woman.

He pushed the longing, the lust and the out-of-control sensations deep, as deep as the wrath. That lost feeling he kept with him to remind him that he couldn't find his way with her. Even a marine knew when he was beaten. He let her go, removing the cuffs. Taking the chance that she wasn't going to leave him behind again, he bedded down and dropped off into slumber, his dreams a feverish jumble of chasing her and just barely brushing his hands against her, getting burned like she was on fire, only to have to chase her all over again, the sense of foreboding looming heavier and thicker as he ran.

He woke up completely when it was time for his shift. It was something that was ingrained in him, and in the field he adapted as easily as breathing. Combat naps were second nature.

Her warm lap was beneath his cheek, her arm wrapped around him across his chest. He enjoyed the moment, like a thief stealing something inordinately precious. He lay still, listening to her breathing, the barely discernable movements as she scanned for danger.

He rose and climbed over her as she scooted to the side and settled down. She yawned and stretched. "It's been very quiet," she murmured.

He looked out into the darkness, the land alive with

red and orange. He scanned beyond the openings. The forest was nearly soundless except for the whisper of a breeze coming through the trees. Not even a monkey or birds moved out there.

He heard the rumble of thunder in the distance, then a flash as the red-orange glow faded into a murky gray.

It was going to be a wet, miserable day.

And it was. He knew all about jungle rain—big, fat drops that drenched you in seconds, making the ground muddy, sucking at their boots. Even with ponchos, they were soaked.

When it just got too murky with water and mist to see, they pitched the tent and crawled inside, changed into dry clothes and waited out the rain. They couldn't cook, so they consumed MREs and drank the water.

"Did the EDL know where you were headed?"

"No. Ugly was too busy trying to get me to give him my name."

"And that name was?"

"Sister Mary Agnes."

He chuckled dryly.

"Hey, I can pass as a nun."

"Not from where I'm sitting. I've never seen a nun like you."

"What is that supposed to mean?"

He ignored the question and countered. "Who came up with this cover?"

"My source in Panama—"

"Marco de Cruz. A resourceful guy."

"Very. Marco is wonderful—he knows the area very well, has a lot of contacts. He found out that Ammon Set and his wife, Lizeth, have a fortified compound deep in the Darién. She's the daughter of Raúl Torres."

"Right, he was apprehended about ten years ago and died in prison. Both her brothers were killed in two separate DEA raids."

"That's correct. You did your homework."

"When it comes to you, Neve, I'm thorough."

She stilled, and he heard how that came out, husky and suggestive. The way she jacked him up at the waterfall, he was still semi-hard, and keeping his composure was getting hard. No pun intended.

"What about your dead guide?"

She shook her head. "Bray knew, but I don't think he had a chance to say anything before the EDL executed him for poaching kidnap victims on their turf."

"Saved me a bullet," he said without inflection.

She looked away, and he was sure she was remembering what it was like to be helplessly bound and blindfolded. That thought made anger stir. His first instinct was to wrap his arms around her.

They spent the rest of the wet, miserable day under cover of the tent, sharing guard duty, and were ready for more trekking at first light.

This area wasn't for the faint of heart, and he was sure that she'd had no idea what she was getting herself into when she'd made the decision to go after Set. But she was a trooper, especially coming off a ten-week recuperation for a broken collarbone.

"How you holding up?" he asked as she shouldered her pack.

"Physically or mentally?" she queried, giving him a smile.

"Both."

"I'm still determined and I'm doing fine. I was in very good shape when I got injured and had a couple weeks in the pool and gym to strengthen my upper body. That's the only weakness right now."

She went to take a step, and he pressed his hand against her shoulder. "Neve. I can get you out of here now. Just a call away. I know people… I've been here before and made friends. No questions asked and you're back in Panama City. Then I can take care of this problem myself."

Her mouth tightened and her eyes went moist. Damn, he hadn't wanted to make her cry; he just wanted her safe.

"I can't do that, Russell. This is my problem, and if I hadn't been so sensitive to what I perceived as a gender issue during that rescue and trying to prove that I wasn't a woman in a male-dominated job with everyone always scrutinizing what I was doing, I might have saved those people. My injury and their deaths, regardless of what the reports say, were my own bias. I'm not going to let you bail me out. That isn't something I do, so I'm seeing this all the way through, no matter what happens. I won't have my family suffer for my actions."

She was stubborn and dedicated, he had to give her that. "The coast guard would have cut you loose if their findings had been against you, Neve. Stop beating yourself up over the deaths of Set's family members. That storm was nasty, and the fact that you even deployed from that chopper in those winds was miraculous and freaking brave," he growled before letting her go and turning away toward the jungle as tenderness filled her eyes and that moist sheen intensified.

"Are you being nice to me, Russell? Wow, the warrior has a heart."

It was clear she was adding levity to an intense moment, but little did she know how much of his heart was tied up with her. "Women," he groused as he pulled out his machete and started to hack.

"Boy Scouts," she muttered behind him, but it was nothing but bluster. The inflection in her voice told him she was damn glad he was here. Didn't make him forgive her and didn't make him drop his guard. It rankled that he still felt he couldn't trust her.

A half mile later they traversed a ridge, a river yards below them, a huge waterfall in the distance. There was a crude cattle path cut into the trees. It would be easier to walk along it, but Rock had the feeling that it was a route used by more than just cattle.

Sure enough, as he took a few more steps, they heard voices and the sound of a Jeep. He ducked and made for the cover of the trees as three men buzzed past them and disappeared down the trail, the back of their vehicle laden with rounded kilos of what was most likely cocaine wrapped in plastic and packed tightly together. Drug smugglers.

They would be killed on sight.

He put his finger to his lips and Neve nodded. They would need to skirt them. But that proved difficult with the sheer drop on one side and the other crawling with cartel members. He was going to have to do some silent mayhem, and prayed they got through before the men he eliminated were missed.

He shrugged off his pack and turned to her, got close. "I'm going to clear us a path through." His breath was warm, and she suddenly clutched at his shirt. If anything happened to him… He covered her fingers. "Buck up, Neve," he whispered. "I'm bulletproof, babe. Nothing beats Rock."

She gave him a wan smile and he growled, "Stay put. Use the weapon with the suppressor and we should be fine." He leaned back. "Wait for me. But if we get separated…" He pointed in the distance. "See that outcropping, the one that looks like eggs at the base?" She gave him a nod. "Head there and we'll rendezvous. Clear?"

"Roger that."

He often heard that from marines, and it struck him as odd coming from her. He stared at her as she crouched near a tree teeming with orange butterflies fluttering their wings. She wasn't a marine, he reminded himself, she was a rescue swimmer who was out of her element. A damn brave one, and while she'd proved herself a tough cookie, she was still not as intensely trained as he was for this type of situation.

He pulled out a compact and painted his face in camo stripes while Neve watched. Then, still crouching, he surveyed the jungle in front of him, his senses tingling. "Don't do anything stupid," he said over his shoulder, and she rolled her eyes.

"I'll give it my best shot, sir." She saluted, and it was his turn to roll his eyes.

He ghosted from their position, his eyes constantly scanning, a sweet adrenaline rush. No pack. No M16, no team. Alone, he worked faster, worried about his own back. Way out here, the security was lax. These guys didn't exactly expect trouble, but they had no idea trouble was in the form of a six-foot-five juggernaut who had every intention of making sure there was a safe path for Neve through this roadblock.

The first man went down easily, and the second. He moved along the ridge, their best bet of getting past this position and farther into the Darién. He estimated they were on the right trajectory to finding Set's compound, then it was lights out for the gunrunner and time to bug out of this death trap.

The sniper watched what was going on below him. Hell of a situation. He took several deep breaths, sick of being wet and hot. He wanted a beer and a cool place to sleep off his combat fatigue. He could see Michaels higher up on the mountainside, and he shouldered the rifle, then peered into the scope. He took careful aim with her between the crosshairs, smiling.

Showtime.

The shot echoed through the valley, and Rock stiffened as the man he was just about to grab and choke turned and saw him. He drew a breath to yell and brought up his rifle, but it was much too late as Rock leaped and drove his KA-BAR into the drug runner's neck, effectively changing the shout to a barely perceptible gurgle.

As soon as the guy was down, Rock sprinted back along the path he'd just cleared, his heart in his throat. *Neve!*

He ran right into her, and she clasped him. "They found me," she said, "but someone…" She gestured back toward where she'd been crouching. Bodies littered the ground.

A narco guerrilla rushed out of the trees and another shot rang out. The man dropped, blood flowing around him. Rock looked up to the hillside. Sniper. Their shadow.

Looked like he was one of the good guys.

He grabbed her hand and headed for a Jeep, but then he heard crashing and shouting and all hell broke loose.

A young girl broke out of the jungle, then turned and streaked across the opening, jumping over forest debris and shifting left and right, heading directly for their escape vehicle, men hot on her tail. She couldn't be more than sixteen, black hair flying behind her, her body willowy, her feet bare, brown shorts and a T-shirt covering her. The girl would never outrun full-grown men. It was clear they didn't want to hurt her... They were going to... do much more. Oh, hell no.

He raced to intercept. It was as easy as calculating the trajectory of a bullet, leading his target. He heard the whip of leaves against flesh and quickened his pace. Then he ducked in behind a tree, he and Neve using the mass as a shield. Rock didn't have time for the rules of engagement and remained hidden, listening to the approaching footsteps. Louder, closer... The girl ran past and he stepped out and grabbed her, snatched her right off the path, covering her mouth and giving her the kind of look he reserved for terrorists. "Not a word."

Her eyes widened, and he passed her to Neve.

Then more footsteps... He rolled around and punched the man in the throat. The guy dropped to his back, choking. Rock grabbed him by the shirt and delivered a blow to his nose. A gunshot went off, zinged past his ear and killed the man behind him.

That was damn close.

When he turned, a man was aiming at Neve. He jumped, and the bullet gouged his upper arm in white-hot pain. Neve brought up her weapon and shot the assailant.

"The Jeep," the girl said. "It's our only chance!" Her English sounded impeccable. All three of them made a beeline for the vehicle.

Luckily, the keys were in the ignition and, bleeding profusely from the wound, Rock turned over the engine and put it in gear.

"Go straight!" she shouted.

Rock looked in front of him, then back at her.

"It's our only chance! Do it!"

He put the Jeep into gear and gunned it, heading for the sheer drop-off.

The engine made a whirring, grinding noise when it went airborne, and his stomach fell out from under him as the bundles of cocaine ejected into the air and they plunged to the foaming river below.

Chapter 9

NCIS Special Agent Derrick Gunn pulled the rifle from his shoulder, unable to believe what he'd just seen through the scope.

He'd never met Russell, but had talked to him briefly on the phone when his brother, Navy SEAL Dexter Kaczewski, and Senator Piper Jones had gone missing in Afghanistan about three months ago.

Russell Kaczewski was evidence that courageous DNA ran rampant in that family. He was one crazy son of a gun.

Shaking off the shock, and with lightning quick speed, he shouldered the rifle, glancing to the jungle below him. He'd downed plenty of the drug runners with suppressed fire, but Neve Michaels had been cornered, and she'd used her weapon with deadly consequences.

Now there was a large mass of pissed off *pendejos*

gathering, some looking over the cliff, others running to vehicles. They were in hot pursuit.

And who in hell was the teenage indigenous girl?

Derrick was completely black, off the radar in an unsanctioned mission that was purely personal. Special Agent Amber Dalton had told him what was happening, worried her soon-to-be sister-in-law wasn't going to sit still as she was directed.

Special Agent Austin Beck and CGIS Special Agent Davis Nishida were busy building a case against Ammon Set, but as Neve had predicted, she and her whole family, including Amber, would be in that bastard's sights.

He'd been watching her ever since she'd left the NCIS offices.

He'd taken leave and called in more than one favor.

His shadowy past had come in handy in this instance.

With his heart pounding, he went down the hillside as fast as he could, picking his way through heavy undergrowth, then farther down to the water's edge.

But as the Jeep sunk, there was no sign of the three people who had gone in with it. He inched back as several men jumped into the water and started to retrieve the floating cocaine. Not even bothering to look for survivors.

Freaking bastards.

He stashed his pack and the rifle into the thick overgrowth, pulled out his side weapon and chambered a round, melting into the forest. He wasn't going to let Amber down. He'd vowed that a while ago.

He'd find them or die trying.

After the initial impact and shock of hitting the water, Neve's training kicked in the minute she started to sink.

She searched for the girl and saw that she was submerged and gesturing wildly, but when she looked for Russell, she didn't immediately see him. She staved off the panic, using her training to sustain her. She dived and caught sight of him sinking, too. The panic broke through her barrier of calm; she was afraid he would drown, and she couldn't get him to the bank for fear they would be shot.

Russell might rule on land, but this was her domain. She stroked strongly for him and as she reached him, she saw the blood trail from a gash on his temple. As she grabbed him, he opened his eyes groggily. The girl touched her shoulder and motioned again. She slipped her arms under Russell's armpit and followed.

Soon, they reached the opening of a submerged cave, and Neve got nervous. It didn't look big enough for Russell to fit. The girl gestured and Neve knew they had no choice. She vowed she wasn't leaving Russell behind. She maneuvered her body through, then with Russell's help, got him through as well, his big chest and wide back scraping the opening. They emerged in a cave under the falls, and all three of them drew deep, panting breaths. She helped Russell out of the water, and they rested.

"We can't stay here," the girl whispered. "We must go."

"Russell?"

She grabbed Neve's arm. "We can't go back. We must go."

"Where?"

"Back underwater. There's another cave. We have to swim. Once we come out the other side. We will be safe. They don't know about either cave."

"Russell. Can you hold your breath? Are you okay to swim?"

He looked up at her and grimaced, nodding. "Can do."

"Are you sure?" She knew they didn't really have a choice, but he looked like he was in no condition to hold his breath, let alone swim.

He pushed up to his knees and stood, a bit wobbly. She caught him against her, and the girl motioned them to the back of the cave. Voices echoed close by, and she gave Neve a fearful, wide-eyed look.

"Come," she whispered. "They're outside. Keep quiet or they might hear us."

At the lip of the pool, they lowered themselves into the water with as little noise as possible. "Take three deep breaths and on the last one hold it," Neve instructed.

She kicked hard and dived, swimming after the girl with strong strokes. She felt the pressure immediately and the rush of water around her as she pressed hard.

The underwater cavern expanded, the blue-white illumination growing bright and crisp as she neared. She looked up at the jagged edge of the pool and swam hard, breaking the surface, then turning instantly to look for Russell.

Her heart froze in her chest. The water stayed level and there was no sign of him. "Russell?" The rush of alarm was so intense that for an instant she thought her heart would stop.

She turned to look at the girl, who had pulled herself up on solid ground. She covered her mouth, worry and concern evident as she, too, searched the water. It was nothing to the fear that sliced through Neve. She took a deep breath and dived back into the water, swimming hard, searching everywhere. Then she saw him floating, her heart suddenly jammed against her ribs, hammering frantically as dread churned through her. Instinct and training taking over, she kicked like crazy. When she reached Russell, she grabbed him and pulled him into the same wrapping hold.

Then she started back the way she'd come. It seemed like an eternity before she broke the surface. The girl reached out for Russell the moment Neve got him to the edge. She pushed up as the girl pulled him hard onto the ground.

Using her hands on the lip, Neve catapulted herself out of the water.

"Oh, God. No." She bent her head and listened for a heartbeat. It was weak, but there.

He wasn't breathing. She tipped his head back and opened his mouth.

Please, Russell. Don't die. Please. God. Please, Russell! she thought, breathing for him. Her heart pounded hard against her breastbone, and she'd never felt this scared.

Of course he said he could make it. He knew she wouldn't leave him and they'd be caught and killed, but he had hit his head and he was woozy.

She focused on counting and giving him rescue breaths and kept it up when she wanted to shout, "Don't die. Don't leave me." How much time had passed? "Russell, come back to me. You're a marine. Don't give up! Breathe, *damn* you!"

He coughed, his body convulsing hard, and she pushed him onto his side as a small amount of water dribbled out of his mouth. He started to shake, and she gathered him

in her arms, rubbing his skin. It was several minutes before he did anything more than breathe, and Neve closed
her eyes, so grateful. She didn't even try to excuse away
her feelings. She didn't need this threat to make her see
the truth, damn it.

"Neve—" His lids lifted, and his eyes were so blue,
so deep with concern. She curled her hand around his
jaw and squeezed, holding him tight with her other hand.
"Breathe deep. Don't talk right now." Fear still throbbing
through her, she closed her eyes tightly as she rested her
head against his. Determined not to let fear overwhelm
her, she made herself concentrate on taking deep, steadying breaths, making her muscles relax.

He coughed again, giving her an almost smile at her
tone. "Yes, ma'am," he murmured huskily.

She let her hand linger for a few more minutes, then
she looked at the girl. Her panic, her fear, her relief at
having him conscious and breathing on his own, came
dangerously close to the surface, and Neve held on to
her composure by a thread, her voice breaking badly. "I
need to get him somewhere safe and tend to his wounds.
How far is your village?" She took a breath, feeling like
she was going to shatter, realizing she couldn't. She had
to be strong and get Russell medical attention. The drug
runners' threat was neutralized, and they had escaped.
She forced herself to pull it together even as Russell
watched her solemnly.

"Not far." The girl leaned forward and squeezed her
arm with sympathy. She was a self-possessed little thing.
"The *traficantes de drogas* don't know me. They won't
follow. They're happy to have their drugs back."

She helped Neve get Russell to his feet and, without asking, took the pack from his back and shouldered it.

He started to protest and she shook her head, her expression fixed and defiant. "I am stronger than you think. Follow me."

Neve kept her arm around him as they walked. She was still shaken, and Russell coughed a few times.

"What are your names?" the girl asked. "Mine is Opal, like the gem."

"I'm Neve and this is Russell."

"Rock," he rasped. "I prefer Rock."

The girl looked at him warily, and it was not surprising. He'd plucked her off the path and put the fear of God into her with that look he'd given her. He was big and intimidating. But geez, that was one of Neve's favorite things about him.

"Why were those men chasing you?"

"Drug runners. They don't like anyone near their merchandise. I got too close and these men…they take what they want. You saved me from a terrible fate. They don't ask permission when they want to be with a woman."

"What tribe?"

"I'm Emberá. My village is not much farther. You both can rest and Rock can get patched up."

"I can handle that. I have medical training." Neve sounded proprietary, but she didn't care.

Opal nodded. "He is a soldier," she said with a matter-of-fact tone. "You're an Amazon warrior, though." She smiled.

Russell chuckled, then coughed. "I'm retired. But she is an Amazon warrior. We're just visiting."

In the distance, as they topped a rise in the trail, Neve

saw structures emerge. The girl picked up her pace, and Neve and Russell followed. Russell wasn't doing too well. His breathing was labored, and he kept stumbling. She was taking on more of his weight. She hoped he didn't have a concussion.

"Retired, my ass," Neve murmured.

As they hit the outskirts of the village, she felt like she was dragging a slab of granite. "Just a little farther, Marine."

He perked up at that. The settlement was not much different than the other village where they'd eaten. The town had a round, thatched, elevated common house, surrounded by rectangular wooden homes with metal roofs. Opal led them to one of the simple houses on stilts. "You can stay here. It's vacant right now. The family has left. I will let my father know that you're here, and will bring you something to eat."

She reached out and touched Russell's arm. "Thank you very much for saving me. I am in your debt."

"You're safe and sound. That's enough for me," he said, smiling. "Driving off a cliff was a new experience." Giving him a cheeky grin, she shoved Russell's pack up over her head onto the porch. She was definitely stronger than she looked.

A harrowing experience, Neve thought. But the girl's quick thinking and resourcefulness had saved them, too. "If you hadn't been there, we would have been in big trouble. So we're even."

Opal turned and ran off.

With Neve's arm steadying him, Russell navigated the notched log that was used for a staircase.

Inside there was one room, a large, wide hammock

that could easily accommodate two people with room to spare and two tables with chairs. Neve slipped off her pack, and Russell dropped into one of the chairs and cradled his head in his hands. She went back out to the porch and dragged in his pack. Opening hers, she dug around inside for the first-aid kit.

There wasn't even a basin inside, so she used the cooking pot and poured in some of the purified water. She started with the worst injury. His upper arm. A chunk of flesh was neatly sheared away where the bullet had just creased his skin. She pulled out the supplies she needed from the kit with trembling hands, trying with all her might to stay professional about this. But it was difficult. This was Russell, and he wasn't some victim. He was… Her throat closed up. Oh, God, she couldn't lose it. While she cleaned the wound with water and then swabbed on some iodine and added a topical antibiotic, Russell stoically suffered through the pain with a clenched jaw and occasional grunts. Swiping the wound one more time with iodine, she wrapped his arm in gauze and taped it up.

With a gentle lift of his chin with her fingers and thumb along his jaw, she tilted his head to get a better look at his nasty gash, red and still oozing blood. His skin was warm, and the bristles of his stubble prickled not unpleasantly against her sensitive pads.

She went through the same process with his minor head wound as Opal returned with food, which she set on the table. When Neve was finished, she went to step away, but Russell grabbed her wrist and drew her face close to his and said, "Thank you."

For a long, drawn-out moment, she stared into his

blue eyes and remembered his body floating in the water of that underground pool—drowning.

He'd known he wasn't up to the task. He knew it was going to get dicey, but the alternative of saying so and cementing the fact that she wouldn't have left him there to die didn't even cross his mind, she was sure.

His courage, his conviction and his ability to melt every bone in her body made her crazy. He was so close, and he smelled so inviting, and suddenly Neve felt very fragile and very shaky inside. Clenching her teeth against her own emotions, she said, "You're welcome." Then she glared at him. "But if you ever…ever put your life in danger again without us having a conversation about it and taking as many precautions as possible, I'll…I'll…" A sob caught in her throat, tears welling in her eyes as a delayed reaction washed over her with concussive force.

She looked down at him and pushed hair off his forehead with unsteady fingers. She tried so hard to be cool and unemotional, but the instant she met his gaze, something inside her just collapsed. She touched the side of his face, his skin warm and alive. He penetrated her soul and made her hurt. "You scared the crap out of me, Marine." The thought of losing Russell hit her, and her throat closed up with a painful cramp, only this time her vision blurred with tears.

"Neve," he whispered softly. "Aw, babe."

She held his gaze, her eyes awash with tears, and Russell brushed his knuckles across her cheek, then tucked her wet hair behind her ear. His expression etched with strain, he let a strand curl around his finger, then swallowed hard and looked at her, his eyes dark and tormented. Then releasing a long, shaky sigh, he shifted and pulled her across his legs, gathering her up in a tight, enveloping embrace.

Neve sagged against him, unable to hold in all the raw and turbulent emotions that surged through her. She'd thought she could hide her feelings, but being held by him, having him share her fear, finally having his arms around her in acknowledgment of those feelings, was just too much to handle, and she huddled in his arms, pressing her wet face into the curve of his neck. The devastation of almost losing him was just too much.

It seemed like an eternity before she had cried herself out, her harsh sobs dwindling to the occasional ragged one. Pressing her throbbing, swollen eyes against his throat, she worked at regaining control, waiting for her emotions to settle.

Releasing a heavy sigh, she wearily lifted her head, knowing that, although a damned good cry might take the edge off, it didn't fix anything. There were still so many complications with Russell.

"Neve…" he whispered hoarsely against her hair. "I know I'm not the man for you…in the long run…"

She covered his mouth, and he kissed her fingertips. That one single, gentle act devastated her, and she caught him by the back of the neck, her hand sliding over silky hair and hot skin. "But life is too short? Is that what you're saying?" It was clear from the look in his eyes and the hard-on she was riding he wanted her. This was about so much more than sex. If it had been just about the physical, this would be such a no-brainer. But she didn't want to hurt him, hurt her brother, break her own heart.

"Yes. That, and you're Tristan's little sister, and I feel like hell wanting this but if I don't have you, I think I'll go insane."

"It's risky. So risky, Rock. We want different things, are on different paths." She shivered when she used that coveted name—so personal, so intimate to her.

He groaned softly at the sound of his nickname on her lips. "I know. If I ever hurt Tristan..." he said, then swallowed, a hollow look in his eyes. She had fought the good fight; she'd thought she had everything under control, but that roughly spoken admission, that statement of commitment, completely did her in. "Right now, in this moment, our paths overlap. Can we agree it's enough for now?"

"On one condition," she murmured.

"What?"

She collected her courage. She couldn't be with him unless something important was resolved between them. "Can you forgive me? Trust me again. No more handcuffs."

He blinked, grinning. "Ever?"

At that teasing glint in his eyes, she gave him a dry, amused look. "That could be up for discussion," she said, her voice whiskey soft.

His eyes flashed, and he went even harder beneath her. "Don't tease me."

"I'm not against submission, Rock, as long as I get to dominate sometimes."

"Damn," he swore softly. His face showing the strain, he took a shuddering breath. "On that condition?"

"Yes?" She was all ears.

"Promise me you will never ditch me again." He rose

with her in his arms and headed toward the wide hammock, the movement of his hips and thighs making her ride against his thick, hard heat. He laid her down, and with the kind of balance that was reserved for sea captains and tightrope walkers, he got in without any scary mishaps. Her heart was starting to pound, and when he dropped his weight on her and she wrapped her legs around his hips as he settled between her thighs, his voice dropped an octave into deliciously gruff. "Promise me you will also discuss putting your life in danger so we can take precautions."

She opened her mouth, but he said, "Shh…just one more thing."

"What?" she asked, her breath hitching. Overloaded with sensation, Neve tightened her arms around him and closed her eyes. Opening her mouth against the soft skin of his neck, she was desperate for the taste of him.

He didn't move or speak for a moment, his breathing choppy, then he said, his chest expanding raggedly, "Tell me you're sorry. But only if you truly mean it."

"I am sorry, so sorry," she whispered, her heart in her voice as she kissed his neck again. "I promise, Rock. You have my word."

He cupped her jaw, and the anticipation was killing her as she met his gaze. It softened to such an intensely tender look, she ached. His mouth dropped to hers, and this wasn't a hello kiss. It was a full-out assault, an I-need-you, real man kiss.

She made a low sound in her throat, surrendering to him as she'd wanted to do so many times. He increased the pressure of his mouth, an eating kiss, his mouth trailing her throat, then back to her lips.

He was huge and muscular, and for someone being held by a guy who pulled a trigger easily, she felt almost fragile in his arms, his kiss tender, as if waiting for her to give him more. Helpless to do anything else, she took the kiss deeper, savoring the hard feel of his erection. The palms of her hands swept up his chest, and she moaned a plea for more, lifting herself against him, counterstroking along the length of him, giving them both what they demanded.

He jerked against her as she yielded all that she had because she could do no less with him. Her Rock. The hungry heat of his mouth drowning her, the feel of his hand against her face destroying her.

He rocked his hips and she responded, his breathing harsh and labored. Locking his arm under her, he dragged in a ragged breath of air, then thrust against her again. Reaching down, she grabbed the hem of his T-shirt and pulled it over his head so she could get her hands on his hard-muscled, bare chest, caressing over the firm, delineated contours, running her hand all the way down to his lower abdomen.

He moaned softly and twisted against her. "Christ, Neve. I don't have anything to protect you. I should have been prepared, but I didn't want the temptation."

Snagging his waistband, she plunged her hand inside and stroked him, and he broke their kiss as he threw his head back, thrusting hard into the palm of her hand, the feel of him so hot and smooth, the tip like velvet.

"It's all right. I'm safe and clean. The Pill…"

His breath shuddered out. "Me, too. I always protect my partner, but it's been a long time." She stroked him again, and he lost his voice. Bracing his hands, he lost control, his hips moving again and again until he grabbed her wrist and went to his knees. "Any more and I'm done," he whispered, "and I want to be deep inside you before that happens."

His hands went to her garments and he stripped her upper body bare, then her lower, dropping her clothes over the side of the hammock.

She tore at his button and zipper and with careful movements, he shimmied out of them, and they were gone.

She shivered when his hard, hot body pressed down on her, the weight of him felt so good, covering her mouth in a kiss that made her sob, made her move against the hardness of him, made her crazy with wanting. Cupping her buttocks, he slid down her body, his moist mouth on her center hungry, wet and wild.

"Come for me, Neve," he whispered hoarsely, giving her unimaginable pleasure.

"Rock," she sobbed, her voice breaking. "Oh, *yes.*"

With an agonized groan, she clutched his head, her hands twining in his hair, tightening, pulling. Relentless, she rocked against him as the sensations inside her gathered and gathered, pulling into one hot, pulsating center. He didn't stop as the sensations converged, and she cried out and arched stiffly against him when it ruptured, the explosion rocketing her off into a shuddering release.

He surged up her body, his mouth taking her throbbing nipples one at a time. Making a low, incoherent sound deep in his throat, he plundered her with his mouth and Neve clutched at him, a jolt of sensation driving her deeper and deeper into the heat of urgency.

He slid his hand heavily down her spine, cupped her

rear and meshed her hips to his. She felt his broad erection, the warmth and the pressure, and she hooked her leg around his, sliding it up to his thigh to his hip. Then she arched into him, urging, her hand sweeping wildly over gorgeous power, her fingertips molding to curved muscle and man.

Her touch slid lower. His stomach muscles contracted instantly as she neared his groin, and his moan of pleasure thrummed through her.

Chapter 10

Rock fell apart. Like a HALO jump, his feelings tumbled over each other with the feel of her warm, silky palm sliding over his erection again.

He curled her tighter to him, kissing her madly, then drew back long enough to murmur. "Christ, you're an addiction."

And she was—addictive from her kiss that twisted him into a pretzel. He didn't know if he wanted to keep her as close as possible or turn in the other direction.

He kissed her ribs, crushing her back, the need to bury himself inside her quickly and appease this wild hunger for her. But it wouldn't matter. She was more than under his skin. She was inside it. And when her hand closed around him, she took him with her—away from danger and isolation, from ignoring everything he'd wanted from the moment he'd laid eyes on her.

Since they'd met, she made him indulge in feelings and sensations. Trapped with her, he gave them freedom. She stroked him heavily, her little hand working him into a frenzy that threatened his control.

Rock gritted his teeth, then grasped her wrist. "What did I tell you about that?"

"You are such a killjoy," she groused.

"No, ma'am. There will be plenty of joy, babe. I'm having my way with you."

"Now you're talking," she said, and they laughed.

"I'm not interested in talking," he whispered, and her eyes glazed over as he bent to taste the smooth texture of her skin, loving the way she sounded so damn sexy.

His gaze slipped over her plump breasts, smoothing the roundness, and then he leaned down again and drew her into the warmth of his mouth, watching her expression of pleasure this time. Her head fell back, her body bending into his. So freaking sexy times two. The motion ground her warm center to his erection, and she thrust back as he licked and scored his teeth over the soft underside of her breast. He held her gaze as he ran his finger around her nipple, cupping her breast, and she watched him taste her.

"Rock. Now I'm really glad you followed me." Her hands roamed over his shoulders, his chest. She wrapped her hand around him, slid her fingers over the moist tip and laughed softly when he groaned, drew in air through clenched teeth.

"Geezus," he said and clasped her hands above her head. "Where are those handcuffs when you need them?"

Her smile was bone-melting, and he swept his palm from her delicate throat to her sleek hip, molding her flesh, his gaze lingering over her, naked and shameless for him. Her eyes held the awareness of her power, her shape slim and supple, wrapping him in her scent and sensation. Rock felt privileged, the moments of denying himself over, kaput, the message driven home as she touched his face, slid her thumb over his lips. It was a simple thing, and he wanted more of it, to connect deeply with her and seal this connection tighter. Screw the thought that he could lose her.

His hand rested on her belly, then slid softly between her thighs. He nudged them apart, loving her quick breaths, yet he taunted, slowly drawing a line up her center, circling the tiny bead of her core.

She thrust her hips enough to put him inside her a bit, and he grunted and cursed, then nudged her thighs wider and slid between. He held himself poised, and a million thoughts ran through his mind, nothing sticking long enough to make sense. He felt privileged and freed, his need beyond passion, beyond control.

She covered his mouth, wickedly plundering him until he was wrung out with the taste and feel of her. His breath shuddered, almost gasping when he leaned back and she straddled his broad thighs; her mouth rolled over his, down his throat, and her tongue snaked to lick his nipple. His grip on her hips tightened as she suckled, and he let his head drop back and savored it till he needed that mouth on his again. He took it, cradling her face and savaging her soft lips till she was gasping and wild on him.

"Russell," she pleaded.

He gripped her hips, his body nail-hard and sliding into her deeply. Her delicate flesh clasped him in a tight fist, her willowy body rocking back and forth like a cord pulling him quickly to climax.

"*Oh*, my. Oh, *man*…oh, man."

Her muscles locked and clawed, and yet she smiled, met him and thrust harder. Her whispers were as soft and wispy as the mist as she made love to him, watching as he disappeared inside her with tormenting abandon.

She quickened, thrusting longer and harder, untamed. her kiss more erotic. Her body spoke to him, urging him with her. He reached between them and circled her.

"Oh, Rock," she said softly, drawing it out. He couldn't breathe, his body beyond his control and in her. His blood hummed, rushing along his erection, and he wanted more, only more of her slick heat taking him inside her, her body tightening with each moment closer to the peak. He pushed long and slow, then quickened, and Rock fought the tension, wanting this to go on, but his body wasn't cooperating.

Her muscles tensed, contracted, her tender grip trapping his hard-on, and he pumped, his control slipping. Scarred and seasoned melted with feminine, wet and hot. Primal. Captive sensations ripped free, roaring through his blood and blinding him.

Her hips rose greedily, quicksilver and sleek, pulling him along with her, and he plunged into her with a frantic, erotic pulse. He met her gaze, her smoky eyes intense as her body took him again and again.

Sitting back on his calves, he crushed her to him as if to bring her into his very core. He pushed on her lower spine and thrust upward, deeply, elongating, and the untamed monster inside him roared free. His groan rose in tempo, melting with her gasps, and they shivered through the shuddering culmination.

He held her tightly, his kiss strong and softening as the pleasure ebbed to a humming in his blood. He slid his hand up her spine to the base of her skull, his fingers sinking into her hair, and she tipped her head back. She met his gaze, and Rock swiped his hand over her hair and kissed her softly.

He'd always known they would be good together.

In the tropical rainforest of Central America, in the most dangerous place on earth, she embedded herself deeper into his soul.

Deeper than he could have ever imagined.

Rock awoke just before the gray half-light of dawn, feeling damn good in spite of the tender temple and a sore arm. But the feeling-good part had mostly to do with the beautiful woman he had tucked close to him, his arm secure around her waist, her breath warm against his neck, and he let his eyes drift shut, loving the feeling of waking up with her in his arms.

He was loving this hammock, gravity pulling them both automatically to the center and right on top of each other. Yesterday was still somewhat of a blur, as was that near-drowning experience he could have done without.

He'd been cognizant enough to know that he was in no shape to hold his breath for thirty seconds, let alone the two minutes it had taken for them to pass through that underwater cave. But she wouldn't have left him, and he couldn't expose her to any more danger. If those drug runners had found them, there would have been no questions or quarter. Just plain murder.

He was a marine. It was either do or die.

And he would die before he let some scum of the earth harm Neve or a young girl with the courage of a lion.

The bro code had been smashed to smithereens, and just like his brother, Dexter, he'd succumbed to his best friend's little sister. In Dex's case, Piper Jones had been Tyler Keighley's older sister, but age didn't matter here.

He was heading for a fall either way. He loved her, had for a long time, and she wasn't going to stay put. Her plan had been and would remain to be a rescue swimmer in the coast guard, which meant pulling up stakes every two to four years and going somewhere new.

When he'd been young, he wasn't like Dex, who could practically breathe and make friends, settle into a new life like he'd always been there. Belonged wherever their father took them, be it somewhere in the United States or overseas.

But Rock hadn't been like that; even in the marines, he'd been a loner until he'd bonded with a screwed up, kick-ass partner named Tristan Michaels. Other than his family, Rock didn't let many people in, and that mostly had to do with protecting himself against getting attached to someone and then having to move again. It was self-preservation.

With Neve, he was fresh out of self-protective instincts.

The bottom line was he didn't want to move every two to four years, especially once he had kids. He'd built a business in San Diego, and it was true he was branching out, but he chose that area because he loved it. He couldn't have both Neve and his way of life; that was a fact.

But he'd ride this temporary fix until the very bitter end. Neve was in his blood, and that was where she would always stay. He hated to think he was ruined for any other woman, but he was really quite immovable on this fact. Once she was out of his life, he would deal. Right now, in the present, they still had a threat to defuse. Personal complications aside, they also had someone tailing them. From the performance of their sniper in that camp, the way he'd kept Neve safe, Rock was inclined to give him the benefit of the doubt. She had to be aware of it now. She stirred against him, and he already had a bad case of morning wood.

A breeze could blow across him and that would set him off, so having all this...woman against him put him on a hair trigger.

He looked down at her, the buzz from his hard-on jacking him a little higher when she cuddled against him, her generous breasts rolling, then flattening against his chest, her face snuggling his neck. Geezus, he could get used to this every morning for the rest of his life. He shifted his arm when she said, "Ow." Realizing he was on her hair, he gathered the thick, mass into one heavy cord. Smoothing it down her skin, the long strands clinging to his hands, he pressed a kiss against the top of her head. Her hair was something else. In a braid, it was as thick as his wrist and stick-straight, so black it looked blue under the lights. But it felt like silk, and it glimmered like satin. When he'd first known her, it had reached past her waist, but now it fell midway down her back.

"I would kill someone for a cup of coffee right now," she murmured, then kissed his neck, trailing her lips up his throat to the curve of his jaw.

Rock grinned, slowly running his hand over the thick, rumpled mess. Shifting his head, he looked at her, lifting a stray strand that clung to her cheek. Damn, she was beautiful, her Inuit coloring and unique almond eyes adding to her magnetism that made men look. But part of that, he suspected, was the way she carried herself, the way she moved. She was tall, five feet eight inches worth of sleek muscles and legs that went on for days. But it was how she moved, with the confident, long-legged stride and the grace and power of an athlete. He could just while away the time watching her.

"You smell good," she whispered. "Almost as good as coffee."

His grin widened, getting a charge out of her groggy ramblings. "I wish I could nip down to Starbucks for you, babe, but the closest one is…oh…about one hundred fifty miles from here."

Her eyes still closed, she smiled against him. "You're a marine. That's a leisurely jog for you."

He chuckled and he squeezed her. "Ooh-rah, I'll be back in two shakes." He shifted as if to rise.

She wrapped her arms around him and when she felt his erection, she murmured, "On second thought, I think I prefer this testosterone-flavored wake-up call to a dose of caffeine."

Still smiling, he ran his hand down the full length of her hair. "Is that so? I'm so damned flattered."

"You should be." Her voice was full of that sassy dryness he loved. "This will be much more physical."

"Oh, really?" he said, just as dry. "Jogging a mere one hundred fifty miles isn't physical?"

She laughed. "It's a small price to pay, a trifle really. Coffee is no laughing matter."

"I'm pretty damned amused right now."

"Be careful or I'll shove you on the floor."

He wasn't too worried. "I'm injured, and you just saved my life, like, twice yesterday, so that's somewhat of an empty threat." He figured it wasn't prudent to challenge her, but he couldn't help it. If she did decide to dump him onto the floor, he would have one hell of a fight on his hands—and he could think of better things to do. Another smile softened his expression. He didn't know how many times they had made love last night, but it didn't matter. It would never be enough. Shifting slightly, he drew her leg completely over his, then began softly stroking her breast.

"Sex maniac," she murmured.

His amusement intensified, and he trailed his fingers down the side of her breast. "Insatiable."

"If you start something here, Marine, you better be ready to finish it. I like things done all the way." She raised herself up on one elbow and shook her hair back, then looked at him, her eyes all smoky from sleep.

"First in, babe. Last out."

"I like the sound of that." She trailed her hand over his face, across his stubble several times. Then her fingers took a journey down his throat and over the rounded muscle of his bicep. She lifted his arm and peered closer at the tattoo there. "Devil Dog?"

"Yeah…marine moniker." He sent his hand over her hair. "*Teufelshunde*. Hellhound…devil dog. Germans weren't too fond of marines."

"I bet the enemy is never *fond* of the marines," she said with a gleam in her eye.

"We don't go in to make friends. But there's some doubt the Germans ever called the marines that now-legendary name." He shrugged. "Doesn't really matter. Those WWI marines fought like devil dogs. Unleashing hell on the enemy is just a perk."

"I do like the chocolate and cream cakes myself." She rubbed her fingers over his collarbone, then traced the swell of his pectoral muscles, enflaming him.

"Are you saying I'm a cream puff?"

"Sometimes," she murmured, her voice dropping to a whisper as she flattened her palm, rubbing over his chest, his nipple. "Completely yummy. And with fewer calories."

He closed his eyes, lost in the soft meandering of her hand and fingers as she bumped over each ridge of his tight abs. When she got closer to his groin, his breath caught and he lifted his lashes. Her admiring eyes flicked up to his, and she leaned close to him, brushing her lips over his mouth. "In fact, I'm sure I'm going to burn quite a few with you."

"I need a workout or two."

"All this—" she indicated his upper body "—says differently. I've always wanted to tell you how sexy I find all this delicious muscle." She ran her hands over both his biceps, careful of his bandage. "Especially these—"

"Guns," he said, grinning like a sappy fool. "You've got me locked and loaded, babe."

She returned one of her own. "Yes, deadly weapons, my friend." She used her nails, sending him into overload.

"I'm not your friend," he growled as she molded her hand over his arousal.

She braced her hands on his shoulders. "And here I thought we were getting along so well." There was nothing better than tits and ass in the morning, but it was ten times better because this gorgeous woman was Neve.

He gave her a lazy grin, slowly running his hand up the back of her thigh, liking the way her black, shiny hair fell around her shoulders, liking the way her eyes got all soft and inviting. "From my excellent and sexy-as-damn-hell vantage point, I'd say that's a foregone conclusion, babe."

"Russell," she said softly.

Experiencing a thickness in his chest, Rock lifted a swath of her hair. Maybe if he wasn't so freaking lost in her he could enjoy this as lighthearted banter and let her go. But she made him laugh, and she had his back. Disconnecting from all the longing, he caressed the swell of her breast with the backs of his fingers. Trying to stay away from all those easily pulled triggers, he kept it light. "Why don't you come up here and say that again?"

Her eyes got dark, the pulse point in her neck beating, and she gave him a smile that he felt all the way to his toes. With the sensuousness of a cat, she slithered on top of him, her hair spilling around them as she straddled his hips, then slowly—so slowly—took him into her, her gaze riveted on his. Rock clenched his jaw, the pleasure so intense it made his whole body respond. Once he was fully inside her, she settled her weight on him, then softly, so softly, she cupped his face in her hands and leaned over and kissed him, her mouth moist and pliant and unbelievably gentle.

He made soft, slow love to her, both of them reaching the peak again, then taking a while to get their bearings.

When she finally eased away, he slid his hand up to the back of her head and pulled her against him, releasing a very shaky sigh.

"How was my response to your challenge?" she whispered unevenly.

"Looks like you put me in my place. You were first in and last out."

Christ, she filled up the holes inside him, holding her like this, feeling as if they had become part of one another. And she understood how much he needed that. There was a time, after his grannie had passed. He'd gotten the news while on leave with Tristan. It was sudden and devastating. He'd never gotten a chance to say goodbye. Neve had found him, sitting outside on their porch, losing it. She stayed with him all night, and he'd never forgotten it. And he never would. He could not have felt closer to another human being than he'd felt with her that night. Or now.

Pulling her hair out of the way, he kissed the base of her neck, then cradled her tightly against him, letting the sensations wash through his whole body. It didn't get better than this. It couldn't. Closing his eyes against the sudden thickness in his throat, he turned his face against her neck and tightened his arms around her. He would take all of this he could get.

He knew when she'd drifted back to sleep. A small smile surfaced as he closed his eyes, listening to the sounds from outside—the distinctive "jungle" noise that was always present—howler monkeys, birds, the rustling of bushes and the wind in the trees. He drew in the soul-deep calm she brought him. He filtered everything through his warrior senses.

The sky had started to lighten, and he could hear the villagers starting to stir, when she stirred and straightened one leg alongside his. "You can start moving anytime, Kaczewski," she murmured against his neck, her voice thick with sleep.

Rock tipped his head back and laughed, then hugged her hard. "I didn't hear reveille."

She threw her head back this time and laughed. Sliding her hand up his neck, she leaned down and whispered in his ear and contracted her leg around him. "Can't you get it up... I mean, get up in the morning?"

He made a soft half laugh, half moan. "Oh, I can get it up anytime, babe."

Grasping her straightened leg, he pulled her knee up, then put considerable effort into a long, hot, wet kiss.

"You are a very wicked man."

"Ooh-rah," he murmured against her mouth, then moved, slow and deliberate. And suddenly it didn't matter that their time was limited.

The rays of the sun were cresting the horizon when reality checked in, along with Opal. She knocked at the panel of their door. He had asked her to come back. They still had a trek ahead of them, but it was time to do some recon. They weren't far from Boca de Cupé, and Neve's contact had said that Ammon Set was in this area somewhere. They could use the village as their base.

Releasing a heavy sigh, he tucked Neve's hair back and nestled her closer, his expression sobering. Sometimes he wondered why he had given in. It only made loving her harder. He sometimes wondered what would have happened if she'd never gotten stationed in San Diego. If, by the luck of the draw, she'd been shipped off to some other station. Maybe he would be married by now, both having gone on with their lives. He looked at her, experiencing a twist around his heart. And again, maybe not.

"Time to move it out?"

His expression solemn, he smoothed her hair into a long fall. "Yeah. We need to talk and plan. Take stock of our supplies with the hope that everything made it through that harrowing drop."

She shifted her head and brushed a kiss against his chest, then she said, her voice smooth and textured like satin, "I want to check your wounds and change your bandages."

"Sure." He knew this was only a temporary thing, that absolutely nothing would come of it. They were on different paths—sometimes they got close enough to touch, but an actual connection was impossible. That's why, after she'd held him after his grannie died, he hadn't accepted another invitation from Tristan to visit Dutch Harbor.

"You go first and be careful, or we'll both get dumped on the floor."

"Too bad we don't have the time to see where that would lead us."

"Get going, bad girl, before I dump you on your ass."

She laughed and gingerly rolled toward the edge, dangerously tilting the hammock. "This is a very tricky maneuver."

Her rear in the air as she went to get her legs under her made him groan softly. "But the view is amazing."

She shot a look over her shoulder, and it was all the warning he got as she pressed down and then let the hammock go. It recoiled, and since he was more toward the other side to give them leverage, the cloth flipped and sent him onto the hard floor.

"Oops. My bad," she said with an innocent look. "Now *that* is a view." She gave him a once-over. He came up off the floor, and they horsed around until finally he gave her a hard, sweet kiss.

She went for her pack. "I'm starving," she announced, pulling on a clean sports bra with a bit of lace around the edges and pair of panties. After slathering on sunscreen/bug repellant, she tossed the bottle to him. "Could you get my back?"

He caught it and walked up to her. Before she turned around, she said, "You are a distracting package, Marine."

He slathered on the cream, enjoying the feel of her skin.

"Thanks," she said when he was done. "Turn around and I'll get yours." Her soft hands roamed over every inch of him, then she slapped his butt. "Done. Get dressed."

"Yes, ma'am."

Playtime was over. It was time to go hunting for more than just Set. There was someone out there shadowing them. He wanted to find out whether he was friend or foe.

Their lives depended on it.

Chapter 11

"What the hell do you mean you lost them?"

"Things got hairy, and they drove a Jeep off a cliff and landed in some deep, fast-moving water. I freaking lost them, Austin. So don't rub it in. Do you think I want to let Amber down? And I like Dexter Kaczewski, by the way. So this off-the-books mission was a no-brainer."

"Aw, hell. What do you want me to tell Amber?"

"Don't tell her a damn thing right now."

"Do you think they're dead?"

"I don't know, but they went into the drink with a young girl."

"This just gets better and better."

"You busting my chops?"

"No. Look, I'm not there, and I trust your judgment. See what you can find out and call me back. But Geezus, Derrick. Be careful. I'd rather not have to explain to Kai why you were in Central America in the Darién Gap when you were supposed to be on vacay. Savvy?"

"I got it loud and clear. No one will see me. This isn't my first covert rodeo."

"Okay, call me when you have more information."

He'd laid low overnight, and it didn't take long for the drug runners to pull up stakes and bug out. They were completely twitchy and probably trigger-happy, but Derrick could have picked them off one by one. He didn't want to draw a lot of attention just now with Rock and Neve somewhere in the area. They were hunting really dangerous prey.

As soon as the coast was clear, Derrick stripped down to his shorts and went diving. The current was strong, but nothing he couldn't swim in. He dived and found the submersed Jeep, but that gave him no answers.

He swam close to the bottom of the river, breathing a mental sigh of relief when there were no bodies. Could the gators have gotten them? It was totally conceivable that they could have been pushed downstream. Just when he was resolved to search along the river in case they had been washed up on shore—he swore softly to himself at the thought—he caught sight of a shadow beneath the falls. Frowning, he surfaced and grabbed several breaths of air and headed for the darkness, expecting it was just a trick of the light.

What he hadn't expected was to find a small cave on the backside of the falls. He pulled himself out and sluiced the water off his face as it ran in rivulets from his body. He padded over the smooth floor to another pool.

He didn't allow himself to breathe a sigh of relief. Not just yet.

* * *

How did she lose her resolve? How did everything get so turned around and even more complicated?

She sat in the common house with Rock and Opal. Looking at him, she sighed. He responded to Opal's question about fruit. It was simple and straightforward, but Rock's voice, the deep, feathered undertones, the easy, measured cadence, stood out like a foghorn. One look at him and she could remember every steely inch of him. Every. Freaking. Inch.

Oh, *that* was how.

Opal's father was graciously welcoming them to the village, and when Rock smiled, Neve felt punched in the gut. Dammit, maybe it was better when he'd been angry at her. Except that had all been resolved.

If she was being honest with herself, she couldn't regret one moment of what had happened yesterday. Being with Rock had been an experience she would never forget. It only made her calculate how many hours there were until nightfall.

"How about you, Neve?"

All three of them were looking at her, and she had no idea what they were talking about because she hadn't been listening. She was stressing over sleeping with him, and that had taken over her brain cells.

"I'm sorry. What was the question?"

Rock gave her an indulgent look. "Papaya, pineapple or fried plantains?"

"Oh, right, breakfast."

"From what I *heard*, she's starving. All three," Opal said, then smiled and left the table, as her father excused himself and also rose. Neve nearly laughed; restraining her amusement, her gaze connected with Rock's. He was sitting with his elbows on the table, his hands resting palms down. His expression gave nothing away, but there was something in his eyes that made her pulse jump into overdrive. The hint of amusement instantly faded, replaced by a glint that was more heated, far more potent, far more intent. Far more male. And Neve remembered that instant when he'd entered her, when she'd experienced the full thrust of him, and she clasped her hands together in her lap, her breath jamming up in her chest.

Rock's gaze intensified, and Neve could feel the heat of his gaze from across the table. Suddenly, she wished they were somewhere dark and private, somewhere…

The sound of the plate being set onto the wood interrupted her thoughts. Rock looked away, the muscles of his jaw clenching, something that excited her flaring in his eyes. She eyed the plate full of fruit, and since there were no utensils, she grabbed a piece of pineapple.

On the table were some flowers that Neve had seen in the jungle. These were a deep pink. "What are these called?"

"We call them *pinzas de langosta*."

"Lobster claws?"

"Yes, very pretty." Opal looked at both of them and said, "Why are you here in the Darién?"

"We're backpacking," Rock said, keeping his voice even and neutral.

She stared at him a moment, then looked at Neve, then said, "I might be sixteen and live in an isolated village, but I'm not stupid. I have seen many soldiers, and it's clear you have military training. You're no tourists."

Neve leaned forward. "We're just taking on the challenge of the Darién. Would it be possible for us to stay for a couple of nights?"

Opal still looked skeptical, but there was no way they were going to give away their tactical advantage. They really couldn't trust anyone. "Yes, of course. You are very welcome," she said eagerly.

After Neve and Rock finished their breakfast, they headed back to their hut. They packed only what they needed for a day trek into the jungle.

"She's suspicious," Rock said.

"I know. What do you think she's involved in that would get drug runners pissed at her?"

He shrugged, looking concerned as he checked over his weapon and chambered a round. "She's working for them maybe? Ripped them off?"

Neve closed the ties to her pack. A muscled arm reached in front of her, and her heart lurched. She went still, giving her pulse a second to settle.

His shoulder brushing against her, Rock grabbed a couple of granola bars and tucked them inside one of the pockets. He snagged her hand. "I guess that's possible." Opal seemed wise beyond her years, but life, even in this beautiful place, wasn't always beautiful.

He caressed her fingers. "You have nice hands," he said gruffly.

Experiencing a heady rush from his caressing touch, Neve closed her eyes, her pulse going wild. She turned her hand, sliding her palm against his. He inhaled deeply, then lifted her hand and kissed her fingertips. Neve turned her face into his shoulder, her strength sapped by the sensations that surged through her. Shaken by the intensity of her reaction, she laced her fingers through his, needing time to get herself together. He had over-whelmed her; with one single kiss, he had simply overwhelmed her. Then she picked up the thread of their conversation. "She seems so young."

"There are drug dealers on the streets of New York City younger than her," Rock said with disgust, rising with her and releasing her hand. "There are no age limits when it comes to trafficking and selling that stuff."

She wasn't under any illusions here. They were on their own; no help would come if they got into a serious situation, and Neve could probably kiss her coast guard career goodbye if it was ever discovered that she came here to a foreign country to kill someone. She would not be given any quarter. Her commander, in particular, already reamed her out for not being a team player. It made her think about that, especially what happened during the rescue of Set's relatives. Even now, she was "teaming" up with Rock, and if she looked below the surface of her reasons for trying to ditch him, she wondered if her tendency to want to go it alone was part of that underlying reason. Why was it so difficult for her to ask for help? Did she think that made her look weak?

"Do you think we should leave?" she asked, dropping her head. It was hard to look at him, especially when he was in that sexy warrior mode. He went still and braced one hand on his hip. His gaze was intent when she lifted her head. His eyes were dark and steady, and she got a tiny dose of the nerves. Really, what was there to be nervous about? This was Rock. It had been so much easier last night, when things had just happened. She wasn't quite sure how to proceed from here, how to handle all… all of him. Mostly her uncertainty.

He stepped closer and everything went haywire. He stared at her, and she tried to curb the feelings she had for him. "No, I'd like to know what she's up to. We don't want to be walking into any ambushes."

Neve nodded. "Agreed."

His compressed expression showed as hard lines around his mouth; his eyes giving nothing away as usual. Then he slipped his hand behind her neck and squeezed. He held her gaze, his hair shining in the sun falling into the room. He looked dark and foreboding and unapproachable, but the look in his eyes made her heart pound and her knees weak, and that was so unlike her. There was a flare of emotion, and he tightened his grip on her neck. His touch put her into sensory overload.

"I want to kiss you right now," he whispered roughly. "But I'm not going to because I'm afraid we won't get out of that hammock for a week. We need to be on point here. Opal is an unknown ally, and we still have the EDL after us, not to mention we don't know what's going on with those drug runners. And we have a mission to complete."

"Then this won't help at all," she said, wrapping her arms around him and planting her mouth on his, kissing him soundly. He groaned softly and she pulled away, smoothing her hands over his shoulders and collarbone. "Sorry. I guess I don't have your willpower."

He stared at her, then a glimmer of amusement appeared in his eyes and he gave her a lopsided smile. "Great, I've never been on patrol with a hard-on before. Oh, wait…no, I have." The husky intimacy of his tone set off a wild flutter, making her wish they were anyplace but here. He gave her a sultry look and reached down and shouldered the lightened pack.

"What a waste," she murmured as she preceded him

out of the hut on a very male, wholly frustrated strangled sound.

As soon as they cleared the village, Neve asked, "So what exactly do you do when you reconnoiter?"

The dirt path was narrow, but still wide enough for them to walk side by side. It was steamy, the rain the night before leaving the jungle wet with wisps floating in the canopy, small, thin clouds of vapor.

"It's all about keeping the enemy off balance, adding an offensive punch to the defense, allowing us to retain the initiative and guard against surprise."

"Looking around and getting the lay of the land."

"That's a watered down version, yeah."

"Then my first suggestion is to head back to the drug runners' camp and see what's going on there. We can slip back through the pools if you're up for it and covertly check it out."

He gave her a quick, assessing look. "That was going to be my first suggestion. See if we have something to worry about from that quarter." He squeezed the back of her neck and said, "I'll make a marine out of you yet."

"The coast guard isn't any slouch, you know. Drug smugglers, gunrunners are all in a day's work for us Coasties. And," she said, nudging him, "I held my breath longer than you did."

"True," he said, chuckling, "but there were mitigating circumstances."

"Excuses," she said as they approached the cave with the pool. Setting his finger to his lips, he indicated that she should go first.

She shook her head and pointed at him, then tapped her temple. He nodded, moving in front of her after giving her an indulgent look.

When he reached the lip of the pool, he slipped into the water; Neve really didn't want to get wet again, but this was a smart move on their part. It was clear that if the smugglers had known about the hidden cave beneath the waterfall, they would have sent some men after them. Neve had to wonder if Opal really did have a reason to seek out the group.

The swim went much better this time, with Rock easily maneuvering the waterway without any problem. Neve couldn't stop the memory of his soft, unresponsive lips beneath hers as she'd breathed air into his lungs.

They emerged on the other side, their boots making very little sound on the rocky floor. Russell slipped down into the opening, and they swam again until they were outside the cave. She followed him as he crawled out of the water into a deep clump of underbrush on the side of the river, then hunched down as they scooted into the cover of the trees.

He got close to her ear. "If they're still here, they would be right above us. Let's go down that way." He pointed to where the path sloped, allowing a short climb back up to the cliff above them. Luckily there was plenty of cover.

She nodded, and he moved toward the incline. As soon as they reached the edge, they heard voices and both of them ducked for cover.

Staying crouched, Rock indicated they should move, and he flattened out on his stomach and started to GI crawl up the incline. She found it was harder than it looked as she followed him. They got to the top, right near where Neve had been discovered by several of the smugglers. Her clothes clung to her, the humid air adding to the moisture, sweat running down their faces. The ground beneath them was rough with plenty of roots and leaf cover. When they moved, the loamy, somewhat moldy smell wafted up to her.

Those bodies were gone, but she could still detect the dark splotches where blood had splattered.

It got her to thinking and remembering as Rock peered out into the clearing.

That had been such a blur of crazy, terrifying danger when those men had suddenly burst through the trees. The shots, now that she was looking at the area, couldn't have come from the direction Rock had gone.

She twisted and looked over her shoulder, calculating the trajectory, then focused on an area high above her.

A sniper?

Had someone rescued her from those men?

The only person she could think of that might be out here sniping could be Tristan. Her mouth tightened. She had specifically asked Rock to keep him out of this. It wasn't like her brother was in the dark about Ammon Set, but it hadn't occurred to her that he might have taken on this mission, as well.

Except Amber hadn't given away anything when she'd talked to her on the phone. And she couldn't imagine Amber wouldn't have talked to her about it. The NCIS agent, her soon-to-be sister-in-law, wouldn't have hesitated to keep Tristan safe. There was no doubt about that in Neve's mind, but if Rock knew about this, or even worse yet, had enlisted her brother's help without her knowledge…

All her insecurities about what Rock thought about her and her abilities surfaced. If she couldn't trust him to tell her about Tristan, then how could she trust him at all? Teamwork meant trust, and maybe that was her problem. She wanted to trust only in herself. That way, she wasn't judged by others' standards or disappointed in her own performance.

Except, she had screwed up. That's why she was currently here in the Darién: to handle the apocalyptic mess she had created for her family. Losing those people in that storm had shaken her to her core. Could she have prevented their deaths?

That thought ate away at her whenever she'd allowed those doubts to surface.

She focused once again on the task at hand. There was no way to question Rock right now. She peered over his shoulder, and this time it was clear. The drug runners had cleared out. The camouflage netting was gone, along with the small tented lean-tos. There wasn't anything left except one Jeep and the cleanup crew.

They were throwing bodies in the back of the Jeep. It was clear they didn't want to leave a shred of information behind them. It smelled like death.

A twig snapped somewhere behind them, and one of the drug thugs paused and stood still, listening. The other man went on guard, as well.

Rock looked behind them, then said so softly she could barely hear him, "Stay here and don't move a muscle."

He slithered off, and Neve watched the men. One of them picked up a rifle and the other followed suit. He motioned to the area behind her, in the direction Rock had taken.

She kept them in her sights. There was no way they were going to harm him while she was still breathing.

He thought she was some untested novice, but Neve knew how to shoot, and her mixed martial arts training was a formidable deterrent to any unarmed attack. She wasn't experienced in taking a man down with a knife, but she had handled her assassin quite handily.

The men split up, and one headed in her direction. She was just about to test her theory.

Derrick couldn't believe it when he turned and saw Rock and Neve break the surface of the water. He'd just scouted the village and had come back for his gear. He was lucky he wasn't in plain view or, even better yet, meeting them in that underground pool.

He was just about to move when he spotted her. She was good, but he was better. She melted out of the water and took up a position right behind them. With a shock, he recognized the teenage girl from their harrowing flight off the cliff yesterday. The one who he suspected belonged to that village he discovered after several hours of searching.

What the hell was she up to, and why was she spying on them?

For just a split second, he thought about warning them. But this mission was supposed to be black, and he'd never gone against mission protocol, even when it had destroyed his world and hurt like a son of a bitch. He'd chosen his duty over his personal life.

He wasn't going to change that now. Rock and Neve had proved themselves resourceful up to now.

It was up to him to get to higher ground and act like the silent and deadly killer he'd been trained to be, the one Amber was depending on. He'd never let a teammate down, either, even when it made him look like the bad guy.

After all that he'd seen and done? He felt like a bad guy.

He slipped out of his hiding place and ghosted up to a better vantage point.

Neve moved off into the brush, so that when the searching drug runner got to her position, she was already primed and ready for him.

As soon as he looked around and then turned his back, she was on him. She jumped on his back and wrapped her arm around his throat, her legs around his waist. She tightened and held on as he dropped to his knees, the rifle falling from his lax hands. In moments it was over.

She grabbed up the rifle when she heard someone moving toward her, and had it cocked and pointed just as Rock burst out of the trees. He stopped. "Whoa," he said with his hands up.

His eyes went to the downed thug, and he gave her a lopsided smile and shook his head. "You are one tough babe, babe," he said.

"Yeah, I think I broke a nail," she said. Now that the danger was past, she was working at keeping her cool. She wanted so much to bring up the topic about Tristan, but it was best to get out of here.

"Looks like they were busy clearing out," he said as he jogged up to her. They went down the incline together.

"Looks like it." They reached the water, and he brushed something out of her hair. She went a little weak at the look in his eyes, but she wasn't going to be some kind of a pushover just because she'd slept with Rock.

Slept?

What a freaking tame term that was.

She'd ravaged him just as much as he'd ravaged her,

and she would be willing to bet everything she had he wanted to do it again first chance he got. That would depend on his answers to her questions.

It was back into the water and the swim from one pool to another and then back out. They walked until they were in a more defensible place and sat down to eat some lunch.

Rock opened a plastic pouch and pulled out a map just as Neve finished the last of her water.

He spread it on a flat stone and pulled out a pen. He studied the map, then made a mark. "Here is where we are."

She nodded.

"And here's where we started, Yaviza. Here is Boca de Cupé."

She looked at the map and was so damned impressed. They had made almost a straight shot toward their destination. She couldn't remember him looking at the map very often, either. "How did you do that?"

"What?"

"Get us this close to our target without wasting a single moment?"

"Compass," he said, as modest as he was handsome.

"Rock," she said. Neve saw his eyes flare. "What?"

"I like when you call me Rock, that's all."

Oh, God. She had, and he knew it was as significant as it actually was to her. She'd always avoided his nickname because it was just too personal and intimate. "Stop changing the subject."

"You stop changing the subject."

She released a breath. "How did you manage to stay so completely on target? You never got lost once."

"Marines don't get lost… I don't get lost. If I don't

have a map and compass, I can figure it out by the stars. You could have dropped me in the middle of damn nowhere blindfolded, and with a compass and a map—screw GPS—I would have known where I was on the planet in a couple of minutes. Guaranteed. Marines are the ultimate Boy Scouts."

"Boy Scouts," she said with a raised brow.

He chuckled. "We don't rely on guides. Even in the Middle East, Afghanistan, Iraq, I knew where I was, regardless of having a guide. The trick is in knowing where we are supposed to be or finding a target that wasn't where anyone thought it was going to be."

"No target, no mission?"

"Exactly, and that is where we are right now. Right in the White Falcon's backyard."

"Lost."

"No, not lost. Targetless at the moment until we figure out where our foe has gone to ground."

Rock picked up his pack as if he was going to put something away. He was close to the edge of the underbrush. Suddenly he lunged and grabbed someone and hauled that someone out of a hiding place.

Opal, her eyes wide at being caught blurted out, "I can lead you to the White Falcon!"

Chapter 12

Rock stared at the girl, but to her credit she didn't flinch. Her chin rose and she faced him down. "I can. I know where his fortress is."

"What the hell is going on here? You were spying on us?"

"Yes, I was," she said defiantly.

He set his hands on his hips and eyed the strong-willed girl. "Opal, this isn't a game. This is serious business."

"She knows that. Geez, Rock, she's been living here a lot longer than we have. You have something on your mind. Why don't you tell us what it is?"

"I didn't just happen on those drug runners. I went looking for them."

"Are you out of your mind? Why?"

"I needed armed men to help me."

"What?"

"I offered them gold, and instead of taking it, they were going to rob me and rape me."

Rock ran his hand over his face.

"Why didn't you go to the government troops?"

She looked away. "I did. They said they couldn't help me. Money talks," she said sheepishly. "I was desperate."

"Why?"

"They have my twin brother. He was...taken to work for them. I have to get him out of there. He's just a boy. Please, will you help me? I can pay you." She reached for a pouch and spilled gold nuggets into his hands.

"This is what you offered those lowlifes?"

"Yes, it's all I have, but I could promise you more if you—"

"I'm not taking your gold, Opal."

"But, I can't leave him there." Tears started to stream from her eyes.

"Rock," Neve admonished. "You are such a *man*."

She wrapped her arms around Opal, who lost herself to the sobbing.

He rubbed the back of his neck. Geez, all he was doing was trying to keep this young girl out of danger. Take her deeper into the jungle? Were there worse dangers than drug runners? The White Falcon had proved himself to be a brutal and merciless man. Her young brother was tied up in this? Geezus. It was bad enough he had Neve in tow. Now a sixteen-year-old guide with enough gold to buy a house in San Diego? For Christ's sake.

At a loss to ever understand women, he sat down on a rock and folded his arms across his chest, waiting for the storm to pass.

Finally, Opal raised her head. "I know it was risky

and reckless, but no one in my village owns a gun, they don't know how to shoot and they don't want to cause any more trouble. But Ammon Set has no right to take my brother into service when he is so young."

"What is he doing for Set?"

"Bodyguard," she said, her lips pinched and fresh tears welling.

"In other words, he's his human shield?"

"Yes. If he stays and gives up his life, Set won't bother us. No, he won't hurt or harass our family, but he'll just cull more boys from our village like it's his personal human sacrifice shop!"

"What exactly were you planning on doing, Opal?"

"I'm going to kill him," she said with conviction.

During this conversation, they had gone back to camp, told Opal they had to discuss it and once again refused her gold payment.

Neve went with a distressed Opal, and Rock stopped at the hut before going to see Opal's father, Miguel.

"Tell me about your son."

The man stood and picked up a container and two glasses. He brought them over and poured. "*Chicha*, corn beer. It's good."

Rock sniffed, and all he smelled was a fruity odor, but the juice-like amber drink was very tasty.

"This is a ceremonial drink, good for celebrations, but you are a guest. José is a very good boy, excellent fisherman and hunter." His face fell. "Then they came and took him. I could do nothing. Tell me, do you have children?"

"No, not yet."

"They are a blessing, and it's not that I don't miss my boy and worry about him, but this Ammon Set is very powerful, has many guns. I don't wish for Opal to go after him, but the girl isn't going to heed my counsel. I fear that I will lose them both."

"Can't the government—"

"They do their best, but Set is very deep in the jungle and fortified. You would need an army."

"Sir, I am a marine."

"Yes, I have heard of these fighting men. I only beg of you to try to talk my daughter out of this folly. Have her tell you where this monster is, and you may continue on your journey."

"If I can't?"

"Then I will lose both my children. I cannot tie her down."

Rock set his hand on the man's arm. "We will do the best we can to keep her safe." It was time to continue their journey, but they needed to take care of some housekeeping. "Where is the best place to wash my clothes?"

"In the river, but I can have that done for you for a small fee."

"Thank you. Could I take the *chicha* with me?" Rock set down some money on the table. The old man's eyes widened.

"Yes, for that kind of donation, it's yours. Before you go, I have something you and your lady can wear for modesty."

When Rock went back to the hut, carrying the two flimsy pieces of colorful cloth, he climbed up the notched stairs. Neve was standing at the end of the hut, looking pensive. "Babe?"

She turned, then froze. Her eyes went over him in a

slow, sultry slide. Her breath hitched, and then she said, "Oh, my God."

He smiled. "It's all they had, and I wanted clean clothes." He looked down at himself. "It covers me."

"Well, it covers up the good parts, if you ask me."

"Yeah?" He walked across the wooden boards, barefoot after dropping his boots near the door. He reached her and held out the skirt and skimpy top.

She eyed them. "You want clean clothes?"

"Yes."

"Then stop being picky," he said.

She frowned. "What's that in your other hand?"

"Corn beer. It's good."

He set it on the table, pulled out a chair and sat. "Have a drink?" he offered.

"You want me to have a conversation when you're dressed…er…mostly…semi…oh, never mind." She sat and he poured two glasses.

"I wish I could get rip-snorting drunk on this, but it doesn't have enough kick."

He went to clink glasses with her, but she wasn't looking at his face. He reached out and slipped his finger under her chin. "This thing doesn't have a whole lot of room to…um, grow. So eyes up here."

She laughed and shook her head, taking a drink. "Oh, this is good."

"Did you talk to Opal?"

"Yes. She won't tell me where Set is, Rock. She insists on taking us herself. She threatened to follow if we tried to leave her behind. She's set on finding and saving her brother."

"You sympathize with her."

"Yes, if it was my twin, no one could keep me from doing something about it."

"She's sixteen."

"She seems to know her way around the jungle, and it would make our trip that much faster. But I didn't even want you involved, and now we have this dilemma."

She rose abruptly. "I should just leave."

He rose and latched on to her arm, pulling her to him. "No damn way, Neve. You made a promise to me."

"That's why I was hoping you would let me out of it."

"No goddamn way." He held her tighter.

"Damn Set, damn him. Damn *him*." She hugged hard.

What was he supposed to say to this? Rock pressed her head to his shoulder, trying to soothe her and being pretty much useless. It was an ugly feeling when you knew someone wanted you dead. Even worse when it included people you loved very much.

"This is all my fault." Her fingers dug into his back. Her body trembled with rage she wouldn't vent.

"I get that."

She pulled away. "I'm not exactly a team player, Rock. I think you would agree. I'm too independent."

"Right, but there were three other people in that chopper, right?"

"Yes. It's a lot of pressure to be one of a few women who have made it to rescue swimmer. You have to be faster, tougher, stronger, smarter. That storm spooked me. It reminded me of what my father used to have to fight against while crabbing. I got defensive, thinking the pilot didn't trust me because of my gender."

"You didn't kill those people, Neve. They were already in pretty bad shape when you got there. You did the best you could, in the face of terrible conditions. Your life was on the line."

"I almost didn't make it back up." Her eyes teared. "That scared the crap out of me and those people died." She looked down for a second, blinking, then met his gaze. "What if it was because of my bias, because I didn't wait and I was impeded by my injury, Rock? You said it yourself. I'm not a team player. What if I'm not fit for coast guard duty at all?" A lone tear rolled down her cheek, and the sight of it sliced through him.

Rock saw doubt in her eyes, and it tore at him, pissed him off. He liked it better when she was ready to chew him up and spit him out. "You saved my life in that pool, Neve." He stepped closer to her, pointed at her. "You." Grasping her upper arms, he squeezed gently. "I think that's all the answer to your question you need."

"You should get away from me." She smoothed her hands up his arms, then wrapped them around his neck, seeking comfort. "Far away."

"No dice, babe. I like that you confided in me, though. I've been waiting a long time for that."

She separated from him, grabbed his shoulders and shook him. "You're a protective fool. I'm trying to keep you alive." Panic radiated off her in waves.

"*I'll* keep you alive, dammit." She stared up at him for a long moment, then finally nodded. He leaned over. He loved her direct, tender gaze. Damn, but he loved this woman. He kissed her, not with the hot fire of passion from before, but slowly and infinitely more cherishing. It was seeking, a soft probe, and Neve moaned, gripping his waist; her hands felt good there, but he wasn't kidding. There was nowhere for his hard-on to go but up and out. He tried thinking about ice and baseball scores.

He softened his mouth and went slowly, drawing everything she had inside her like a ribbon wanting to tug at her soul. He framed her face in his big hands, his attention only on the kiss, on telling her what he couldn't say.

Then he pulled back, breathing hard, stunned by that, too. He pressed his forehead to hers.

"Russell," she murmured.

He picked up the clothes. "Trot down to the river and find Lupe, change into these and you'll be happy I coerced you with alcohol and promises."

Her brow rose. "Alcohol, I got. Promises?"

He whispered in her ear, and her fingers tightened on his shoulders. She looked at him with her mouth open. He used his index finger to close her jaw. "This is a limited time offer."

"You are a…wicked…wicked man," she said, her face flushed.

"While you're gone, I'm going to make a perimeter run."

She looked him up and down, arched an eyebrow. He just smiled.

She let out a breath and left.

Regardless of what he was wearing, Rock moved like he was invisible. Combat boots, bare feet, battle dress uniform, loincloth. It didn't matter. Even naked, he was still a marine. The only problem with the loincloth was there was no place to tuck his gun. But it fit quite nicely in his hand, his KA-BAR snugly tucked into a sheath strapped to his ankle.

He stopped without making a sound and went to one knee. Boot prints, fresh ones. He looked around.

"I know you're out there," he said, low and threatening. "I don't like to be followed."

There was no answer.

Damn, this guy was good.

The back of his neck prickled. He was sure there was someone watching him. But this had to be someone who was on his side. He didn't care. He never did like surprises.

But he'd saved Neve's life.

Yeah, right. He'd shake his hand and give him a medal after he punched him in the mouth.

Everything around the little village was as quiet as could be, except for the usual jungle noises; no two-legged predators walked. Didn't mean Rock would let down his guard.

He headed back to the hut, his stomach grumbling. As he entered the village, the smell of cooking fish made it twist even more. He would go get Neve, and then they'd get a meal.

When he entered the hut, it was his turn to freeze and send his eyes over her. She had on a halter top, but it hadn't been made for a woman with such—how did he put this?—full breasts. She flowed over the top of it, the swell of her breasts creamy and inviting. The short, colorful skirt snugged around her waist, set off her beautiful tanned skin, the length of her legs making his mouth water.

"The top doesn't fit. Did you do this on purpose?"

He couldn't have planned it any better. "You make me crazy with all that beautiful skin showing."

"Really? My skin?" She looked down then back up. "I don't think it was exactly my skin you were looking at, so can it. I'm starving."

She turned to leave, but he grabbed her arm and swung her back around.

"What do you think you're doing?"

"You're not going out dressed like that."

"Oh, for the love of God, you wanted me decked out like this for a little scintillating role-play?"

"Not exactly, but it turned out damn fine for me."

"You are such a man."

"I know." He pulled her against him and she stumbled hard, colliding with his chest and pressing all her sweetness up against him. "I'm guessing that's what you like about me."

"Rock, we don't have time for games."

"We have time to let Opal cool her heels and think about this reckless plan of hers. We'll talk to her in the morning and get the information out of her, then be on our merry way. In the meantime, I'll get us some dinner. You, stay."

"What? Did you just order me to heel?"

"No. I asked you to please stay here."

"I think all this skin is making you a little disoriented."

"Haha." He kissed her soundly as she pressed on his chest. "Actions speak louder than words," he said huskily as he headed for the door and some of that delicious-smelling food. "Be right back."

The fish, vegetables and tubers were excellent, along with the fruit. He decided to make one more perimeter run, and when he got back, Neve was sprawled across the hammock, facedown and naked. The gods were torturing him, he thought. He stared as any red-blooded man would. Her hand dangled off the edge, her hair covering her face. He pushed it back, his gaze traveling over her long slim body. He grew hard instantly, painfully, and yet he let her sleep. He poured himself some more of that fruity-tasting beer and sat down in a chair. He propped his feet on the other chair and laid his gun on the table.

Maybe he should have contacted Tristan. He had to wonder what his best friend would think right now as he sat here and ogled his baby sister. It seemed almost a betrayal, but Neve... God, she was so damned beautiful.

Rock jerked awake, his body stiff. He must have slept for a while. He slapped his hand over his gun, instantly aware. He slipped off the chair, tracking shadow and moonlight with his eyes, then relaxed when he saw her. She stood at the low rail, the balmy jungle breeze pushing her hair back along with the T-shirt she wore.

One of his.

Hell of a sight, he thought, like a fantasy played out: hair flying, the thin fabric whipping and molding to her body in the moonlight.

"Neve." She didn't open her eyes, but from her posture he could tell she knew he was there.

"I didn't mean to wake you."

"That chair wasn't the most comfortable."

"You should have come into the hammock with me."

He came to her, leaving the gun on the table. "I wanted to make sure we weren't followed."

She smiled softly. "Always vigilant, huh?" she said, staring out into the night. "This is a beautiful place."

The jungle stretched out before them, a verdant, living, breathing green monster, dripping in moisture under a canopy of twinkling stars. "I guess."

Neve smiled. "Spoken like my true alpha marine."

He wished that was so and he could get her out of

here, but she wouldn't acquiesce to him because she was more an Amazon warrior, yet she proved to be his ultimate temptation. Everything he wanted in a woman. He'd sat there watching her sleep and knew it to be true, but that fact was evident years ago when he'd first set eyes on her. He wished he could tell himself she was the best screw he'd ever had and that was all it was. But that would be a complete lie, and playing games with himself was never his style.

He didn't want her body; he wanted her soul.

He took a step, crossing over the line for the millionth time and moved behind her, sliding his arms around her waist.

"Nice backrest," she murmured, leaning back and sliding her palm over his hand.

Just to feel her soft length against him was enough to make him rock-hard. The sleek curve of her throat beckoned him, and he pressed his mouth there, feeling her pulse beneath his lips. It nurtured something in him, this need to close the distance between them, and when she twisted enough to kiss him, pushing his hands where she wanted, Rock wanted her more than ever. He slipped his hands underneath her T-shirt, exposing her warm skin to the moonlight, circling her nipple with his thumb, his free hand sliding down to lay flat on her belly. She wiggled in his arms, pushing his hand, deepening his touch. He slid lower, his fingers diving between her legs as she melted and moaned beautifully, a delicious purr as she pushed back on his erection. She turned, sliding her hands across his chest, then her mouth was on his nipple, lips tugging.

"The jungle is not the only beautiful thing here tonight," she whispered, cupping him through the flimsy cloth that covered his groin, sliding her tongue over his nipple as his world shuddered.

Her hands at his waist, she pulled at the swath of material and it fell off his body.

"Oh, I like the easy access, adds a new meaning to the word *package*."

"You won't hear me complaining," he said on a gasp as she flowed down with the rectangle of cloth now in a pile at his feet. She wrapped her hand around his erection, stroked him his full length, then closed her mouth over him.

"Neve, damn." She worked him over until he was breathing hard and wanting more from her, then he dragged her up the length of him.

His mouth came down on hers hot and heavy, making his already labored breathing more intense, electrifying his nerves. The power of it drove him back against the rough wall, and his mouth left hers, storming a path down her throat to her breasts. He tasted her, the flavor of her groan exquisite; he was sucking her as if starved, taking it deep, then pulling.

Neve writhed, her hands running over him as if she couldn't get enough of the feel of his skin, her hands tugging and pulling, urging him, wanting the thrust of him. Her body bowed with each contact as his mouth wet a path to her center. She gasped, a soft inhalation that turned him on all the way, and he pushed her thighs wider, and knelt.

Her scent was heady, arousing, and he took what he wanted, glad that in the process it was good for her. She gasped for air as he tortured her, each stroke deepening with pressure, her climax a forgone conclusion.

"Rock," she pleaded.

He rose, his breathing as harsh as hers, wrapping his hand around her knee and lifting her leg to his hip. He didn't need to respond as her eyes met his.

He thrust, sliding deep, his penetration making her groan as she flexed against him and the wall, moonlight limning their bodies, his muscles thick and heavy, hers sleek and supple, both of them gleaming. He withdrew and thrust again and again, her flesh tight and silky against his erection. He smoothed his hand down her body, pulling at her nipples, teasing her sensitive core.

She leaned up and he cupped her behind, pulling her legs around him, then he pressed his back against the wall and slid down. With a soft cry, she took control, straddling, her hands on his shoulders. A slender beauty undulating in the dark. He'd never forget seeing her like this, her ripe body ribboned with passion. He looked down and watched her move over him, taking him inside her with abandon, wondering why it felt so amazing with her, and then he didn't give a damn. He kissed her, gripping her hips, and pulled her harder and harder. She cradled his face, her gaze locked on him as she came, pulsing with him, shuddering and flexing as the eruption ripped through her like a creature of madness and hunger.

He groaned, his kiss all-devouring, his hips uncontrollable in a wild ride till he caught up with her—and burned. Rock's mind went blank, sensations hammering him, and he fell back with her, cupping her behind and trembling for long delicious minutes.

She turned her head so that her mouth was against his ear. "You really know how to storm those beaches," she murmured and he pulled her close and laughed softly.

Chapter 13

Cradling her face, laying a sweet kiss over her mouth that made her heart turn over, he said, "You are a piece of work, lady."

"Right back at you, Marine." He did things to her, erased old pain and loneliness. She knew this was a time out of time and couldn't last, but discovering Rock and being with him was one of the most profound experiences of her life. She didn't want to give her emotions free rein because so much was up in the air with them, least of all the outcome of this dangerous and risky venture they were currently on. Even though she didn't want him in harm's way, she couldn't, at this moment, wish for him to be anywhere else.

In a powerful move, he rose off the floor, carrying her, still intimately locked with him, to the hammock. He backed into the suspended bed with the kind of balance that astounded her and maneuvered them down into it where she slid against him tightly.

"That was pretty impressive," she said, using both hands to massage his shoulders, and she felt him smile.

He brushed back the hair at her temple, then lowered his head and kissed her. "I do have skills."

"I wasn't talking about the sex, but that was good, too." He laughed as she sighed.

Neither of them spoke for several moments, content with gentle stroking and even gentler kisses. Finally, Rock eased his upper body away from her. Neve smoothed her hands up the contours of his biceps, her voice husky as she whispered, "Rock?"

Bracketing her face with his hands, he leaned down and kissed the bridge of her nose.

"Uh-huh?"

"We have to find a way to get the information out of Opal and keep her safe. We owe that to her. She really saved our bacon."

"She's not going to be easily swayed."

"She's stubborn."

"Like someone else I know."

She pinched his waist and he pulled her tighter to him. After a comfortable silence, he tucked in his chin and brushed a kiss against her forehead. "Neve?"

Drowsy with contentment, she sleepily watched the shadows of the leaves on the wall, comfortable in the cradle of his arms. "What?"

He hesitated, then said, his voice quiet. "You could stay here with her, encourage her to tell us where the compound is, and I could go take care of it."

She lay absolutely still for a split second, then she rose on one arm, bracing her hand on his chest as she looked down at him. "No freaking way am I going to let you do this alone," she said fiercely.

Meeting her gaze and smiling so softly it made her heart turn over, he carefully tucked her hair behind her ear. His tone gruff, he said, "Pretty much the response I expected, but it was worth a shot." Taking her with him, he rolled onto his back. Making room for her knee between his, he nestled her head on his shoulder, his touch gentle as he stroked her arm.

Cupping his jaw, she caressed the curve of his cheekbone with her thumb. She didn't know what was going to happen tomorrow, but she knew she was never going to allow him to take on Set without her.

She'd rather die trying to save her own life than cower in the dark and wait for Set to make his final move against her.

She really hadn't let go of the incident with the drug runners. It had been pushed to the back of her mind, but she needed to bring it up to him.

"Rock?"

"More sleep, less talk," he murmured.

"Just one more thing."

"Okay." He let out a deep, tired breath.

"I think someone covered me from the ridge when those drug runners were closing in on me."

He didn't give anything away, but he was quiet, then he said, "What makes you think that?"

"I didn't kill all of them. I had help."

Covering her mouth in a drugging kiss, his fingers snagging in her hair, Rock pulled her head down, distracting her. "It was most likely a crossfire. We're just lucky as hell you weren't hit. I don't even want to think about it."

Catching her by the hips, he drew her fully on top of him, then settled her between his thighs, running his hands along her rib cage until he reached her breasts. His touch sent spirals of sensation through her, and Neve closed her eyes, yielding to his mouth. She could trust him. Rock wouldn't lie to her.

She could trust him.

Neve didn't make it up before him, but she saw her meager stack of clothing all dried and folded on the table. She rather liked the pretty skirt, so she donned that and one of her tank tops.

This whole trip had been a time of discovery for her. She'd found an astounding physical intimacy with Rock. That had empowered her, and he had uncovered a sensuality in her that she hadn't even known she possessed. Being part of a team, really part of a team, was also something of a surprise. She found that she enjoyed it, that giving a little didn't mean she couldn't still be strong, power in flexibility, bend in rigidity.

But even with this wonderful connection, at some point she was going to have to deal with reality. But right now, with the future unknown and dangerous, she would take this time with Rock as a gift. She was smart enough to know that there were countless complications, and any one of them could destroy something so fragile and new. That realization filled her with such cold, hard dread that it sat like a rock in the pit of her stomach.

And there was Rock himself. He was still a bit closed to her, and she worried that there was something more to that incident at the drug runner camp, more to Rock than he was voicing. The only thing that was for certain was the here and now. She made up her mind that she was

going to cherish the gift she had been given for as long
as it was hers to hold. She would make the most of what
she had today and worry about tomorrow—tomorrow.

She left the hut, and as soon as she was steps away
from the stairs to Opal's place, the sky split, letting loose
torrential rains. Neve ran for cover, the mud splashing
on her calves. She climbed the stairs, then knocked.

"Are you the second wave?"

Neve tilted her head and said, "Rock's already been
here?"

"Yes, and he was very…intense," she groused, pushing past Neve to sit on the edge of the porch.

"Was he successful?"

"In getting me to tell him where the White Falcon is?
No. I won't leave my brother to him, and I won't give up
going myself. I have to. This is my fault."

"How is it your fault?"

"I was panning for gold. I wanted to go to the city
and make my way there. I like clothes and wanted to
maybe see about designing them. I encroached too close
to his compound and when he caught us, he took José
as payment."

Neve curled her arm around Opal and squeezed her
close. "This is not on you, hon. It's on Ammon Set. I
think you can trust us to handle this for you and get your
brother back. Just tell me where to go."

Her shoulders slumped, and she looked out into the
jungle, tears tracking down her face. "I will think about
it and have an answer for you this afternoon." She turned
to Neve, her face earnest. "What do you want with the
White Falcon? Why is he a threat to you or Rock?"

"I failed to rescue his family from the sea. I work for

the coast guard in the US, and they were all killed in a boating accident off the coast. He blames me."

"For trying to rescue them? That is sick and twisted. For what it's worth, I'm sorry that happened to you."

Neve hugged her harder. "We promise to bring your brother back safe and sound. Rock and I are a team, and we'll make sure we get him out of there and back here to his family."

Opal rose and smiled softly, "I know you mean that, and it's not that I don't believe you. It's not about you two at all. It's about me and my responsibility to my brother and my father. I need some time to make peace with this. After the celebration tonight to wish you well on your journey, I will give you an answer."

Neve stood, too, and nodded. "All right, Opal. Rock and I will wait until then. We can't stay here any longer. We've got to move forward."

Derrick sat up straighter; he'd already sweated through his T-shirt, but he barely felt the heat as he watched a young girl, moving stealthily to the edge of the jungle. She stopped and looked around, then pulled out a knife. It looked like a KA-BAR. Had she lifted Rock's? He looked closer at her features through the scope. The girl from the drug runners' camp.

What was she up to?

She spent a few moments carving something into the tree, then she sheathed the knife.

The hair on the back of his neck stood up, and his shoulders stiffened. She turned and looked directly into the scope of his sniper rifle and did a little salute.

He reared back and swore softly. How the hell?

Oh, she was good.

She pushed through the overgrowth, and he felt a tinge of fear for her as the jungle swallowed her whole. He waited, but when she didn't return, he broke cover and, crouching low, his senses on full alert, he ran to the tree.

Carved into the bark was a message.

For Rock.

The kid was heading into some harrowing danger, and Derrick was torn. She was young, but seemed pretty resourceful. Even if he wanted to follow her, she wasn't part of his directive. He clamped down on his instinct to find her and hog-tie her for Rock to find.

Rock and Neve.

His past came back to send guilt, anger and an incapacitating pain to tie his gut into knots. He wasn't here to protect a sixteen-year-old girl.

He gritted his teeth and melted back into the underbrush. He was relatively sure Rock and Neve would be headed this way.

Neve walked over to the communal hut, where she found Rock eating. When he looked up and saw her, his eyes lightened. "Good morning."

She sat next to him, the husky intimacy in his tone setting off a wild flutter inside her, and she wished this wasn't a…communal hut. "Good morning." He looked at her hopefully. She shook her head, and he swore softly. "Not so good. She said she would tell us her decision after the celebration tonight."

"Right, the hoopla we don't need."

"Don't be rude. These people have been kind and generous."

"I just don't need the pomp and circumstance. We

need to get a move on and hunt this guy down." He moved closer to her as she nodded her agreement. "Do you know you have your tank top on inside out?"

Neve looked down, feeling like an idiot. Dammit, how had she managed that? Restraining a sigh, she gave him a level look. "This is your fault."

He grinned and looked innocent. "How?"

Conscious of the other people in the room, Rock set his forearms on the table and leaned forward, making her remember all the ways he'd made her moan last night. "You know how," she whispered.

He reached out and poured her some juice, but when she went to take the glass, he didn't let it go. She looked at him, the intimate gleam in his eyes making her heart speed up. "I think," he said, just loud enough for her to hear, "I'm in the same boat. I might not have my T-shirt on wrong, but you do that to me—turn me inside out."

Neve wanted to hug him so much that she could hardly stand it, her senses overdosing on the scent of him, on his closeness.

"Good to know I'm not the only one."

He flashed her an amused look, pulling on the tag on the side of her top, his eyes crinkling up at the corners, the intimate glimmer setting off fireworks in her midriff that made her pulse skip and falter. He held her gaze, that almost-smile in his eyes, then lightly touched the small gold stud she wore in her ear. The movement made her aware of the adhesive bandage on his arm.

"We should make a trip to Puerto Fluvial and stock up on supplies, get ready to move out," he said.

"How far?"

"Not far. We can take a boat up and back."

"We'll have to be on the watch out for the EDL."

"All right, but make sure you don't tell anyone you're a nun."

"Got it."

They left the communal hut and walked back to theirs. After gathering up what they needed, they headed down to the dock and rented a boat. They stepped down into the seats, Rock taking her hand, steadying her as they settled on the narrow seats.

Once on the water, the evidence of deforestation was clear. There were many banana plantations along the way and thirty minutes later, when the boat sidled up to the next dock, an honest-to-God town. They stepped out and paid the driver.

Walking down the docks, Rock kept his eyes constantly moving. They headed in the direction of a general store, where they picked up what they would need. There was a cooler with cold drinks; they bought a couple and found a place in the shade of a tree to sit.

The town was small, but it had paved sidewalks, even as both the walkways and the buildings were a bit worse for wear, but she suspected that wood, especially untreated wood, wouldn't fare well in this kind of humidity. It was god-awful hot and she was constantly sweating.

"And I thought I came from a small town," she said, sipping. The cold swallow iced down her throat, quenching her thirst.

"Dutch and Unalaska are pretty small, part of the Aleutian Islands, but thriving metropolises compared to this small, jungle hole-in-the-wall."

"Where are you from?"

"All over. My family pulled up stakes every couple of years. I spent most of my time in San Diego, then DC, once my dad went from combat to administration."

"That must have been exciting, moving and seeing new places."

"No. Not for me. For Dex it was—he was home wherever he laid his head. Always popular, never felt out of place. He's a remarkable guy."

She turned to look at him, the sound of his voice tight. That meant Rock was trying to hold back.

"I attended nine different schools and had to move twice in high school. I played football, so it sucked that I had to be tested all over again when I was a junior. But I soon taught them I could play defense with no damn problem. And don't get me started on academics. I was either behind and had to catch up or ahead and got bored out of my skull."

"Yet you joined the marines?"

He shrugged. "I didn't have much of a choice or control over the moves. It was for my dad's work. Couple that with him being gone a lot and having just my mom, it was tough. I'm considered military royalty, and we step in time and march to the beat of our family history. I was expected to join."

"Would that have been your first choice?"

"I don't know. I never really thought about it. It was my path from the time I could remember."

"And sporting goods? Your own business?"

"I got a business degree while I was at the US Naval Academy in Annapolis—that's in Maryland. I also love the outdoors, every aspect of it. As a marine, I spent a lot of time outside in all kinds of weather. Learned a lot and what folks who want to do it for fun might need or want. It was a way to put down roots."

"What's your favorite thing to do for fun?"

"White-water rafting is at the top, climbing would

probably be a close second and camping, of course. What about you?"

"I love adventure, something new and different. I like the challenge of rising to the occasion and making a difference. So the coast guard is perfect for me."

"I don't want to be on the move anymore. I had enough growing up and during my deployments. I love San Diego. It feels like home to me, and that white picket fence idea suits me fine."

One more thing that they disagreed on, another gap in their relationship. Rock was grounded, and Neve wanted something more. She left home to pursue adventure and opportunity. She hadn't been thinking about settling down or children. Not on her radar. But now that she was getting older, those thoughts crossed her mind more often. She just wasn't ready to make anything permanent. She wouldn't physically be able to be a rescue swimmer forever. She was aware of that. She couldn't always jump out of helicopters.

Rock stiffened when he saw a man with an automatic weapon eyeing them a little too closely. Neve looked like she fit in here. He didn't.

They rose and headed toward the docks and caught a ride back to Opal's village.

As they walked up the incline on the dirt path, Neve said, "Do you think she'll give up the location?"

"I'm going to encourage her to do that."

They did a quick washup and went onto the celebration. There was plenty of dancing and drumming, and Neve sat next to Rock, in the curve of his body. It felt so good to be close to him and sad to know that they were from different mind-sets, different worlds and surely wanted different things. She started to worry all over again what would happen if they got too involved and if there would be a rift between Rock and Tristan. It would break her heart to come between them, not that who she dated, slept with or spent her time with was any of Tristan's business. It just added a layer of difficulty that he and Rock were so close.

As the celebration wound down, Neve noticed all of a sudden that Opal was nowhere to be found. She rose, getting a bad feeling that the girl was missing. She looked at Rock and he asked, "What's wrong?"

"Opal isn't here."

He sat up straighter. "Let's go check her home."

They left as discreetly as they could, and once out of sight of the communal building they ran to Opal's house. Neve knocked, but unlike this morning there was no sullen teenager inside. When they entered, the place was empty.

Opal was gone.

It didn't take too much brain power to figure out where she was headed.

"Son of a bitch!" Rock said.

Chapter 14

He swore again. "She's as stubborn as you." Probably not the smartest thing he'd ever said to Neve, but he was frustrated and scared for the young girl.

"I'm going to let that pass because I think you're worried about Opal."

He prowled around the room, but found nothing that could help them in their search. "I am worried about her."

"How long do you think her head start is?"

"The last time I saw her was this morning. God, she could have seven to eight hours on us. She's young and fast."

"Can you track her?" Neve asked.

"Yes, I can, but first we have to find out where she went into the jungle. I have no idea what direction to head. It could cost us a day to recon."

Her lips pinched into a moue. "That's not good."

Rock ran his hands through his hair. "She doesn't have a chance, Neve. What is she thinking?"

"She's thinking we're going to follow her, and if that's the case she would have had to leave us some kind of clue."

He slammed his hand against a post, and then he saw it, the rough wood. Something was carved into it. He read it and swore again.

"Bread crumbs," he murmured when Neve frowned at him.

"Do we look like Hansel and Gretel?"

"No, and I'm not playing damn games."

"Looks like we don't have much of a choice."

"She's gone northeast."

"How—"

He tapped the post.

"Oh, bread crumbs. Isn't she a resourceful little Girl Scout?"

"She's a pain in my ass. Let's go," he said, memorizing the coordinates she'd carved. On their way out of town after grabbing all their gear, Rock stopped at Opal's father's hut and explained to the clearly horrified man what Opal was up to. He shook his head and pleaded with them to find her and bring her back. Rock remained noncommittal. He couldn't guarantee her safety, especially when she was being reckless.

Neve gave him a scowling look, but he shrugged it off. There was much more at stake here than a young girl getting herself killed—a fact he would do everything in his power to stop—but they had to keep their eye on the ball.

She didn't say anything until they were outside the

camp. She grabbed his arm. "Really? We're not going to try to help her?"

He gritted his teeth. "We came here to kill the White Falcon—Ammon Set. That is why we're here. She wants her brother back, and she knows where the compound is. This will save us days. If I can do something about her brother I will, but our objective is clear. Ammon Set."

She closed her eyes as if she was pushing back the need to rescue. It was, after all, her job. "I'm not going to throw her to the wolves, Rock."

"I didn't say we should, babe." He stepped closer and grabbed the back of her neck and squeezed. "She's got more courage in her little finger than I've seen some men in combat situations. She's got her mission, Neve, and she wants our help. Since we refused to agree, she's doling out her information piecemeal and forcing our hand. I don't like to be manipulated."

"I agree, but she's trying to save her brother. You know if that was Nova in there, I would move heaven and earth."

"Same with Dex. I would not rest until he was safe. How about we agree to cross that bridge when we get to it?"

She stood there for a minute, then gave him a curt nod. "All right. How is this going to work?"

He searched around the area and saw the message on the tree. He pointed. "There's another clue." Approaching the trunk, he peered at it and again memorized the directional instructions. Pulling out his compass, he took the reading. Then he sucked in a few breaths. "Let's go. It's time to hoof it."

"Lead on."

He didn't wait for her, and unaware if Neve was keeping up or not, he ran, his senses on alert and searching the jungle for any sign of the next clue. They had to make up time. If that kid got into trouble, she was going to need backup. He knew from experience that this was a dangerous area. EDL and government troops were currently duking it out for dominance. If Opal ran into either of those groups, he had no idea what her chances were. He stopped, listening for any type of human sounds or movement, and Neve touched his arm. They were going to have to be very careful. He scanned the area, saw that he was on the right track. The disturbed earth showed just enough scuffing to indicate one person came through here, then on a parallel path, he sucked in a breath, went to one knee. Swore soft and low.

"Rock," she said into the silence.

He glared at her and thumped a finger to his lips.

"Are those EDL boot prints, you think?" Neve whispered in his ear.

He nodded. Now she understood why he swore. They traipsed some more and came to a narrow stream.

He waded into the water, his machete in his hand as he turned back for her. She moved slowly but steadily. He grabbed her hand, pulled her the last couple of feet to the shore. She smacked into him, her nose to his chest. She met his gaze. *Thank you*, she mouthed exaggeratedly, and his lips curved.

He turned away, kept the steady pace and was floored by the sheer amount of denseness. Everywhere he looked…just more jungle. Rock listened for Neve's footsteps instead of looking behind him. She barely made a sound. For the umpteenth time, he thought, *What the heck did Opal think she was doing?* Right now, finding her was essential. He didn't want to be noticed by the government troops, and pissing off the *federales* wasn't good any way you looked at it.

When he felt they were due for another clue, he stopped. Neve slammed into his back. He twisted, grabbing her before she fell. She was winded, sweating, which wasn't unusual in this country, but she looked like a drowned cat. Wisely, he didn't say so.

"Okay, Marine, you're gonna have to cut the pace a little." She bent over, her hands on her knees as she dragged in air.

"It was only a mile."

"At top speed when it's a hundred and ten out here?" She tried to put some force in her words, but it just sounded like whining to him. "I've run five miles, three times a week, for years. But you…you'd clean up in the Olympics."

"Keep up, babe. We have to make up time," he said with a nudge, then frowned as he looked around, and there it was. He read the coordinates and got his bearings while Neve groaned.

"You're cute when you're handing out orders. I'm just too winded to salute."

"That would make my freaking day, but we have more pressing matters. You need to get the lead out, Neve. Let's go."

"You're going to pay for that, and I've been convalescing, pushy," she bit back.

His gaze flashed to hers. "Sounds like excuses to me. Last one there has to do twenty-five push-ups."

"You're tough. One-armed…"

He grinned and took off. Damn she was sassy, and damn if he didn't love that about her.

Whatever he couldn't plow through, he hacked. After

running for a while, he called for a stop. Both of them were sweating heavily. He pulled out water and drank, Neve doing the same. He pointed at the tree straight in front of him. More coordinates.

The area he entered was dark, dusty and sweltering. In the distance, he could hear the commotion of a number of men—raised voices, barked orders—and he wondered if Opal had already gotten herself nabbed by them. But then he shook his head and pulled Neve toward cover. Guerrilla tactics—this was definitely a shakedown, and from the sound of it one faction wasn't happy with the other. *Great. Caught in the crossfire between two sets of hostiles.*

Behind him, he heard the sound of someone running. He leaned back and took a quick look just in time to see a man with a rifle skid to a stop at the edge of where they were hiding and lower himself into a crouch while he checked the forest floor. The gun-toting guy rose, his eyes going over the expanse of the jungle, his intent gaze focused straight ahead. Then Rock's eyes snagged on it—a crude bag with a woven cord. Dammit, that was Opal's gold bag. Looks like someone had snagged her and they were out of time. Well, hell, so much for Opal's skills. He just hoped she was still alive and the drug runners hadn't hurt her or worse. Rock prayed the guy wouldn't guess right about their hiding spot. The hostile moved forward, and if he didn't change his trajectory, he was going to walk right into them.

He was forcing Rock's hand. Rock picked up a rock and tossed it. The guy whipped around and went toward the sound; Rock rose quickly and grabbed him around the neck and squeezed. As soon as the enemy dropped the rifle, he motioned for Neve to get it.

When the guy went limp, Rock bent and got him draped over his shoulder and headed away from the shouting, increasing his pace once he heard a gunshot. *Looks like the negotiations were over.*

He traveled a fair distance and set the guy down. He pulled out the cuffs and manacled his hands, then tied his feet. Slapping his face repeatedly, he roused the guerrilla.

The other man shook his head; his eyes were a bit glazed, then they cleared. He opened his mouth, and Rock shoved a sock inside. He couldn't remember if it was one of his clean ones.

If looks could kill, he would be dead.

Rock reached for his knife and pulled the blade from its sheath. He set it against the man's throat. "I'm going to ask questions, and you're going to give answers. That's going to be the extent of our interaction. *¿Comprende?*"

He nodded. "Good. You speak English." Rock reached down and snagged the bag. He opened the pouch, and his mouth tightened when he saw it was almost full of gold.

Rock pulled out the gag. "Where did you get this?"

"Girl. We have her back at camp."

"Who are you?"

The man looked up at Neve and his eyes widened. Anger suffused his face and he struggled. The knife nicked him, blood welling, and he stilled. "Sister Mary Agnes," he spat. "You are a dead woman."

"EDL."

He drew Neve away from the man, tucking the pouch into his pocket, and said in a low voice, "We're going to have to get her out of there. I doubt they will ransom her."

"What do they want with her?"

He looked back at the soldier.

"Entertainment." He smirked.

Neve blanched. "Do you think she's still alive?"

"Let's hope so."

Rock bent and untied the man's legs. "You're going to take us to the camp." He pulled him to his feet. *"¿La tienes?"*

"I get your drift," Rock's captive snapped.

Rock shoved the sock back into his mouth. "Of all the baddies here, we have to get ourselves a comedian."

"Yeah, a laugh a minute," Neve said.

Rock shoved him, and he started to walk. Neve, looking like she wanted to shoot him, shouldered the rifle and stepped up behind him. "She better be alive," she whispered, and Rock thought, *Damn, she was getting the hang of being a marine.*

It was clear the armed conflict was the distraction they needed. Rock, Neve and the EDL member easily approached the camp, where there was a skeleton crew, fully armed and on guard.

That was in their favor. He led their captive to a tree, unlocked one of the cuffs. "Give the tree a hug," he ordered.

When the man hesitated, Neve placed her pistol against his back and said, "Do as he says."

He hugged the tree as Rock grinned. He snapped the cuffs on and pulled out a bandanna, then tied it around his mouth so he couldn't work out the sock. The EDL thug's eyes shot daggers, but Rock turned his back and slipped out of his pack. He checked his gun and chambered a round, tucking it into the small of his back.

"Shoot—"

"—anyone who gets too close."

He grinned for real, grabbed her by the back of the neck and gave her a hard kiss. He felt the heat radiating from her body, and he could taste sweat and delicious Neve on his mouth. He released her and gave her another rueful grin. "That's my girl. There's so much gunfire, it'll mask the sound."

She nodded.

Rock pulled the knife from its sheath and said, "I'll be back with her. Be ready to bug out."

This time she grabbed him by the back of the neck and kissed him quick and hard. "For good luck."

He rose and slipped up to the edge of the EDL camp. There were only three drug runner guards, and all of them were facing toward the sound of gunfire. He assessed how far apart they were, their reaction time and his plan of action.

When he was ready, he snuck up on the thug closest to him and knifed him nice and quiet. One of the guards started to turn. Rock flicked his wrist, and the guy went down. The last man was spinning, bringing up his rifle, but before Rock could even clear his weapon, the guy went down. "Courtesy of my friendly neighborhood sniper-man. Thanks, pal."

He retrieved his knife, wiping the blood on the guy's shirt, and checked the nearest tent, but no Opal. He then looked into the others until he found her in the next to last one, bound and gagged. Her eyes were closed, and she had developing bruises on her cheek, and up and down her arms. He cut her bonds and picked her up, slinging her light body over his shoulder, angry at her treatment.

She weighed almost nothing.

He stepped out of the tent and stopped dead. A steely-eyed man shoved a rifle in his face, and Rock put up his hands. Someone pulled Opal off his shoulder and he tried to stop them, but he was shoved back. Rock, his fists clenched, hauled off and hit the guy square in the jaw.

"Stand down."

His head jerked around, and he stared for a moment at the middle-aged man with a head of thick hair starting to gray at the temples, handsome features and intelligent, dark eyes.

The distinctive sound of a rifle being cocked broke the silence, and he heard Neve say in a deadly quiet voice, "Don't move a muscle."

"Son of a bitch."

Derrick sighted down the scope, noted the scuffle and calculated how many he could pick off; he figured five right off the bat.

He noted Neve Michaels getting the drop on them, and the limp girl snatched from Rock. He checked the wind and waited for Neve to make her move, his finger hovering over the trigger.

Then Rock took two strides, and he and the dark-haired man were holding each other in a huge bear hug. They talked for a few minutes, then Rock turned to Neve and pushed down the barrel of the gun.

Derrick sat back, breathing out a hard breath. "Must be the good guys," he muttered.

Rock reached out and drew Neve over. "This is Captain Alejandro Garcia. He's in charge of the government troops in this area."

"Let's move out of here. We can talk once we get to base and we can get the girl some medical attention."

They marched through the jungle for about thirty minutes until they came to a fortified government checkpoint near the river.

The man carrying Opal took her to the infirmary, and Rock and Neve were escorted to the office. Finally, after a few minutes, Alejandro came into the room and closed the door behind him.

Okay, this was the moment when the crap hit the fan, and it was all going to come down on them. Armed Americans in a foreign country, one of them on medical leave from the coast guard. Neve would be lucky if she wasn't busted out of the service.

No political sanctions, no gray areas. Just black and white clear.

If they were shipped out of Panama without taking out the White Falcon, Neve and her family wouldn't survive. Even now, they were in mortal danger.

Alejandro took off his cap and hung it on a hook just behind his desk. He sat and leaned back in his chair, wiping his wrist across his forehead. He leaned forward and held out the dangling cuffs. "I suspect these belong to you."

Neve went to open her mouth, and Rock reached out and squeezed her hand. It was silent code for "keep your damn mouth shut and let me do the talking." His other hand took the cuffs with a swift and noncommittal half smile.

"Rock, you can't imagine my surprise to find you hoisting a young girl over your shoulder in the wilds of the Darién with a very beautiful woman in tow. What are you doing here, my friend?"

"Sightseeing."

Alejandro's brow rose and he laughed softly. "I suppose the girl is your...what...guide?"

"Bingo. I've always wanted to come back here. The last visit wasn't at all pleasant." He glanced at Neve. "We've heard so much about the Darién, and we wanted to test it for ourselves."

"And you, *señorita*? What is your business here?"

"I'm with him, and I...wanted to see the howler monkeys, oh, and the toucans. The only ones I've ever seen are on the boxes of Fruit Loops. You know, Toucan Sam."

"I wouldn't know," he said dryly. "I prefer Frosted Flakes. They're great."

"Look, Alejandro, can't you just look the other way?"

"I'm afraid not. You are being detained."

"Alejandro—"

"Detained, Rock, until I hear a story that doesn't have sightseeing, monkeys or...toucans in it, especially ones that talk."

Neve feigned laugher to mask her deep frustration at this setback, covering her mouth and looking away.

"Don't leave camp. This man will escort you to lodgings. Whenever you want to talk, let him know."

"You owe me—"

"We're done for now, my friend. Don't push your luck."

The man assigned to them escorted them out of his office and across the base to a small building.

"Wait here."

They went inside, and Rock sat in one of the chairs. "This looks like an interrogation room."

"Alejandro is being subtle," she said. "Does he really expect us to stay here until we talk?"

"Yes. He doesn't bluff."

"I want to know how Opal is doing."

Rock went to the door and said, "The girl who was with us. Could you find out how she is?"

The man nodded, spoke to another soldier who was walking by. "He will ask and report back."

"Could we please get some water?" Neve asked as the man flagged down another guard, and a few minutes later the water and two plates of food arrived.

It smelled delicious. They settled on the cot and started to eat. "Maybe I should use my Sister Mary Agnes passport?"

"Alejandro is going to be skeptical you're a nun. He will check—"

"Marco will back up my story as Father Abernathy."

"You had all your bases covered, then."

"Completely. Marco planned very well."

There was a knock at the door and the man put his head inside. "Your young friend is doing fine. Just a knock on the head, but the doctor is going to keep her in the infirmary under observation until tomorrow. You might as well get comfortable."

"Does the door lock?" she asked, and he nodded.

"If you'd like to secure it, I'll be guarding outside. If there is anything that needs your attention, I will knock, but it is getting late" the guard said.

After he closed the door, Neve walked over and locked it. "I'd prefer we didn't have company we weren't expecting," she said. "I am so frustrated we haven't found Set and that Opal is involved in this. Now we're being detained. I just want to get this over with so that my family is safe."

He turned toward her and nodded, reaching out and

squeezing her shoulder. "I know. We're tired and hungry. We'll get some rest and get back at it. Alejandro will let us go. I'm sure of it."

Rock removed the sleeping bags and spread them out, untying his boots, and Neve sighed and did the same, slipping out of them with a groan. "My God, you can really eat up the ground."

Rock smirked. "Wasn't there something about one-armed push-ups?"

"There was," she said, laughing. "But who really won? Can you give me a definitive answer?"

"No, and I'm too damned tired to worry about it right now. I have other thoughts on my mind, but this isn't exactly the most romantic place for them."

Her eyes flared and she looked at the door, then back at him. "Are you worried about our privacy?" she asked.

"A little," he murmured, reaching out to her and pulling her against him, to feel her down the length of his body.

"I don't want to wait to be with you again, Rock."

It was his turn to feel the fire.

The contrast of her midnight hair against her skin made him want to lick every creamy, smooth inch of her skin. He wanted her to respond to him at the most basic level; then, from there, he could take her to places accessible only to those who felt more than physical pleasure. She'd come to understand what he knew was there, because she would no longer be able to deny it. He'd imagined it wild and tender, carnal and sweet. A roller coaster of sensation, emotion and primal responses, where barriers of any kind could no longer exist. In that moment, she would be as defenseless as he was. Sometimes a person had to take the only moment available and find a way to make it work. They'd be on the hunt all too soon, and the job would take center stage again.

What he wanted her to see was that there were treasures far greater in this lifetime than the pursuit of rigid goals. And that sharing victories made them doubly sweet. He leaned down and gently bit her neck, sucking gently at her skin, while she arched against the need for his touch. She moaned, and her legs moved restlessly against his, while he fought an equally challenging battle against going ahead with this and risking losing it all. "Neve—" he began, only to be surprised when she lowered her chin and claimed his mouth.

He hadn't been expecting an offensive maneuver, and it caught him off guard just long enough for her to make serious inroads into destroying whatever common sense and rational thought he might still have. And he wasn't too certain he'd ever had any of that around her.

After all, he was campaigning for the affections and possible commitment of a woman who was already gone. She gently bit into his bottom lip, making him groan, then pressed his body along hers as he plunged his tongue into her mouth and gave in to his raging need to consume her.

She met his thrust with a sinuous kiss of her own, taunting and teasing him with her tongue, becoming the woman he craved. She slid her foot along the back of his calf, urging him to snug his bulging erection tightly between her thighs. She gasped at the direct contact, the increased pressure, and he silently swore, wishing he'd removed his clothes before he'd started unbuttoning hers.

He pushed her against the wall, sliding his hands down her arms and back up again, and wove his fingers into the soft strands of her hair, holding her where he wanted, so he could taste those lips, plunder that mouth, fully and completely. She responded in kind, sinking her slender fingers into his hair, lightly raking his scalp with her nails, making him shudder in pleasure as she drew them down to his neck and urged his tongue more deeply into her mouth. He grunted with the need to free himself, constrained as he was now to the point of serious discomfort, but unwilling to leave her long enough to take care of it. Instead, he dragged his mouth from hers, biting her neck again, harder this time. She groaned when he slid down to roughly strip the shirt and bra off her and take a nipple into his mouth.

She arched into him, kissing his temple, molding her hand over his arousal. He moved to her other breast, needing to taste her like a man starved for food. Sweet, so damn sweet. He rolled one nipple between his fingers while teasing the other with his tongue.

Neve groaned and moved against him, her hips pressing up, pushing at him, demanding he push back. This, they knew how to do, this almost mindless need to mate, to join, to give and take pleasure. This, they could give themselves over to completely. Actually, it was as if they almost didn't have a choice in the matter.

She pushed at him, and he moved downward, trailing his tongue along the delicate line of her abdomen as he used his fingers to continue teasing her nipples. He dipped his tongue into her navel, then along the lacy edge of her panty line. He could already breathe in the sweet scent of her and knew she'd be wet and wanting when he finally worked his way there.

He slid his hands along her waist, lifting her hips so he could press his mouth against the damp silk covering her. She sucked in her breath on a little gasp, then moved beneath him. He knew just how wet she would be, just what it would feel like to sink into her, to feel her take him all the way in, holding him so tightly, so perfectly. He thought he might burst behind the zipper of his pants, but he wasn't about to leave her now.

He knew that if he pleasured her this way, brought her screaming right to the edge, then pushed her over, let her tumble, fall, regroup, then pushed her over again, even when she thought she couldn't, when he climbed up over her body and thrust himself into her, she'd keep coming, and the way her body would grip and convulse around him in an almost constant roll of aftershocks would jerk him so hard and fast over the edge he'd see stars.

Mindless. Primal. Basic. Essential.

That was what this was. And yet he wanted so much more. And he planned to push, and push plenty hard. He slid his hands down, taking her panties with him, all the way down and off, trailing his tongue along the inside of her thigh, the back of her knee, the sensitive spot below her ankle. He yanked off his shirt and, finally, blessedly freed himself of his pants, while nipping the side of her hip, biting her belly, making her squeal and laugh. Then he teased his way back up the inside of her other leg, making her gasp and moan.

She was twisting now, writhing as he drew closer and closer still, panting, knowing what was coming. He wondered if it made it twice as good for her, already knowing how fantastic, how deeply, insanely pleasurable it was going to be.

It did for him.

And it was the knowing, the wanting, that made it possible for him to take his time, when all he wanted was to climb over her and slide back into the one place he'd wanted to be since the moment he'd first entered her. If this was the only way to get to her, to get to any part of her, then he was going to get to all of it that he could. And that meant taking his sweet time. Knowing the reward that awaited them both made that an easy decision to make.

Grasping her wrist, he pressed the throbbing length of his erection into her palm, accepting the delicious friction only making him crazier for her. He nudged her legs a bit farther apart, then dropped the softest of kisses along the inside of each thigh, so close, but not brushing against where she wanted him most.

Her fingers twined into his hair, playing with it, toying with the ends, sending little skitters of pleasure through him, but not directing him or pushing him, trusting that he'd take care of her. It wasn't long before she was shuddering and moaning, going over the edge. He slid his thumb over her and kept her vibrating as he entered her and pulled her calves around his waist, then thrusting into her so hard it drove them both crazy.

She cried out, and he grunted as she took him, held him, moved beneath him, matching him stroke for stroke as she continued to pulsate and shudder around him. He had no recourse, no way to stop the climax rushing to overtake him, and didn't even try. She sank her nails into him, her heels digging into his lower back as he came with a long, jerking groan. It was as if he couldn't get deep enough, couldn't pour enough of himself into her.

He stood there panting, both of them dealing with the aftershock. He then let her slide down his body. Walking over to the sleeping bags, they folded down to them, arms sliding and holding, hands caressing.

He kissed her once, gently, but firmly, then again,

more slowly, softly. "Promise me," he murmured against the side of her cheek, keeping her nestled closely, "that you won't take any unnecessary risks when we get to this bastard's fortress."

She shifted, so that their noses bumped, before pulling back just enough to look at him, but not enough, he noticed, so that she wasn't still tucked under the crook of his arm, her leg casually hooked over his. "If you make me the same promise." There was a tender edge to her tone and in her eyes, but along with that tenderness was fear, whether she thought he could see it or not.

"Okay, babe," he said, knowing that he would do anything in his power to keep this woman safe.

Even make the ultimate sacrifice.

Chapter 15

In the morning, Neve woke up early and just lay there, memorizing Rock's face. Scruffier than when she'd met him in Yaviza, his hair short and tousled. Beard stubble darkened his jaw; the planes and angles made her knees weak and her heart pound. She would recognize him anywhere—a firm, sensuous mouth that she wanted to kiss, and those eyes, deep, cobalt blue under dark lashes, absolutely clear, absolutely unwavering. She remembered the first time she'd ever seen him. She'd heard enough from Tristan that he was bringing a friend home. He'd made sure everyone was aware that he wanted to make a good impression on Rock. She'd thought from his nickname he would be huge, muscular, immovable, expressionless, boring.

She'd been completely wrong. The morning after he'd landed in Dutch Harbor and she'd gone downstairs, she'd been startled to find him in the kitchen. He was huge, but so beautifully formed, with his thick muscles, immovable all right, but not expressionless; his gaze was absolutely locked on to hers. Soulful, that's what she'd thought of his eyes five years ago. And he was far, *far* from boring.

In fact, she was falling in love with him then, and now, well, she might have already hit the damn ground. Even when it was impossible, complicated and messy. Even when she wasn't sure she was going to get out of this alive. She wasn't sure what scared her the most— that she would never see him again, or that she would. His lids lifted, and she was staring into his hot eyes. He was far from soulful right now. His gaze was piercing, fierce and unnerving the hell out of her. *Geez*. Her heart thudded in her chest. *Russell*.

"Are you all right?" he asked, coming up on his elbow, smoothing his hand over her hair. She leaned toward him and kissed him.

No. She wasn't all right. She would never be all right again because it was like she was looking into the face of the man meant for her, formed for her, given to her by fate. He was hers.

"I'm not used to sleeping on the ground, but I'm adapting. You make a comfortable bed."

He flashed her a grin. She rolled out of the bag and grabbed her clothes; he watched her get dressed, his eyes caressing her from head to toe.

"Come on. We really need to resolve this and get out of this base."

"Do you want to tell Alejandro that we're here illegally and under false pretenses, are hunting and planning on killing Ammon Set, one of the most dangerous men in the world?"

"When you put it like that, ah, no."

He rose and leaned toward her, stark naked and way too devastating first thing in the morning. "Well, Sister, you better start praying…"

She shoved his arm and giggled. "That's not funny."

There was a banging on the door, and Neve almost jumped out of her skin. "Open this damn door!"

Rock hastily pulled on his pants, and went to unlock the door. It flew open and banged against the wall. Captain Alejandro Garcia stood there breathing fire. He grabbed the door, shoving the guard behind him out and slammed it.

"Are you out of your mind?"

Rock stepped back at the vehemence of his friend's words. "Alejandro, calm down."

"Calm down? *Madre de Dios*, Rock. You're going to assault one of the most dangerous men in the Darién Gap with a nun and a child!"

"Wait a second! First off, Neve isn't a nun. She's posing as one. She's coast guard. And secondly, Opal is the only person who knows where he is hiding. Her brother has been kidnapped, and she ran away, leaving us a bread-crumb trail to follow."

Alejandro rubbed his hand over his face. "Oh, that's much better."

"Look, Alejandro, we go way back and I helped you when I was here. Can't you just look the other way, forget you ever saw us? We have to see this through. He's threatened Neve and her family, had sent an assassin after her."

"And your government does nothing?"

"No, they are investigating and building a case, but that takes time, and even if they find him and manage to arrest him, what's to stop him from threatening us from prison?"

"Nothing. He is a ruthless, merciless bastard. I would love to see him eradicated."

Neve stepped forward. "Then let us go," she pleaded. "I can't leave here without completing this mission."

Rock stepped forward and said, his voice low and firm, "You of all people know what he is capable of, and all we're asking is a chance to neutralize a threat."

"I do know what he is capable of and I hate the man with a passion, but let two Americans and a young girl walk into certain death?"

"We're not going to take any unnecessary risks." He looked at Neve, and she held her breath. Rock was always so persuasive, and he was 100 percent on her side. This...*this* was what it was like to be part of a team.

She dropped her head for a moment, overcome by his commitment to her, overcome by his sacrifice, his vow that he wouldn't let her do this alone. She realized it wasn't just for Tristan. It was for her...because...he cared deeply for her.

Alejandro set his hand on her shoulder. "I know what you're up against, and it may be possible for a small force to do what we haven't been able to do. But if there is anything I can ever do to help you in this quest, please let me know. You both are very brave." He turned to Rock. "I will never forget what you have done for me. When I lost my son in that terrible battle, you were there during the most difficult time of my life. I will look the other way. *Vaya con Dios.*"

"Thank you, my friend." They shook hands, and Neve breathed a sigh of relief.

"Take the time to clean up and have a hot shower, breakfast and restock. You are all free to go. Your friend Opal is ready to be released from our infirmary."

Neve kissed him on the cheek, gathered up what she needed and asked to be directed to the shower, Rock right behind her. When they entered and he locked the door, she smiled. "Are you going to wash my back?"

"Ah, yeah, and anything else you let me."

She laughed as he pulled her against him, the sensual mouth she'd been staring at this morning coming down on hers and making her sigh.

Derrick watched the base while perched in thick undergrowth on a high-rise. Rock, Neve and the teenager had been taken here, and he'd only caught a glimpse of them as they had been escorted across the base. He wasn't really keen on storming a SENAFRONT post and demanding they release Rock and Neve.

He was just about to contact Austin, then his senses went haywire, but he wasn't fast enough. A gun cocked behind him, and Derrick already had his slim throwing knife in his hand, the razor-sharp blade lethal against his palm.

"Keep your hands where I can see them," a male voice said, and Derrick swore low and fierce. "Turn around."

He did as he was told and turned to face the man who hadn't made a sound traveling through the jungle, up an incline with loose rock and getting the drop on him.

"Russell 'Rock' Kaczewski." Damn, that sucker was big. Up close and threatening with a gun he so knew how to use, his big hands looking ready to pull the trigger if he didn't get the right answers. It was Derrick's job to keep him ignorant. It really was bliss.

"You know me?" His features tightened. "I don't know you."

Derrick tilted his head. "You kinda do."

"Who are you?"

The tone of Rock's voice was clear. Derrick was lucky he wasn't shooting first and asking questions later. "The Easter Bunny," he deadpanned and wondered if he was going to have to take the big guy on.

Rock eyed him and scowled. "You're missing those big, floppy ears and that cute cotton tail," he said, gesturing with the gun.

Derrick just smirked. "I'm in disguise."

"Why are you following us?" His dark blue eyes narrowed dangerously. "Protecting us?"

He shrugged. "I'm not at liberty to say." There was something very unnerving about the bore of a gun pointed in his direction. He really preferred to do the pointing.

"Ah. 'I have no recollection of that event, Senator.' You're trying to avoid any official questioning in case this comes to light?"

"You're really good at that."

"Your voice does sound familiar, but I can't place it."

"Best to forget where you heard it. I was never here."

"And I never held a gun on you, you never saved Neve's life and you aren't shadowing us."

"Now you're getting the gist of it."

"CIA?"

"Nope. Easter Bunny. Remember?" He shifted and looked over his shoulder. "Does Neve know about me?"

"No."

"Let's keep it our little secret."

"Plausible deniability."

"You must have been at the top of your class." Derrick needed all the intel he could get. "What's with the kid?"

"She had the coordinates and is trying to save her brother, José. She won't listen to a word I say." Rock holstered the weapon at the small of his back. "They're the priority. Neve and the kids."

"Got it," he said as Rock turned away and disappeared. But there was no way he was going to let Amber or her decorated fiancé down. He especially wasn't going to let Dexter down. That SEAL had put everything on the line for Senator Jones. All of them were walking away from this.

"I need to rest," Opal said. "You are hard to keep up with, Rock."

He pulled water out of his pack and handed it to the girl. They had been walking for about two hours.

"We're almost there. The compound is hard to detect because it's so well concealed." She shielded her eyes and pointed. "They have this canopy that is hanging over the structure, so it's very hard to distinguish from the jungle."

"Opal, how did you find it?"

"I followed them when they took my brother."

"That was very brave."

She shrugged, wiped at her forehead and tipped her chin up and looked at Neve. "You would do no less for your family. That's why you're here. ¿Si?"

"Yes. It's exactly why I'm here. I have a sister and two brothers, and I could never leave them to that kind of fate."

"Let's set up camp and wait until nightfall. I'll do

some recon, and you two stay put." He touched Neve's arm and it was clear he was in pure marine mode here, giving off warrior vibes. He pulled a pair of binoculars out of his pack and tucked them into one of his cargo pants pockets. Grabbing a couple of energy bars, he turned and jogged into the jungle.

Neve got busy finding a good hiding spot. Setting up the tent, she and Opal crawled inside for the shade it offered.

"No cook fire. It's MREs."

Opal eyed the package dubiously, scrunching up her nose. "What are those?"

"Meal, Ready-to-Eat. The military uses them for combat missions."

"Is Rock your man?" Opal asked with the innocence of youth, opening her package and taking a bite. She wrinkled up her face, but must have been much too hungry to stop eating.

Startled, Neve looked at Opal. "What?"

"I just see the way he looks at you. It's clear he cares about you very much. I hope for that kind of joining when I'm older."

"He's not my man. We're just friends."

Opal snorted. "He doesn't look at you like he wants to be your friend."

"That subject is closed, missy."

Derrick had set up with a beautiful view of the fortress below him. He could see Neve and Opal disappear into the trees to set up camp and track Rock as he moved away from their location. He decided to stick with the women. Rock could take care of himself.

He sighted through the high-powered scope, pray-

ing for the White Falcon to walk right into his scope,
and two pounds of trigger pressure later, Petty Officer
Michaels's problem was over.

There was only a whisper of sound to warn him as he
rolled away and the knife meant for the back of his skull
missed, scraping against rock instead of his brain stem.

He brought up the rifle, but the assassin batted it away
and went for his throat. They grappled for the weapon
and rolled across the rocky ground. Derrick threw some
hard punches and took a few to the jaw, fighting for the
weapon.

They rolled again, then again, and found nothing underneath them. Breaking apart, they crashed toward the
jungle floor.

The trees shook in the distance, and Neve shaded her
eyes and peered, wishing she had binoculars. It was most
likely monkeys, she thought. She bided her time walking
around the camp, getting the lay of the land, planning a
couple of escape routes. When Rock hadn't come back
after thirty minutes, Neve was beginning to worry. She
strapped on her gun and told Opal to stay out of sight.
Moving as carefully through the jungle as she could,
Neve climbed over a huge felled tree. She crouched and
got her bearings. Just as she was going to rise, a hand
covered her mouth. She struggled and almost got free,
but froze when she felt a pistol against her temple.

She went to turn her head, and she glimpsed a man
carrying a limp Opal over his shoulder. A second later,
the electrical charge of a Taser lit her up like the Fourth
of July.

Oh, God. Had they killed Rock?

* * *

It seemed like an eternity before she opened her eyes. Like lingering static, energy reverberated down her body. She sat perfectly still for several moments, waiting for it to pass and wanting to sink back into the oblivion where nothing mattered. A scent came to her; it wafted on the gentle breeze that blew...smoke across her nose. Cigar.

She forced her eyes open and started upright, only belatedly realizing that her hands were tied behind her back. She blinked, confused and shaken, her stomach dropping away to nothing. She was in a comfy leather chair, and across from her, seated behind a large, shiny mahogany desk was the White Falcon, Ammon Set. There was a cigar sitting in a heavy ceramic ashtray on his desk, the smoke curling up and disappearing into the air.

Neve drew a deep stabilizing breath, reaching down deep for control. He had coal-black hair with eyes to match, a wicked goatee on his chin that cast his features with a sinister look.

He was attractive, his cheekbones high, his eyes slightly tilted at the sides; he wore a multicolored silk shirt with parrots on it, the shirtsleeves rolled up.

"Petty Officer Neve Michaels. You saved me the trouble of shelling out the money for that obviously incompetent idiot I sent to kill you."

"He took a terrible fall," she ground out. There was no way she could talk her way out of this, and she was helpless.

She was a dead woman.

He smiled in self-satisfaction, his eyes narrowing in menace. "You have come so justice can be served."

"That's exactly why I'm here. I had nothing to do with

the deaths of your family members." Her voice was unsteady when she spoke. "I was doing my job." Her insides in turmoil, she experienced a light-headed feeling.

"You were incompetent, and because of you, my brother and sisters died," he spat, the mask falling away and the hatred burning like pitch in his eyes. "Because of you I have no family left. This is going to be your fate before I end your life with my own hand." He picked up a file and opened it. "Nova Michaels, born May 5... Cinco de Mayo... Ah, that is your date of birth, too. I see. You're twins. That will be particularly distressing, to lose someone so close to you not only in age but with such a connection." He picked up a photo. "She is very pretty. I see that she is also in the coast guard." He picked up another file. "Tristan Michaels."

She remained closemouthed. The light-headed sensation turned into something close to motion sickness, and the blood drained from her face. Suddenly the room was very, very hot. Her palms clammy, she drew a shaky breath, then schooled her face into a blank expression, her heart beating like a wild thing in her chest. He focused back to his file. "Engaged to Amber Dalton. NCIS agent. That is a shame... She is a federal agent and that could cause me some problems. But it's not like I haven't done away with federal agents in the past."

Her stomach turned at how easily he talked about murdering the people she loved.

"Thane Michaels, another military member, this time a lieutenant in the Navy who teaches at Annapolis. I hear he was recently in a car accident." He shook his head, giving her a look of mock sympathy. "And your parents. Your father is very robust. Fisherman. Dangerous profession, and your still very beautiful mother."

"Leave my family out of this."

He rose, and the breeze from the open door carried with it the taint of salt, the overhead fan whirring with each gust of wind and revolution.

He came from behind the desk. "This is the deal for you. Give me the address of the safe houses, and I'll make your death painless and quick."

"I don't know," she said. "I didn't know they were moved into safe houses. NCIS must have thought that was necessary."

He backhanded her across the face, and she tasted blood. Then he leaned forward and began to describe exactly what he was going to do to them. "I don't believe you."

Knowing she was approaching emotional overload and knowing she couldn't handle many more graphic details without coming completely apart, Neve swallowed and closed her eyes. God, it was so awful, so horrible—and unbearably painful. "Leave them alone!" she shouted.

He looked completely unaffected at her outburst. "If you're hoping for someone to save you, the little girl you brought with you and the sniper are all neutralized."

"Sniper?"

"Yes. Oh, you didn't know about him?" he sneered. "I don't believe you. We'll find the other man with you. It's only a matter of time."

Rock had lied about him? Why? Oh, God. It must have been Tristan, even after she'd asked him not to involve her brother. She could only wish she could get a chance to find out from him. It was good Set hadn't captured Rock. That was something she could hope for— Rock figuring out how to save them.

He kicked the chair over and Neve hit the rug, the back of her head impacting so that she saw stars.

As he moved near, sweat pooled at the base of her spine, at her temples. The clamminess of her skin reeked of fear. She had nothing in her favor. For a moment, she simply lay there, absorbing the pain.

"You will give me what I want, then you will know my agony."

She worked her jaw and glared. "I will never betray my family." It was the wrong thing to say. He called out, and when a man entered the room, he motioned to the flunky, who dragged her off the floor and shoved her into the chair. Then Set grabbed her face in a punishing grip. Neve's defiant gaze met his. He wanted fear, terror. He wouldn't get it.

"We will see about that. When I'm done with you, you'll be begging to tell me."

Chapter 16

Rock approached the camp and saw an ambush had been set up. Pulling out his KA-BAR, he went to work, eliminating the threat. But Neve and Opal were gone. His lungs suddenly so tight it was impossible to get air into them, he realized their sniper must have been eliminated or he would have protected Neve. A rush of emotion jammed up in his chest, and he looked off into the distance to the exact location he would set up for a perfect shot at the Falcon. God help him, he had to keep his head on straight. And he had to do right by her. Because, in the end, her life depended on it.

There was no room for error here. His next steps were to get to Neve and Opal and get them out of there. They had to regroup and take a different tactic. But he knew where this bastard lived; he still had contacts in the marines. He would call in favors and would eliminate the threat to Neve one way or the other.

He wanted to check on the sniper. If there was even a chance he was still alive, that would give them all an advantage, but he couldn't waste a moment.

With all the skills he'd learned as a marine, he made it back to Set's fortress undetected. It was heavily fortified, and he would have to take the time to find a weakness. There was always one he could exploit.

He only hoped they could hang on until the path inside was uncovered.

Neve sat against the wall, the floor beneath her nothing but dirt, damp, muddy dirt, the kind that soaked into her clothes and left a clammy, gritty feeling against her skin. Bars separated her and Opal, and they had huddled together for comfort as close as the metal would allow. The teenager was scared; the light of it was in her eyes. But she put on a tough front and Neve was thankful for her strength in the face of these overwhelming odds. She breathed a sigh of relief when she saw that Rock wasn't in any of the cells. Opal confirmed that she'd overheard two guards who said the marine was being elusive and had killed a contingent of men who had gone to their camp to ambush him.

If anyone could get them out of this, it would be him. She had complete confidence in his abilities. The door rattled open and she heard footsteps, then a teenage boy, looking furtive, approached Opal's cell.

"José," she said fiercely, her voice filled with joy. She rose and ran to the cell, gripping the bars.

"Opal. What are you doing here?" His voice was strained.

"I had to come for you, José, I had to. I brought friends, but we messed up and got captured."

He shook his head, his expression one of sick fear and worry. He was the spitting image of Opal, and Neve immediately thought of Nova and how mad she must be right now to be holed up in protective custody, unable to fly rescue helicopters. She squeezed her eyes shut as the two teenagers conversed, missing her sister, worried that Tristan could be dead if he had been the sniper they had taken out. She burned with the need to do something.

"Neve," Opal said, motioning her over. "This is my brother, José."

He nodded in her direction. "He's going to get us out of here."

"I will come for you tonight. It's best to escape when it's dark."

"I have a friend outside the walls. He's a marine, and his name is Rock. He will help you."

"I won't be able to get outside," he said reluctantly. "Set doesn't realize right now that Opal is my sister, but if he makes the connection, he'll throw me in here with you. I don't want to take the chance that he'll remember. We need to leave as soon as possible."

The sound of the door opening made him look quickly over his shoulder. "Be ready," he whispered as he concealed himself. A man came down the short hallway, and as soon as he passed José's hiding spot the boy melted out of the shadows and ran down the hall. Neve didn't even hear the door close behind him.

The guard ignored Opal and went right to Neve's cell. The key made a jingling sound, then a grinding noise as it turned in the lock. A second man appeared at the end of the hallway and trained a gun on Opal. It was clear if she tried anything, he would shoot Opal.

Neve scowled and thrust out her arms for him to

snap on the cuffs. He grabbed her by the upper arm and marched her to a room, then closed the door behind him.

There was a chair and a table. It looked like an interrogation room, everything bare and dirty.

Finally, the door opened and Set entered. "Your man appears to be quite elusive. It's no matter, we will have him soon and then won't that be fun…for me. If you won't give me the information I want, you can watch while I carve his heart out."

"You'll never catch him. He's invisible as air."

"I suspect that girl out there is nothing but a guide and doesn't mean as much to you as your family, but let's see what we can do before we have to resort to bloodshed."

"It doesn't matter what you do to me. I'm never giving you what you want."

He hit her dead center in the solar plexus, and she buckled over, gasping for air and fighting the pain expanding to her limbs.

The door opened, and two men entered with a barrel, water sloshed over the side. Water. This was what the first round was going to consist of—drowning.

Neve told herself not to be afraid. Not to give an inch. Even if she had the information, he would never get those addresses. She would keep her family safe as she'd vowed she would do when she came out here to eliminate the threat.

And the most important thing was…Rock was still out there.

He forced her to stand, holding tight to her manacled hands, then shoved her to the ground. She rolled to her side, and he moved around to the front of the barrel. He motioned for one of the guards to proceed, and he grabbed her by the hair.

"The addresses."

"Go to hell." She started breathing deeper, taking in oxygen for the plunge. Set had no idea who he was dealing with when it came to water. Neve loved it, and it was her office. This would be nothing compared to thirty-foot waves.

Lifting her off the ground, he shoved her face-first into the water, but she'd already prepared herself. He held her down hard, the edge of the barrel cutting into her stomach. After a minute, she barely felt the effects. After thirty more seconds, her heartbeat started to resonate in her ears. It was all she could hear beyond the strain to hold her breath. Her lungs grew tighter by the millisecond, and she desperately wanted to exhale. She let out more air through her nose—she had to—and when she didn't have any more, couldn't hold it in, she faced her death. Just when she started to relax, she was yanked back.

Neve drew in a long harsh pull of air, coughing. She'd barely cleared a lungful when the guard pushed her back under again. He repeated the torture, just long enough to fill her lungs less and less each time. The question was always the same, and her answer was more breathless, but firm, until they were no more than words scattered in the air, random and angry. Then Ammon Set took over, holding her down longer. Neve felt her energy slipping with each plunge. Oxygen starved. She'd be brain dead before this was over. If she lived.

The first fingers of sunrise painted the bellies of the fat, cumulous clouds with pink and purple, the angle of early-morning light stretching the shadows and making the dew sparkle, the trees dripping with moisture. Facing the sunrise, Rock perched on a thick, sturdy branch, his shoulder propped against the trunk, his knees bent in a crouch. The only thing missing was a steaming cup of coffee cradled in his hands. It was not quite 5:00 a.m., but even after getting out of the marines, he was always up by then anyway. He attributed the success of Rockface to his early hours. It was his favorite time of day. He liked witnessing the sunrise, the beginning of a brand-new day. And he liked that particular stillness that came with early morning. But most of all, he liked soaking up that quiet as he watched the sun rise over the bay on the east side of the house.

But here in the Darién it was far from quiet, with the monkeys and the birds, a cacophony of sound he now had grown accustomed to and didn't register.

He knew where they were keeping her, and he'd found a vulnerability he could exploit. He was currently watching the fortress, and he'd pinpointed the jail. Ammon Set had gone in and, a few hours later, he'd left. Rock was vibrating inside thinking about what the bastard must be doing to her. He wanted to take the man apart, but storming in there now would be suicide and wouldn't help Neve.

Hold on, babe. I'm coming for you.

He would wait until nightfall, and then he was busting her out of there. As he watched, he saw the furtive movements of a boy, and the kid looked familiar. Wait…was that Opal's brother? And if it was, what was he up to?

He watched the kid for another thirty seconds and smiled softly. Oh, he had a plan, and he was putting on this show solely for his benefit. "I got you, kid," Rock whispered from his position in the trees. Set's troops had moved below him several times, never thinking to look up. He'd eliminated a couple of patrols. They were sending out fewer.

Rock grinned. He was in his playground, and he wasn't about to give up any of his toys.

If any of them came into his kill zone, he wasn't going to hesitate to gain the odds in his favor.

A thick feeling unfolded in his chest, and he tried to push away the frustration of waiting and watching. They were the very things that were going to make this a victory. He had to be patient. He locked his jaw and closed his eyes, a thousand feelings lumbering through his chest. Neve. His best friend's sister. It was as if giving in to his need to get closer to her was eroding his old defenses.

He couldn't.

As if under enormous pressure, his heart felt suddenly too big for his chest. Closing his eyes, he swallowed hard and tightened his hands around the binoculars, years of rigidly suppressed feelings boiling up inside him. The memory of having her in his arms—with her entire body pressed against his—was almost more than he could handle, and he remembered every contour, every dip, every gorgeous curve. Christ, it was as if a dam had broken loose in him, and every single feeling he'd ever had for her came raging out. He'd known that giving in to this impulse would be the worst mistake he'd ever made, and he'd also known he was going to pay dearly for it. There was no way, not after experiencing the feel of her body molded against his, that he would ever be able to beat down all those long-denied feelings. Never in a million years. She was such a miracle. And he *loved* her. With absolutely everything in him. He knew he had no business feeling that way, but he did.

*I'm so sorry, Tristan, for crossing the line with her...
with you.*

But nothing—nothing—was ever going to change
that, not even his shame. His throat tight and his eyes
burning, he clenched his jaw.

If he could, he'd take her right inside him and keep
her there forever. She was everything to him. Absolutely
everything. As if unloading some terrible stored-up pain,
he gritted his teeth and endured.

Hold on, babe. I'm coming for you.

He was coming for her. There was no doubt in her
mind.

He would never leave her here to die.

Never.

Neve had to endure two more rounds of near drowning and several blows to her face. Her eye was swelling,
and her cheek and jaw were bruised and throbbing. Set
was getting impatient after the last round as night was
descending. He'd shoved her so hard into her cell, she'd
fallen and scraped the heels of her hands to break her
fall. She lay there for a few minutes while Opal cried
softly, calling out to her, asking her if she was all right.

Neve gathered her strength and pushed up to her
stinging hands and knees, then dragged herself over
to the bars that separated them. Reaching through, she
wrapped her arms around the distraught girl and held
her close, her fearful and sympathetic sobs tearing at
Neve's heart.

"It's all right, Opal. Your brother is coming for us.
Rock is coming for us. We'll get out of this."

She prayed she was right.

About thirty minutes later, a guard came into the jail

and shoved two plates and two bottles of water under the doors to their cells. Crawling forward, her lungs and throat raw, her neck and shoulders sore, a strip of her stomach bruised from being held under, Neve grabbed the plate and ate everything, downing the water. She was going to need the strength to run. Once Rock got them out, that would only be the beginning.

Opal leaned her head against the side of the cell. "He is out for revenge against you, and he won't stop. But my brother did nothing. Our village minded our own business. We just wanted to live peacefully."

Neve nodded. "I was doing my job."

"Sounds like you did everything in your power to save those people. It's a tragedy that they died, but you don't deserve this kind of treatment. This isn't your fault."

A knot untied in her, loosening up the bonds she had used to bind herself to the guilt burning in her. Out of the mouth of babes. This journey, getting closer to Rock, understanding what true teamwork was—it all made her realize that Opal was probably right. She couldn't quite believe that she was blameless, but the storm had hampered her ability to carry out her job. True, she had let her bias influence her, but it was more out of eagerness to save those people than it was out of proving herself. In the future, she would put the people she rescued first and foremost without factoring in how each rescue affected her. She would work harder to connect and support her team members as they did the same for her. Without that kind of connection and commitment, what was the point? She might as well swim alone.

And now, she didn't want to go it alone anymore.

In her professional or personal life.

But the stark reality was that she couldn't reconcile

herself to staying put in San Diego and giving up her chance to see her new vows fulfilled. She had an obligation to the coast guard, to her country and to herself to see her duty through.

Regardless of how it would break her heart.

She was half asleep when José came into the jail so quietly she didn't hear him. One minute the front of the cell was empty, the next he was there.

"Opal," he whispered. They both rose and he put his hand up, then pulled out a squeeze bottle. He squirted what looked like cooking oil on the hinges and the door lock. Then he moved to Neve's cell. He waited a few more minutes and twisted the key in the lock. It made a soft snicking sound, and the door swung inward on a quiet hiss of air.

The siblings wrapped their arms around each other for just a moment, and tears pressed at the back of Neve's eyes. The minute she was able, she was going to see Nova.

She took the keys from him while he went to stand guard and unlocked her cell. But as they went to head down the hallway, José rushed into the room. "Someone is coming," he hissed.

He picked up a piece of a table leg on the ground and stood at the ready, his face ferocious with his resolve.

The man moved silently and swiftly. As José swung, a hand came out and halted the wood from impact. He stepped into the light, and Neve sagged in relief.

"Thank God," she whispered.

Before she was even aware of moving, she was in his arms. Unable to speak, she sobbed his name against his neck. She heard Opal quickly introduce Rock to her brother and felt him nod as he held her tightly to him. When they parted, his eyes ignited with murderous rage as he surveyed her face. "Son of a bitch," he said vehemently beneath his breath. "He's a dead man."

The solemn expression in his eyes altered, changing to a heart-stopping look that made Neve's heart roll over. "Babe," he said, his tone husky. "I came for you." He brushed back a wisp of hair, his touch soft and sensual.

"Took you long enough," she groused.

That glint in his eyes turned to amusement. "I was too busy dodging bullets and guys who were trying to kill me."

"Is that all?"

Loving his lopsided smile, but sobering at the shadows in his eyes, Neve pressed her lips to his, even though she knew they didn't have the time.

He opened his mouth and kissed her back, his lips pliant and moist and tasting sweeter than anything on the planet.

"Come on," José said, taking his sister's arm. "We've got to get as far away as we can before they realize you're gone."

On an uneven intake of air, Rock broke off the kiss, his heart pounding beneath her hand. He stared down at her, one hand still around her waist, then bent his head, drew his hand across his eyes and exhaled sharply.

He caught her hand and held it tight, and they ran for the exit, stopping to make sure the coast was clear. Two guards lay slumped near the door, and Opal looked at her brother with new eyes. "José…"

"I did what I had to do," he said tightly.

She nodded.

"I've found us a way out of here," Rock whispered, and they all nodded.

Pulling the door open, he waved them through, and

they stayed in the shadows on the back side of the jail-house. The walls were still warm from the heat of the sun.

"Can you run?" he asked.

"Hell, yes." She gave Rock a cheeky grin. "But don't ask for any push-ups—one-armed or otherwise," she said, so strongly Rock chuckled softly.

"We should go by twos," Rock said. "I'll take you one by one. Opal, you're first. On my mark." Rock watched and waited and the minute the guards were facing the other way, growled, "Now."

They started across the yard, and as soon as they hit the fence at the perimeter of the compound, Opal crouched down to minimize the chances of being seen by guards. Rock moved unseen across the expanse, and then took José across. But before he could come back for her, from behind the ammunition dump, Ammon Set stepped out into the open and they all froze. He had a pistol trained on Neve.

"I know where you came from, José. Did you honestly think I wouldn't suspect you'd betray me? The resemblance is uncanny."

"Let us go," Opal said. "You have no right—"

"This is my domain, little girl," he scoffed. "I don't need the right."

He pointed the pistol and fired at José at the same time as Rock brought up his weapon and squeezed off a shot. The ammunition dump exploded with a boom-ing blast that threw them all to the ground.

She saw José grappling with Set, punches flying. Then Opal threw herself into the fray as Rock barreled toward them. There was another explosion, and all of them were separated, knocked to the ground. Neve's eyes were on Rock's unmoving body.

Neve cried out and rolled to her feet, running for Rock, but Set caught her ankle and sent her sprawling.

José shook Rock and helped him up as Ammon grabbed her by the hair and dragged her back to her feet.

Neve's and Rock's eyes met and for a frozen moment in time, something aching and desperate passed between them. She saw the truth in his eyes, a terrified, anguished sight that she would never forget, a revelation that she would take to her grave.

He loved her.

He had always *loved* her.

Another explosion threw them back, and when Neve pushed up to her elbow, Russell, her Rock, her warrior, was illuminated by the fire's glow. "Go," she screamed at him. "Please, go!" He turned toward the teenagers and freedom, then turned back to her. His face contorted, anguish so deep, so clear that it reached out and grabbed her by the throat. She watched him disappear from sight, her vision blurred, so many emotions breaking loose inside her that she couldn't distinguish one from another. She stared at the spot where he had been, feeling as if her insides might disintegrate.

Set was rigid with rage as he violently slapped her and kicked her in the ribs. She folded in on herself until one of his blows connected with her head.

Darkness, suffocating and black, swallowed her up whole.

Chapter 17

Rock tore down the path he'd made earlier in the day as they crashed through the jungle, feeling raw, unable to control the emotions breaking free and squeezing his heart, his lungs, as helpless rage washed through him.

He had to leave her behind! Son of a bitch!

"Stay alive, babe. Stay alive," he chanted as he came to the end of the path and a sheer drop-off. There was nothing below them but a black nothingness.

"Are you out of your mind?" José said.

José and Opal, their faces showing the same kind of anguish at having to leave Neve behind, looked down, then back at him.

The shouts of men chasing after them heavy on the wind, Rock shook his head.

"Jump. It's our only way out of here. I trusted you, Opal. Now you're going to have to trust me."

Gunshots exploded in the night, causing a din of howling monkeys and squawking birds, a mass of winged bodies taking flight into the dark sky. Bullets made the same sound as rain did as they smacked into leaves around them, making a whizzing noise as armed bodies broke out of the trees.

Without another word, Opal turned and flung herself off the cliff into the darkness. *"Madre de Dios, ayúdenos,"* José whispered, making the sign of the cross. Then he jumped.

Rock followed shortly afterward, leaping into a darkness as deep as the one covering his soul.

Stay alive, babe. I'm coming back for you.

He plunged, his body weightless as the wind tore at his hair, whipping his clothes tight to his body, his stomach falling away. It was like riding a bike, as Rock had performed plenty of such low altitude, low opening jumps. Also referred to as LALO, these jumps gave troops the advantage of being quickly dropped into an area, but because of the low altitude they were one of the more dangerous jumps to execute. Normally there was a line that automatically pulled the rip cord when the plane was over the jump area.

And that usually meant the jumper was wearing and getting the benefit of a parachute, not jumping blind into the air and hoping for the best.

Minutes later he hit the water, and then he was fighting, clawing for the surface. "Opal, José?"

"Here," they said in unison, and they all started swimming for the shore of the wide lake. They pulled themselves onto dry land, and Rock lay there for a moment absorbing his loss, berating himself for not planning better, for his failure in making sure Neve was safe.

I'm sorry, Tristan, he thought, the anguish even deeper when he thought about how his best friend would react if he wasn't able to get back in time. There was only one course of action, one that would take time. But he had no choice now. He pulled the two of them close and started issuing orders.

Opal rose and with a quick hug to her brother, she took off. José watched his sister disappear into the jungle, then he gave Rock one last supportive look and went in the opposite direction.

They all had a role to play. Because there was something he was damn sure about. He wasn't leaving that compound without Neve.

And if Set had harmed her…he was taking the man out, no matter the risk.

Neve woke up back in the cell, and she wanted to cry; she had been so close to freedom. This time there was a guard outside her cell and, she figured, one outside the door.

She allowed herself a few tears, then surreptitiously wiped her face with the heel of her hand. Then she swallowed hard, struggling to achieve a degree of self-control.

Neve had been fighting the good fight and thought she had won until she remembered Rock's face, the wrenching feeling of loss when he'd looked away, the look on his face when he'd turned back. Unable to see through the blur of tears, unable to remain quiet, she wrapped her arms around her and rocked back and forth, her shoulders shaking.

The night wore on. Finally her sorrow eased and she

fell asleep, dreading the morning. She could only be thankful that Set no longer held any prisoners to use as leverage against her.

She would never give up any information about her family.

She was going to die here.

She woke in the early light of dawn at the sound of running feet and gunfire. A lot of gunfire. The guard outside her cell went to the window and looked out. Whatever he saw unnerved him because he whirled, looked at her and raised his rifle, pointing it directly at her.

Neve backpedaled into the corner of the cell as he brought up the rifle. She had nowhere to go as the barrel came up, so she closed her eyes and heard the sound of breaking glass just as the gun went off. The bullet thunked into the wall just to the left of her.

She opened her eyes to find him lying dead on the ground. At first she was confused. But then realization dawned.

The sniper.

Tristan?

There was no sound, except those of glass shattering and a bullet hitting the cell door. The door slid open silently, the vegetable oil from last night greasing its hinges.

Neve rose and used the cell bars as support to make it to the door. Her ribs were throbbing, and there were so many places on her body that ached she lost count. Once she started moving, her limbs loosened up. Bending, she retrieved the rifle the guard had dropped. Looking out the window, she made out the uniforms of the government troops.

A smile broke out on her face from the sight of the cavalry coming to her rescue. She recognized Alejandro among the camouflaged green-and-tan uniforms. She hobbled toward the door, still dismayed by how many of Set's thugs were between her and safety.

She stayed close to the wall, deciding the best course of action was to go out the way Rock had. As soon as she got to the back side of the prison, she went to dash across to the wall, but an arm snaked out and grabbed the back of her shirt, knocked the rifle out of her hand and put a gun to her temple.

"We have a score to settle," Set spat as he used her as a shield and headed toward a Jeep parked in the back of the compound.

The tide of the battle turned as more of Alejandro's government troops fired on his force. He dragged her kicking and screaming away from freedom and toward sure death.

He pressed the gun hard to her temple and hissed in her ear. "Stop fighting me or it's over here."

He turned to head toward the Jeep and Rock stood there, blocking their path.

"It is over, Set."

"For you," he said, as he raised the gun and pointed it at Rock.

In the distance, Derrick Gunn took a breath in and held it, then breathed out; he sighted his target and slowly pulled the trigger. The Emberá boy lay on the ground next to him. The rifle recoiled into Derrick's shoulder, making very little sound, as the suppressor muffled the noise of the bullet leaving the barrel.

Derrick smiled and said, "We're done, kid." He heard

the sound of his ride in the distance. His job was done here, and freaking A, it was well done.

He grabbed up his pack and helped the boy up. "Get going."

There had been no gunshot, no sound, but blood blossomed at his forehead and he'd gone limp as he'd tumbled to the ground. For a moment, Neve looked down at the man who would have destroyed her world, blood pooling beneath his head.

She looked off into the distance, put her fingers to her lips and blew a kiss to the sniper.

Then she ran for Rock's arms. Collapsing against him, she held on to him as she heard the sound of a high-powered stealth chopper, watched as it landed and a man ran for the vehicle, the blades ripping at his hair, a rifle in his grip. He stopped and saluted them both before he got in.

The Black Hawk took off and was soon lost in the distance.

That wasn't her brother. Who was it?

Then another chopper's rotors beat the air as the powerful machine landed in the compound. José ran for the slight girl who climbed out and they embraced. With Rock's arm firmly around her, Neve limped toward them. They enfolded her in a hug as all four of them got inside the vehicle and it took off.

Neve was flown to Panama City and admitted into the army hospital there. She was told by her doctor that her wounds were mostly soft tissue damage, but she had to get a couple of stitches in a gash at her temple and had her face cleaned and bandaged. They wanted to run tests on her, so she was forced to remain there.

After an hour of being prodded and poked, she got a meal delivered to her and slowly ate it. When the door opened, she'd expected to see someone arriving to take her tray away, but instead it was Rock. He had showered and changed into a pair of dress slacks and a light blue, short-sleeved shirt, the cotton molding over his powerful chest and broad shoulders, the bandage from his flesh wound on his upper arm just barely visible.

He was carrying a bouquet of flowers. She didn't know why, but she felt overcome, breathless, and her throat was already tight.

He smiled at her; she closed her eyes and burst into tears.

The sound of quick footsteps and then his warm, strong arms going around her was all the medicine she needed.

His throat tight and his eyes burning, Rock held her head against him, his jaw clenched.

As if unloading some terrible stored-up pain, Neve finally cried herself out, and she turned her head against his shoulder. She pressed her hand against his shirt and whispered, "I got your shirt all wet." He couldn't resist the urge to hug her, so he gave her a reassuring squeeze. His own voice was low and rough when he answered.

"Aw, babe, it's over. You're safe."

"José and Opal?"

"Safe and sound." He'd sent Opal to SENAFRONT for Alejandro's help and José to find the sniper, banking on the fact that his shadow was still alive and ready for action. "You're all safe." Loosening his hold, he swallowed hard and braced himself for her to pull away. But Neve never did what he expected. Instead, she nearly knocked the foundation right out from under him when she slipped her arms around his waist, rested her head on his shoulder and stayed right where she was. She released a long sigh, as if expelling the last of her tears. With her warm and soft against him, Rock locked his jaw and made himself take a deep, slow breath, the heat from her body making his blood thicken. Ah, but it felt so good to hold her—so damned good. Imperceptibly he tightened his hold, committing every single sensation to memory. Sensations to call up and remember after he was gone.

The room was quiet except for her soft gasps. Neve finally stirred. Releasing a long sigh, she flattened her hand against his back and shifted her head. And just as imperceptibly she tightened her hold. "You saved my life so many times," she whispered unevenly. "Thank you for being such a stubborn marine and ignoring everything I said."

Her honesty made his heart roll over and his chest clog up. Feeling as if he might turn inside out at any minute, Rock closed his eyes and rubbed her back. His throat was so tight. He couldn't have spoken if he'd wanted to. He had never expected this to happen, this precious love he had for her. And he had never let himself even think about it because it had always been so far out of reach. It still was. Aware of every curve and hollow of her body, he continued to hold her, wishing this moment could last forever. After a long silence, Neve sighed and pulled away, then looked up at him, her face still puffy from crying, so bruised and battered. He wished he could resurrect Set and kill the bastard all over again.

With so much gratitude in her eyes that it nearly broke his heart, she met his gaze. "Thank you for everything, Rock," she said softly. "I don't know what I would have done without you." She leaned forward and kissed his cheek, then his mouth.

He stepped back as she reached out and clasped his hand. He paused and smiled. "You take good care of yourself, babe. I guess I'll see you when I see you."

She nodded as their fingers held on for a few more fleeting moments. He turned and left the room, his heart shattering and his footsteps reluctant. But as he walked away from her room and the sad, resigned look on her face, he was sure he made the best decision for both of them.

They wanted different things, and neither one of them could compromise and be happy. Didn't stop him from feeling as if someone had just dropped a boulder on his chest. Inside the elevator, he tipped his head back and swallowed hard. He knew he would relive that interlude thousands of times in his mind. If he survived to be a hundred, he would never forget it. His jaw locked as the doors opened and he exited the elevator, walked through the lobby to the street. He raised his hand and hailed a cab, recognizing the handsome devil who got out of a tricked-out Jeep behind him. Marco. At least she'd have a friend with her now that he was leaving.

He got inside the cab and said, "Airport," wondering how in hell he was going to make it through the next couple of hours, let alone the rest of his life.

Back in San Diego, Derrick went to work the next day, and as he got out of his car, he saw Amber walking toward the NCIS building. She stopped when she saw him. He closed his car door and ambled over. She stood there for a minute just looking up at him, taking in the bruises on his face from the life-and-death battle with one of Set's men. His shoulder was still a bit sore, but the gunrunner's flunky had cushioned his fall.

"Derrick," she whispered, then she wrapped her arms around him and hugged him hard. "Thank you."

He nodded. There wasn't anything he wouldn't do for the people he cared about, and after working with Amber for a year now, she definitely fit into that category.

"You're welcome," he said, aware that taking out some gunrunner barely caused him one moment's lack of sleep. It was the innocents, the ones who didn't deserve to die, who haunted him. And along with the blood of his enemies, there was more than enough blood of the innocents on his hands.

Inside the NCIS office, he saw Austin at his desk. He rose when he saw Derrick and offered his hand. Derrick clasped it and for just a moment, Austin tightened his grip, then let go.

Amber smiled at them.

Then their boss, Kai Talbot, walked in, and Derrick faced her. She'd known what was going on, and she'd sent that Black Hawk for him. He wasn't sure how she found out, but at this point it didn't matter. They were a team. She stopped in front of him and reached out and clasped his shoulder, giving him a little squeeze.

"What are you three doing standing around? We have a dead sailor in Oceanside. Grab your stuff."

She winked at him as they all headed for the elevator.

Chapter 18

Six months later

Neve stood on the balcony of her sister Nova's rental on the coast of Oregon, about fifteen minutes from US Coast Guard Air Station Astoria. Soon after returning from the Darién and after getting cleared for duty, Neve had been offered a temporary assignment at the air station. Raw from her experience with Rock and unable to handle being in close proximity to him, she'd jumped at the chance to get out of San Diego.

When Neve returned, NCIS had already been briefed by the sniper, and they were satisfied with the outcome of the mission. NCIS informed CGIS, but kept the sniper's identity, as well as Neve's involvement, confidential. CGIS marked the case closed. Ammon Set was no longer a threat to her family, and they were all released from their respective safe houses. Alejandro Garcia rounded up all the members of Set's organization that hadn't been killed in the raid. With Set out of the picture and the case strong against his wife, the DEA and ATF moved on her operation, dismantling her organization in the process. Set's wife was killed in the gun battle, further alleviating any threat of retribution. With Set's upper-level leadership and many of his wife's key lieutenants casualties of their respective raids, Neve could finally relax. Even her brother Thane was doing well and out of the hospital.

But she missed Rock like crazy.

It was early morning, and the ocean here had a rough personality, choppy and as unpredictable as…love.

A coffee cup materialized in front of her, and she smiled and turned to find Nova, like Neve, dressed and ready for work. "Thought you could use this after your rough night."

Nova knew it all. Neve wasn't able to keep anything from her. When they had found themselves working out of the same air station, Nova had used her knowledge of how to snag the best accommodations to get herself this wood-and-glass house that belonged to another Coastie who was on assignment in Clearwater, Florida. It was clear the two of them were involved. But Nova told Neve it was just casual and easily deflected questions about her love life to focus on Neve.

"Thanks." It was second nature for each of them to know when the other was in turmoil. "You always know what I need."

She nodded and hip-bumped Neve. "How are you doing? You're looking out to sea, like your captain is never coming home."

"Maybe running away from a situation isn't always the best idea."

"I think you'd better try to understand exactly what you want to do." She leaned against the rail. "Tristan says he's miserable, Neve," she said softly.

"It hurts to hear that." Memories of Rock assaulted her, and she searched her soul for the answers, but all she found were pieces of herself scattered around, too fragmented to pull herself together. "He is…steadfast, tough, freaking scary, with the kind of warrior skills that make you happy he works for the United States. He never gave up, and he saved my life and the lives of our family."

"He did, Neve, and we're all so very grateful for what he did, but especially that he made our business his business. Except I'm pretty sure his motivation to keep you safe had nothing to do with his deep friendship with Tristan. Take the time you need to make a decision. But—" she slapped her sister's butt "—make one."

Neve rolled her eyes, turning away from the turbulent ocean. "Thanks, sis. You're such a big help."

Nova smiled. "Anytime." She pushed off the railing. "Ready to go?"

"Yes." They bumped fists and left the balcony. After finishing her coffee, Neve set her cup in the kitchen sink and got into Nova's car for the quick trip to the station.

Her sister was a search-and-rescue pilot, and she flew one of the three all-weather, medium-ranged MH-60 Jayhawk helicopters. They were never allowed to fly together because they were siblings, and Nova could not have direct supervisory responsibility over her sister.

They arrived on base and walked inside the red, flat-topped building adjacent to the long stretch of blacktop that served as the heliport. Since she had downtime, Neve went to the swim shop, where she did tasks to support future missions. She was twining rope around two supports when her beeper went off and the loudspeaker announced two surfers were caught in a cavern northwest of Tillamook Bay. Neve headed to the locker room to get ready. She donned her bright orange dry suit.

When she climbed aboard the Jayhawk chopper, she greeted pilot Lieutenant Raymond Smalls, copilot Seth Mars and flight engineer Eric Sharp.

As they took off, Lieutenant Smalls made sure they were all on the same page. "Two surfers are in the water in a cavern, both of them in distress. We're not going to be able to drop you in the water, Michaels. Find a good spot to egress."

"Roger that, sir," Neve replied as they reached the destination and looked down to the swirling water below, the cavern off to their right. They were above Cape Lookout, the back of the cavern a sheer wall of rock that rose about four hundred feet above the surfers.

The flight engineer lowered Neve down to the ground. Unhooking the hoist cable from her harness, she saw two young men running up to her. "They got sucked in. We were surfing the gnarly waves from the storm. They're back there." He pointed to the rocky outcropping that formed the wall of the cavern. It arched away from the beach toward the ocean.

"Stay here and stay calm. We'll do everything we can to save them." Neve pushed back her fear when she got within viewing distance inside the cavern and saw what she was about to enter. Her determination didn't waver; there were two lives to save inside. She looked up at the hovering aircraft, confident that these men were here to support her, and they would do everything in their power to make sure they all came out of that churning hell alive. There was no doubt in her mind that she would survive and perform her duties to the utmost of her abilities, no matter the cost.

"Michaels," a grave voice said through her radio. "We need to move as fast as possible. If the tide comes in, things are going to get even rougher. Over."

"Copy that," Neve said. As a matter of procedure, before they left base, she'd gone over the weather reports and estimated the tides and currents for the search area. She knew she had thirty minutes until the tide would roll in and increase the magnitude and power of the waves and currents.

This was dangerous, there was no doubt about that, but she didn't hesitate. Her suit would protect her from the Pacific's cold embrace and the threat of hypothermia. Armed with her gear and her determination to save these men, she moved to the entrance.

Walking along the rocks, Neve saw both men curled up on a small ledge toward the rear of the cavern, across two hundred feet of churning water. Toward the back was a spinning vortex to be completely avoided, a smaller opening that led to another tunnel. This area acted like a suctioning funnel, pulling in debris and then spewing it out with destructive force.

Observing the waves and their rhythm, she decided when to enter the water. She dropped into the sea between twelve-foot waves, flinching at the frigid temperature and the immediate turbulence. Aided by the heaving ocean, Neve swam along the rocky wall toward the men. When she finally got there, she immediately checked the first man for injuries, then the second—mostly cuts and bruises. Both of them were dressed in cold-water wet suits, which were staving off hypothermia. There were a couple rips and tears in the neoprene, but all and all they had been smart and gotten themselves out of the water.

"Hi, I'm Petty Officer Neve Michaels. I'm here to help you get out of here safely. You're going to be okay." Worried eyes latched on to her. The trembling men nodded. One had big, blue eyes and short blond hair; the other one had curlier hair with a set of green eyes that were just a tad calmer than the other man's.

"I'm Ben Compton and this is my brother, Mark," the curly-haired guy said, his voice firm and telling her he was ready to leave.

Conditions were epic. The sheer force of the water picked up debris and tossed it around. The air in the cavern whistled like the sound of a nor'easter through the cracks of the damp walls that made way for the Pacific saltwater forcing its way in. The intensity of the surf was gearing up to get even nastier, the winds gusting to twenty-five and thirty knots while the tall waves broke at the coastline.

"They are conscious and in pretty good shape with cold-water wet suits," she radioed to the chopper. "Swimming out of here is iffy, sir. With the surging of the water and the backlash as it's sucked out of the cavern, we're going to get pretty battered."

There was no answer from the chopper, and Neve looked over her shoulder to see the vehicle listing to the side. Something was wrong. The Jayhawk disappeared from view, and she took a breath.

Suddenly, she heard a female voice through the radio.

"Rescue swimmer, this is 6568. Tail rotor out on 6478, over."

That was her sister's voice. With the rotor out on Neve's helicopter, Astoria must have deployed Nova's chopper, since it was the only place in Oregon they could send out another Jayhawk. Flying time from the air station was only fifteen minutes and it was imperative they get these guys out of the water as soon as possible. In light of the dire circumstances, it was preferable to allow her sister, Nova, to fly the mission. That information flashed through her mind like lightning as Neve pushed everything but the rescue of the survivors out of her mind.

"Roger that, 6568. Repeating…swimming out of here is iffy. With the surging water and the backlash as it is sucked out of the cavern, we're going to get pretty battered. Two, that is *t-w-o*, survivors, both conscious. Advise, over."

"Stand by."

It seemed like an eternity before Nova's voice came back through the radio. "We're coming in. Basket drop, but you'll have to get them closer to the entrance."

"Roger that."

Neve turned back to the two men and said, "We're going to have to swim out of here to the center of the cavern, where they're going to drop a basket. Listen to me—you're going to have to swim hard and fast. These waves are going to push us back in. Stay with me." She removed her vest and strapped the two of them together, instructing them to put their arms through the armholes and grab hold of their waistbands. "I want you to lock elbows, and whatever you do, don't give up. We stay together, we get out of here together."

Neve turned around and caught her breath. Her sister was flying the chopper between the walls and below the top of the cavern roof. Her chest swelled with pride for her sister's skill, thankful she was such a talented pilot.

Now comes the hard part, Neve thought as the two men slipped into the water. Immediately one of them let go and started to thrash. Neve punched him twice to get him under control, then she shouted in his face over the roar of the waves. "We're not going to survive unless we work together. Now hook your brother's elbow and don't let go again. Kick with everything you've got." She felt like she was channeling Rock, and the thought of him strengthened her determination to get out of this situation.

Mark nodded, his breathing harsh, exchanging a desperate look with Ben, who, still steadfast, gave his brother a nod. "We're going to make it," he said. Mark took a shuddering breath, resolve settling over his features. He gave Ben another curt nod.

Slipping her arm underneath the vest, she got them into a swimmer's carry. By this time, Nova had the whole helicopter inside the cavern, hovering above the water, keeping the vehicle so steady it was like they were standing still.

Rolling waves struck them, and Neve yelled for the two men to kick. They were pushed back, then the backlash of the waves propelled them forward, but swamped them and they went under. With sheer force of strength, she pulled both men back up, bouncing to the surface.

Then it was as if she hit a wall that she couldn't get through, like some crosscurrent was causing a solid barrier. Waves tossed them up and back and they went under again, but the guys held firm as she swam back to the surface, the drag of their weight minimized by their strong kicking.

She figured the waves rolling in and the heaving ocean dumping out of the cavern were causing a pressured reaction. The combination of the crushing collision obstructed their forward momentum. There was only one course of action. They had to swim under it. She screamed at them to hold their breaths; they were going under. "Kick like hell!" She submerged. The breakers rolling above her, she swam, her flippers giving her strong propulsion and the survivors helping. She calculated she was past it when her lungs were close to bursting. Popping back up to the surface, she almost cried in relief when she saw the USCG lettering on the chopper's underbelly.

Nova explained what they were going to do. The flight mechanic lowered a basket along with two trail lines equipped with a simple loop called a strop that went over the head and was secured under the arms. She assisted Mark into the basket and settled her vest onto Ben. Then she grabbed the lead line, and as quickly as she could in the heaving seas, secured the loop around Ben, then put the second around herself. Wrapping her hand into the steel mesh, she instructed Ben to do the same. "Hang on."

"Don't let me go," he said in a strong voice.

"I've got you," she reassured him. She gave the flight mechanic a thumbs-up. Then she wrapped her arm around him.

Nova dragged all three of them out of the cavern, just high enough, their feet skipping over the waves like stones. Once they were clear of the treacherous swells, Nova lowered them back into the water as aid was deployed from the chopper. When Nova's rescue swimmer hit the water and swam over to them, he clapped Neve on the back.

"That was freaking amazing! Good job," he yelled. Though Neve was exhausted from the rescue, with his help, they got both men loaded into the Jayhawk, and then both rescue swimmers were hoisted up one at a time, with Neve first.

As soon as she hit the deck of the chopper, Nova turned around and lifted her visor, her eyes warm and relieved. "Welcome aboard." Her sister's voice was filled with the same pride that only minutes before had surged through Neve.

"Thanks, ma'am."

Nova grinned, radioed into base and turned the chopper toward Astoria.

It had all been about teamwork. Back at the base, Neve helped the other rescue swimmer with the survivors until he insisted he check her out.

Feeling raw, as if some protective outer layer had just been peeled away, Neve closed her eyes and couldn't stop the rush of tears. Crying was a result of release for getting herself and these surfers to safety, gratitude for these men and women of the coast guard and her pride to be one of them. It was all about teamwork and she finally got it. She didn't have to prove anything to them or to herself. She'd already done that by making it into the elite rescue-swimmer ranks and, with that, she realized she'd taken a new turn in her life, just like she had when she'd let Rock help her and even take the lead.

The majority of her tears came because she'd made her decision and it was an easy one.

* * *

Three days later, she was called into the commander's office.

She faced him across the desk.

"Exemplary work, Petty Officer," he said. "We're awarding you the Coast Guard Medal for your heroism. Quick thinking, ingenuity and teamwork got you through. You can now have your pick of assignments. Think about it when you get back to San Diego."

Back home, she and Nova spent the evening together, and that night she couldn't stop the tears. They were residual from the rescue, but most of them were because she had been a fool.

Rock had left her in Panama City, and she hadn't stayed there long. The nightmares had started when she got home. Feeling so many times as if she was suffocating, she'd wake up, gasping with the memories of the fear, panic and pain of being tortured by Ammon Set. She could only breathe when she focused on Rock. He was like a solid lifeline, and she reached for the phone so many times to call him just to hear his voice.

But each time she resisted, not sure what to say.

She'd buried the truth. She'd never been forced to recognize that, but she'd been doing it for a long time.

The truth was, she was a coward. She had never seen herself in that light before. Because of the way she'd grown up and the things she'd done with her father, she'd always thought she had a fair amount of backbone. Proving herself, using her physicality and her steadfast vow to duty, was a way to avoid handling the emotional side of her life, especially when it came to those deep feelings.

Feelings she'd buried because of the horrible danger

her father, then her two brothers, were in every day. It was easier to push the softer side away and hit head-on the things she thought would make her even tougher, mentally, physically, professionally.

She'd had feelings for Doug, her high-school boyfriend, but not as deep or as wide or as profound as she had them for Rock.

The truth was that hiding from him was easier than confronting him.

Nova was right. It was time to make a decision.

Shooting Range, San Diego, California
One month later

"You can't shoot worth hell," Dexter said, and Rock laughed. Tristan was leaning against the partition, his gun by his side, the safety on.

"What are you talking about, man? His groupings were dead-on," Tristan said.

Dex grinned. "I bet anyone in here could shoot better than you can."

Rock laughed, fist-bumped Tristan and said, "Bring it on, little brother."

Dex motioned to a slight figure next to them, most of her features and lithe body blocked by the partition.

Rock shrugged like he didn't care who his opponent was. Truth be told, he was just managing to get back on track after leaving Neve in Panama seven months ago. He'd heard from Tristan how she'd rescued two men from a cavern off the coast of Oregon, and his chest swelled with pride for her. They were awarding her with the coast guard's highest prize for heroism.

He missed her like hell, but when he'd gotten back

to San Diego and faced Tristan, his heart had felt like it had been ripped to shreds.

He'd told Tristan everything, and his best friend had not only thanked him, but gave him a tight hug that had them both pretending they had something in their eyes.

Tristan negated the guilt he'd felt betraying him when he'd told Rock to go after Neve. Tristan had said he couldn't have wished for a better man for his sister.

Rock had only said that they wanted different things, but Tristan had only laughed at that. He'd told Rock to give her some time. That gave Rock hope, confidence that if Neve wanted him, she knew where she could find him. They hadn't spoken about her since, but it was no secret that Rock was still deeply in love with her.

Dex dodged around the partition, and Rock gave Tristan an "I've got this" look. Tristan's eyes twinkled.

Dex came back around and said, "She's ready to go. She wanted to make sure you could handle being beaten by a girl."

Damn, that sounded like something Neve would say.

He stepped up to the shelf and set his gun down, reloading it and getting it ready to fire. He looked over to the woman, only able to make out dark hair and a delicate jaw. He said, "Ladies first."

She snorted, lifted her arm and sighted down the pistol. *Bam, bam, bam, bam, bam, bam.* Six rounds into the target. She set her gun down, flicked the safety.

"Your turn," Dex said.

Rock brought up his weapon and prepared to fire, his focus on the targets, when a movement caught his eye and he looked back over to his opponent. She'd taken off her goggles, pulling a holder out of her long, black hair.

His hand shook, and he depressed the trigger, emptying the gun. Without even caring how well he'd done, he set down the weapon, put on the safety and pulled off his own goggles.

Dex stepped out of the way, and she was standing there.

Neve.

Dex and Tristan melted away, and it was just the two of them. Rock set his hands on his hips, clenching his jaw, his throat thick. He heaved a breath, and Neve made a choked sound as he looked up. Her face twisted with emotion, and she slammed against him as he crushed her to him roughly, holding on to her as if she were his next breath. His chest expanded as he clutched her tighter, his voice raw and shaking. "Babe," he whispered raggedly. "I'm never letting you go again."

Burying her face against his neck, Neve clung to him just as tightly. "Sounds good to me."

He wasn't sure how they got out of there or how he'd gotten them to his house, but she was there, and he dragged her upstairs as they stripped until they fell together in a heated rush onto his bed.

Later, she sat on his mattress, looking mussed and thoroughly sated, her knees drawn up with her arms locked around them, watching him intently.

Amusement flickered through him. She looked like a pampered and lazy cat, sitting there with her chin propped on her upraised knees, her black hair a wild tangle around her face.

She didn't say anything; she just gave him that drowsy smile. He reached for his shorts and got out of bed, throwing her his robe. It was way too big, but she looked adorable in it. He wondered if she knew how messy her hair was.

Her face went serious. "It's time to talk now," she said.

"Downstairs," he said. "I can't concentrate here."

He sat on a stool as she ran her fingers along his kitchen counters, then looked at the fridge. She pulled down the colorful picture taped to it, and still he was afraid to speak. Afraid that she wasn't staying, that this was goodbye instead of hello.

"Who did this?"

"I'm a Big Brother—the kid I'm mentoring did it."

"Kid. Georgie, cute," she said softly and then put the picture back on the fridge.

She walked out of the kitchen and out into the pool area. The sun was setting and night falling. He came up behind her and knew that it was now or never. He didn't want casual sex with her. He wanted her. Time to lay it all on the line. "Neve, I love you."

She whirled, and her face went soft and tender. She closed the distance between them and cupped his face in her hands. "I love you, too. I've always been afraid of that…love. I was a coward because it always scared me how deeply you can love someone and how fragile life is, how easily you could lose them. But with you I can't be afraid anymore. I love you so much, and I'm willing to do anything to make this work between us."

Her husky, heartfelt tone did him in. He closed his eyes and slid his hands down her arms to clasp her hands and bring them to his chest, a knot of emotion climbing into his throat. He waited for the aching contraction to ease, then said, "Do you know how much I love you?"

She smiled, her eyes full of joy, clearly transfixed by a host of emotions. Rock took her face between his hands this time, his expression strained as he held her gaze. "I want you to marry me, Neve. I want us to get married and have some kids and make a home."

Neve stared at him, unmoving. The look in her eyes was open and certain. Tightening his hold on her face, he took a deep, unsteady breath and gave her a little shake, then said, his voice catching, "Marry me."

She stared at him for an instant, then her eyes filled with tears and she hugged him like there was no tomorrow. His throat closed up completely, and Rock shut his eyes and turned his face against her, hugging her back. Maybe there was still room for miracles. Maybe.

Trying his damnedest to get rid of the big lump in his throat, he ran his hand up her spine. "You have to know I love you, Neve. I've loved you from the moment I saw you."

She made a sound somewhere between laughter and tears, and she hugged him even harder. "I've missed you so much. So damned much."

Wrapping his arms right around her torso, he totally enveloped her and turned his face against the soft skin of her neck. Feeling lighter than he could ever remember, he gave her a tight squeeze.

She whispered against his skin, "You're going to forgive me for being an idiot? Just like that?"

"Yes, because I'm a nice guy."

She moved her hips slowly and sensually against him. "Yes," she whispered huskily. "You are."

"Before you stir up something else here," he added at her frown, squeezing her tighter, "maybe you'd better give me your answer. Tell me you love me. I need you to say the words again."

"I love you and I will marry you. I know your concerns about children and my career. But I can't jump out of helicopters forever, so if you're willing to move around a little bit before the babies, I think we can come to a perfect agreement. After all, they also have to grow to school age."

"I think we can negotiate that. I have stores I want to open up… Let's see where that takes us."

"Right now I'll be in San Diego for another four years. I chose to stay here when they offered me my pick of locations."

Hooking his knuckles under her chin, he lifted her face and coaxed her with a gentle smile, his touch slow and provoking. "Say it again," he commanded softly.

Tears appeared and she looked at him, her heart in her eyes. She drew a shaky breath, then said, her gaze steady and unguarded, "I love you, Russell Kaczewski. You're my Rock." With tears glistening in her long lashes, she touched his face with infinite gentleness, then leaned forward and kissed him, whispering against his mouth, "I love you. I'll marry you, and we'll be together forever."

His throat thick and his chest chock-full of emotion, Rock caught her by the back of the head, his fingers tangling in her hair as he opened his mouth to hers, taking all that she offered. She gave him what he wanted, then she pressed her hand against his face and eased away.

She pulled at the tie of the robe with a mischievous look on her face. "How about a quick swim?" The robe dropped into a pool of burnished satin at his feet. He laughed as she snapped the waistband of his shorts. "You won't need these."

She went outside and jumped into the water, and he removed his shorts and dived in, then swam up to her.

She wrapped her arms around him and kissed him, her lips soft and wet. He got hot and bothered all over again. Pressing her back against the pool, he took her fast and hard.

A little while later, she stirred on the bed. "Now that you've taken care of one kind of hunger—twice…" she murmured, running her hand over his chest.

"You're taking a lot for granted, aren't you?"

She gave him a sugar-wouldn't-melt-in-her-mouth smile. "What do you mean?"

"You expect me to feed you?"

She cocked her head and gave him a smile and a nod.

He watched her, liking the way she held his gaze, liking the intimacy in her eyes. "You're a piece of work, you know that?" Rock said.

She watched him, that same sleepy, satisfied look on her face. He caught a glint of amusement in her eyes, and her mouth lifted a little. "You're the coffee-cake king. So get your hard, gorgeous ass in the kitchen, Marine."

"You expect me to do the cooking, don't you?"

"Yes, in the bedroom and in the kitchen. Just make sure you're barefoot…and naked."

"Well, I think I've got the bedroom covered, but I'll need an apron in the kitchen so that I don't get stuff all over me."

Her brow arched, and she gave him a cheeky grin. "Don't worry about that. I'll lick anything off."

She gazed at him, her eyes dark and slumberous, her mouth still moist from his kisses, and Rock's pulse skittered and caught. He wondered if he would ever get enough of her.

Hell no. But he didn't have to worry about that now.

He had her, and she was going to be his for the rest of his life. He could handle a little naked cooking now and again.

Epilogue

Two months later

Tristan and Amber's wedding was in full swing, and Neve was getting a thrill out of showing everyone at the reception her ring, a huge diamond set in platinum with a spectacular sparkle and shine.

Then a guy walked in, and Neve recognized him immediately. The sniper. For most of the mission she'd thought the one shadowing them had been her brother Tristan. She broke away from her friends and family, putting herself right in his path.

"Hi, Neve Michaels." She thrust out her hand.

He stopped and stared at her, and she realized he wasn't going to say a word. She guessed he was probably former CIA. Those guys never owned up to anything.

"NCIS Special Agent Derrick Gunn," he said, gripping her strongly and letting go.

"Been to the jungle lately?"

"What? Down to Central America? No way. I don't like roughing it, and I hear it's pretty dangerous down there."

Yeah, for the bad guys and anyone who got into this guy's scope.

"Why would you do that when you could be sipping drinks with umbrellas in them on a white, sandy beach?"

"Exactly." He flashed her a devastating grin, and she suspected that there were many women who would easily sink under his don't-mess-with-me-if-you-want-to-stay-safe charm. But she was immune. She had Rock.

"Can I have this dance?" she asked and he obliged her, moving smoothly onto the dance floor, as suave as 007. He looked the part in that tux, one that wasn't off the rack. They danced for a few minutes, making idle small talk.

When the music ended, Neve snagged and squeezed his forearm, gratitude in her eyes. "Thank you."

"For the dance?"

"Yeah, *right*, for the dance."

As Rock approached, he nodded to her big, beautiful fiancé. "Glad to have been of service," he said, then disappeared into the crowd.

After acknowledging Derrick one warrior to another, Rock slipped his arm around her and dragged her close. "Your brother looks so happy. I can't wait until our wedding day."

She looked over at Tristan, who was dancing with a beaming Amber. "He is happy and we will be, too."

She turned into his arms. "You look pretty good in this tux, and I'd say you were the best man here."

He smirked. "I saw what you did there. Yeah, I clean up good."

"I do have to say that I kind of enjoyed our decadent jungle sex."

Stroking the wisps of hair at her temple with his thumb, he gazed at her, a heart-stopping smile in his eyes, then he lowered his head and kissed her. "We can be just as free and unrestrained here."

His eyes held the kind of glint only Rock could give her. She remembered every moment of their time together in the wilds of the Darién. "Oh, you were pretty amazing in every way."

"Damn straight." His eyes really started to dance.

She laughed softly.

He slipped his arm around her waist and looked toward the door. "Wanna see some more of my moves right now?"

"You are so bad," She gave him a little push, and he caught her to him, pulling her closer.

"One hundred percent pure marine badass to the bone," he agreed, kissing her. "I'm bulletproof, babe. Nothing beats Rock."

She couldn't argue with that.

* * * * *

Allison raised her head with every intention of stepping away from him. But his arms pulled her closer to him and his lips crashed down on hers.

The kiss erased all rational thought from her mind. Instead, all her senses came gloriously alive as Knox's mouth made love to hers. His tongue swirled with hers as his scent suffused her, and the heat of his hands on her back invited her to melt against his broad chest. Their bodies fit together perfectly, as if they had been made for each other.

He finally left her lips to slide his mouth down the column of her throat. As her knees weakened with desire, rational thought slammed back into her. She jerked back from him, appalled by how quickly, how completely, he could break down all her defenses.

His eyes radiated a raw hunger as he held her gaze intently. "Despite everything that has happened between us, I still want you. There's always been something strong between us, Allison, and you can't deny that it's still there."

No, she couldn't deny it, but she also wouldn't admit it to him. "It doesn't matter." She took two steps back from him, needing not only to emotionally distance herself but to physically distance herself, as well.

"That kiss was a mistake. I don't feel that way about you anymore." Okay, maybe she could deny it, but she could tell by the look in his eyes that he didn't believe her.

"In any case, anything like that between us would be foolish and it would only complicate things. We aren't going there again, Knox, and now I think it's time we say good-night."

She breathed a sigh of relief when he nodded and turned to walk to the front door. Her legs were still shaky as she accompanied him.

"I'm sorry about my little breakdown," she said.

He turned to face her and before she could read his intentions he grabbed her and once again planted a kiss on her lips.

It was short and searing and when he released her his eyes sparkled with a knowing glint. "The next time you try to tell me you don't feel that way about me anymore, say it like you really mean it," he said, and then he was gone into the night.

Don't miss
COLTON'S SECRET SON by Carla Cassidy,
available March 2017 wherever
Harlequin® Romantic Suspense books
and ebooks are sold.

www.Harlequin.com

REQUEST YOUR FREE BOOKS!
2 FREE NOVELS PLUS 2 FREE GIFTS!

ROMANTIC suspense

Sparked by danger, fueled by passion

YES! Please send me 2 FREE Harlequin® Romantic Suspense novels and my 2 FREE gifts (gifts are worth about $10). After receiving them, if I don't wish to receive any more books, I can return the shipping statement marked "cancel." If I don't cancel, I will receive 4 brand-new novels every month and be billed just $4.74 per book in the U.S. or $5.49 per book in Canada. That's a savings of at least 12% off the cover price! It's quite a bargain! Shipping and handling is just 50¢ per book in the U.S. and 75¢ per book in Canada.* I understand that accepting the 2 free books and gifts places me under no obligation to buy anything. I can always return a shipment and cancel at any time. Even if I never buy another book, the two free books and gifts are mine to keep forever.

240/340 HDN GH3P

Name	(PLEASE PRINT)
Address	Apt. #
City	State/Prov.	Zip/Postal Code

Signature (if under 18, a parent or guardian must sign)

Mail to the **Reader Service**:
IN U.S.A.: P.O. Box 1867, Buffalo, NY 14240-1867
IN CANADA: P.O. Box 609, Fort Erie, Ontario L2A 5X3

Want to try two free books from another line?
Call 1-800-873-8635 or visit www.ReaderService.com.

* Terms and prices subject to change without notice. Prices do not include applicable taxes. Sales tax applicable in N.Y. Canadian residents will be charged applicable taxes. Offer not valid in Quebec. This offer is limited to one order per household. Not valid for current subscribers to Harlequin Romantic Suspense books. All orders subject to credit approval. Credit or debit balances in a customer's account(s) may be offset by any other outstanding balance owed by or to the customer. Please allow 4 to 6 weeks for delivery. Offer available while quantities last.

Your Privacy—The Reader Service is committed to protecting your privacy. Our Privacy Policy is available online at www.ReaderService.com or upon request from the Reader Service.

We make a portion of our mailing list available to reputable third parties that offer products we believe may interest you. If you prefer that we not exchange your name with third parties, or if you wish to clarify or modify your communication preferences, please visit us at www.ReaderService.com/consumerschoice or write to us at Reader Service Preference Service, P.O. Box 9062, Buffalo, NY 14240-9062. Include your complete name and address.